Euphrates Dance

A Novel

Dance

Euphrates Dance

A Novel

Hussein Hussein

Parkhurst Brothers Publishers

MARION, MICHIGAN

www.parkhurstbrothers.com

Parkhurst Brothers books are distributed to the trade through the Chicago Distribution Center, and may be ordered through Ingram Book Company, Baker & Taylor, Follett Library Resources and other book industry wholesalers. To order from Chicago Distribution Center, phone 800-621-2736 or send a fax to 800-621-8476. Copies of this and other Parkhurst Brothers Publishers titles are available to organizations and corporations for purchase in quantity by contacting Special Sales Department at our home office location listed on our website. Manuscript submission guidelines for this publishing company are available at our website.
Printed in the United States of America

First Edition, 2017
2017   2018   2019   2020 10 9 8 7 6 5 4 3 2 1

Library of Congress Cataloging in Publication Data: [Pending]
ISBN: Trade Paperback   978-1-62491-092-0
ISBN: e-book 978-1-62491-093-7

Parkhurst Brothers Publishers believes that the free and open exchange of ideas is essential for the maintenance of our freedoms. We support the First Amendment to the United States Constitution and encourage all citizens to study all sides of public policy questions, making up their minds independently. Closed minds cost a society dearly.

Cover and interior design by   Linda D. Parkhurst, Ph.D.
Proofread by   Bill and Barbara Paddack
Acquired for Parkhurst Brothers Publishers and edited by   Ted Parkhurst

052017

To the woman who blesses me with true love and happiness,
my dearest lovely wife,
Zaineb Albayati,
for her loving patience and generous support during my writing.

Contents

CHAPTER ONE

The Nightmare

THE SUN DISAPPEARED BEHIND NASIRIYA'S WESTERN DESERT DUNES. Black arms of darkness hugged the houses, extinguishing all evidence of human life. The night silence, sharp and frightening, was broken only by the occasional barking dog, or drum sounds drifting in the wind from the date-palm forest on the small, southern Iraq town's northern edge.

Nasiriya always yawned and closed down at sunset. People rushed home, like a flock of birds exhausted from their long migration. In the streets and alleyways, darkness became the master. The night's strange muteness controlled the town, seizing its spirit, bringing an indefinable siege of horror, as if many hidden eyes watched and waited for the moment to attack. This deathlike silence's ominous force frequently left Nasiriya's people in a deep, hypnotic trance.

Very rarely, on a Thursday night, a wedding ceremony or a boy's religious rite of circumcision took place. Then the city could be overwhelmed with loud ululations and songs, giving the people a sense of security, granting them a rare whole night of uninterrupted sleep.

The townspeople never talked publicly of their fears, but terror etched their faces as the sun's last rays would vanish. Strange whispers and hushed voices filled the night, warning of death's constant presence. Some people related stories of the cemetery's ghosts rising, haunting the forest and Nasiriya's streets. These ghosts, they would say, wandered without legs, each sporting a beard hanging to its waist. Goat-like ears framed their otherwise nondescript faces. Each ghost wore a long, white gown with sleeves draping their distorted forms, piercing screams seeming to streak straight from their mad, sunken eyes. Legend held that the night forest, dark and ominous, hid a massive army of ghosts ready to sweep down on the town.

Inside the houses, Nasiriya's children have always shuddered to stories told by old grandmothers, keepers of tradition. Each long Iraqi winter night, they related scary tales of the cemetery's fairy people, genies, or the hyenas haunting the streets, kidnapping undutiful children to devour their hearts. Grandmothers would whisper in wonder, "Do you know that only children's hearts can give the hyena longer life?"

On those winter nights, families would hasten to huddle around their fires burning in heavy iron grates. Adults would slurp strong black tea poured from the steaming teapot, which was then placed back on the coals. Continuing their stories, the proud grandmothers happily watched their families' terrors subside.

If she could tell the scariest story, the night would be all the more entertaining. The grandchildren's eyes glittered with fear. Some of the grandmother's stories made the children burst out crying. They squirmed and fretted, and carried their fears to bed. The next morning, every bed would be wet, each child having been too scared to creep to the bathroom.

In every adult's heart, a terrible story still survived from their childhood, planted there by the grandmothers long ago. This was one familiar to all Nasiriya's townspeople: A monster called Tental came at night to haunt the town, searching for a new bride to steal. Tental, according to the townspeople, could change forms, and would attack anyone and anything—unless a person carried a piece of iron. Anyone who carried iron was safe. Tental would never draw near.

One night, arriving at a house where a family was hosting a wedding, Tental kidnapped the bride. The new husband, shocked and miserable, went to an old witch who lived outside the town. The husband begged her to help him find his bride. But the old witch fell in love with the young groom and asked the groom to forget about his wife and marry her instead. She promised to make him the richest man in the world, and always happy, if only he would marry her.

The witch explained the only way to bring his wife back: kill Tental. Since no one could kill the monster, then the groom should give up on his wife and marry her instead. But the young man refused to marry her. So the angry witch cursed him and turned him into a hyena.

Ever since, as each night fell, the witch unleashed the hyena to haunt the town, to kidnap and kill children, so she could eat their hearts. The more hearts she consumed, the longer she lived, and the stronger she became. The unfortunate hyena had to do this every night until the witch died. Then, the hyena could turn back into a man, and search again for his wife to save her from the Tental.

Legend said in each generation a man was cursed like this bridegroom. He existed only in Nasiriya families descended from the ancient folk of Ur. As these families moved from Ur to the newer town of Nasiriya, the curse followed and survived among them.

The capital of the Dhi Qar province, Nasiriya was named after the Turkish leader Nassir Pasha, who conquered Iraq in the 1800s. He commanded that Nasiriya be built and carry his name. So it stood to this day, a small town with tree–lined, wide streets still haunted by ghosts born of violent death. Every summer, treacherous sand storms attacked the town, clogging people's throats, burning their lips, swelling their eyes, and causing emphysema among the elderly and asthma among children. Nasiriya's streets of crushed gravel mixed with sand added to the airborne assault. Nasiriya was covered with suffocating dust on scorching days. The few asphalt streets displayed their decrepit age with potholes and cracks choked with dagal thorns and sea heath, plants that camels fondly graze upon.

Remarkably, daytime in Nasiriya often proved peaceful. Each morning, the call to prayer—a gently lilting song heard from four directions—assured all that night had ended and rewarded anxious souls with tranquility. Roosters' cries flooded the daybreak, welcoming the waking residents. The abundant date palm forests stood tall and elegant, guarding the town by day, extending to the desert in the west and north, and spreading to the east for hundreds of miles, and to the southeast toward Basra. The Euphrates nourished Nasiriya, splitting the town in two as it flowed toward its mate, the Tigris. These rivers passionately embraced, forming the Shatt Al-Arab at Basra after which the two waters carried on like restless lovers all the way to the Arabian Gulf.

At daybreak, people from surrounding villages swelled Nasiriya's streets, selling chickens, milk, fruit, vegetables, and lambs. Okra, potatoes, eggplant, radishes, celery, lettuce, cabbage, beans, cucumbers, beets, and melons traded hands at inexpensive prices. By sunset, the villagers' marketing cries had died. They rushed out of town just ahead of the darkness.

The townspeople prided themselves in their shops, businesses, schools, and temples of worship. There were two coffee shops, a single post office, a high school for boys and another for girls, two elementary schools, one medical clinic with limited facilities, and ten mosques. Fridays were the holy days when people gathered in mosques to pray, to share their anxieties, and to hear the latest opinions and rumors. Before the religious services began, the townspeople would linger in the coffee shops, drinking tea and breaking bread together.

Few were rich in Nasiriya. The majority lived in poverty, while only a small middle class of barbers, tailors, taxi drivers and bakers accounted for the rest of its population. The poor depended on farm work, growing vegetables and fruits. Some fishermen plied the Euphrates with their nets, selling their catch in the market. Several kinds of fish—shabbout, bunni and gittan— were threaded through their gills, strung just as they had been when ancient Sumerians plied the river. Interestingly, the types of fish that swim in the Euphrates and appear in the market have not changed in three thousand years. Weavers gathered tree branches and leaves from plentiful date palms to form baskets, rugs, chairs, and boxes of all types for fruits and vegetables. A small number performed as blacksmiths, carpenters, butchers, and stone masons. Most occupations passed from one generation to the next by apprenticeship. The handful in government positions enjoyed exalted prestige in town, even though they earned lower wages than laborers. For instance, the old police officer brought home barely half of what a young carpenter or stonemason might earn, forcing him to struggle, only able to buy one new uniform each year.

Nasiriya's houses were built of light brick or mud, lending them an aura of sameness. A house might possess a small window, or more often, no window at all. Large families found protection from the night in homes lacking privacy as well as modern comforts. Each house usually featured a small open patio in the middle, used as the family's living room. On summer afternoons, they gathered before supper there for tea and homemade kleicheh (Iraqi cookies). Kleicheh are usually round or half-moons stuffed with tamer (dates), hazelnuts, or coconuts, and flavored with cardamom and rose water. My grandma used to color and scent kleicheh with saffron and glaze it with egg yolk to give it an irresistible smell and a golden yellow face. A stairway led from this patio to the roof where the family slept during the summer when temperatures soared. To avoid the pesky mosquitoes, tents and nets provided protection.

In one middle-class family lived a boy, Salim, with his five brothers and mother, Monira Ahmad. Salim's father Wissam Jawad was a truck driver, who spent most nights away, hauling goods from Nasiriya to Baghdad, Najaf, Basra, and Mosul. Salim's mother provided the family's structure and authority in her husband's absence. A midwife and fortune teller, Monira was a beautiful woman, thin and of medium height. Her fine-boned, tanned face shone with dark, confident eyes and a ready, warm smile devoid of any antagonism or conflict. A quiet middle-aged woman, her intense gaze penetrated daily commotion, as if casting it into another world.

Like many women of her age, Monira wore black from head to toe. She wore traditional flowing apparel which provided a degree of decency and respect. However, her black veil and gown also cast a false appearance. Usually silent, she seemed somber and mournful. Only family and women friends knew of her true faithful and caring nature. Monira was well-respected, having helped hundreds of women through the agonies of childbirth. She was always ready to perform her duties regardless of the weather or the hour of the day or night. Many times Monira would not even request payment for her services, particularly when she realized the family was too poor to pay. Consequently, Nasiriya's people loved Monira. She, in turn, received much pleasure from her work, in spite of the meager support it provided her family.

Like others in the small, conservative town, Monira and her husband Wissam recognized the importance of family reputation. Both strived to raise their six children to be considerate, appreciative, and kind to everyone. They instructed their children in the basics of their Islamic faith—to be honest, kind, and sincere. Monira had always told her boys, "Family honor is as fragile as a glass pitcher; once broken it can never again hold water. Remember, our family's reputation is our crown. It's the border between honorable and dissolute Muslims. Family honor must remain as pure as the moon on a clear night."

Adultery loomed as the worst sin a person could commit in Nasiriya. Marriage was the only means to sexual fulfillment. Despite the risks, however, a man would occasionally form a secret relationship with a divorcee, a widow, or even a married woman. If the woman was caught, her reputation was instantly ruined, and might not be repaired for generations. She might even be killed. People were merciless, holding an indiscretion against a woman for decades. Adultery could lead to a terrible disaster, like the one that befell the widow Fahima. Fahima lived a few houses away from Monira and her family. She was young and gorgeous, with shining black hair flowing to her slender waist. Her ebony eyes were sensuous and alluring, made even more powerful by her gracefully sculpted nose and luscious, ruby-red lips.

When she was only fifteen years old, Fahima's parents had forced her to marry a wealthy man four times her age. He had lived only five years after the marriage, dying from cancer. He left Fahima a rich woman, yet one starving for love. Her bank accounts were full, but her bed was empty, a private desert of undulating linens. Alone for years, Fahima longed for a strong, decent man to propose to her, to make a family with her, to overwhelm her life with passion, love, and kindness. She and Monira became close. Over tea and biscuits, Fahima poured out all her heart's bitterness to her trusted friend. Monira loved this young woman, giving her attention, admiration, and respect. Monira considered Fahima the daughter she had never conceived.

Other neighborhood women, jealous of Fahima's wealth and beauty, intensely despised the young widow. If she wore a new dress or a different kind of perfume when the women gathered at Monira's house for a chat,

Fahima's jealous foes would gossip behind her back. One day, when Fahima arrived looking particularly attractive, several women choked with envy and anger. Seeing jealousy in their glaring eyes, Monira exclaimed, "Fahima, you are so beautiful! You are the most gorgeous woman I have ever seen in my life!"

Most of the women had to agree with Monira. But one, a poor woman not graced with beauty, could not hide her jealousy. "She is beautiful! It is too bad that Fahima has only her pillow to hug at night in her cold bed."

Another woman growled even more hatefully, "Fahima, how would you like to borrow my husband for a night or two? You need a bull like him to satisfy you, and he is killing me every night. When it comes to sex, I swear he is an animal! That's what you need, Fahima, don't you?" Their tension released, the women laughed hysterically.

But Fahima had been hugging more than a pillow. Secretly, discreetly, Fahima had found a haven in her anguish. She no longer felt victim to the love tornado that overwhelmed her heart every night. Her tender heart, thirsty for love and kindness, was by then brimming with the joy of intimacy. She had found flaming satisfaction in a bed of passionate lust. Unbeknownst to her critics, Fahima had met a handsome man and had fallen in love. After he had promised to marry her, they had begun meeting frequently. In a small town where residents even know what their neighbor is cooking for lunch, such an affair could not remain concealed.

Townspeople began spreading rumors, gossiping and seeking vengeance upon her love affair. Families encouraged their children to fling rocks at her door and write insults on the walls outside of her home. Even happily married men seemed driven insane by jealousy. The rewards of respectability somehow felt hollow. Finally, as the fury of jealous women grew, a concerned neighbor invited them to a meeting. The righteous wives determined that Fahima had to go. They also demanded that their husbands force Fahima to leave town—after being threatened with death.

On the day of her departure, Fahima peered from her half-opened door, petrified. Her legs could barely hold her as she stumbled toward the waiting truck. In that moment, Fahima resolved to face the injustice, alone and proud. A miserable fate had stolen away her happiness. Everybody else seemed to enjoy a love that symbolized an ever-fruitful life, but not her. When the mob of children saw Fahima, they began throwing pebbles and stones, until she bled and staggered. Townspeople had crowded the streets about her house watching Fahima's disgrace. A loud crowd of angry women pushed toward her, singing, dancing, and ululating, taunting her for her sins. The entire town was celebrating her downfall.

Monira would not tolerate the shunning of her friend. She stepped forward and gently escorted Fahima to the truck. Monira sheltered her friend lovingly, defiantly, until Fahima sat safely in the truck, and watched it pull away and out of sight. Long years passed, yet the townspeople never forgot Fahima's humiliation. The man who had sinned with her remained safe from harm; no one bothered him. He lived a peaceful life in an adjacent neighborhood, as if he had never even offended a sand pebble. Fahima alone suffered all the blame and paid the cost of humiliating banishment.

Meanwhile, time flowed by as Wissam and Monira watched their sons grow into men. Eventually, the time came to prepare their youngest son, six-year-old Salim, for the tradition of religious circumcision. In Nasiriya, a circumcision was a highly celebrated event, confirming a family's faithfulness to Allah and to their community.

"Salim, tomorrow night will be a great night to celebrate two wonderful occasions: our Prophet Mohammad's birthday, and your circumcision," his mother told him. "You know that we had to put off your circumcision to summer vacation so that you can stay home and not have to go to school. Now, I want you to go with me to the market for shopping."

"All right, Momma, I'll be ready in five minutes," responded the excited boy.

"What do you want to buy?" Monira spoke to her son from her room as she changed her clothes. "Is there anything special that you'd like? Just choose what you really want, regardless of the price. We've been anticipating these two celebrations."

"A bicycle maybe?"

"A bicycle suits me fine. You've got it, son."

"Thank you, Momma! Tell me again what we'll be doing tomorrow night?"

"Well, we will happily commemorate the Prophet's special birthday by offering prayers to God, and will exchange gifts with each other. You're going with me to the market now to buy what we need for the party: the candles, incense, ribbons, cards, and flowers. Your father will slaughter a sheep to roast for the many guests to our feast, to thank God for His endless bounty and to bring grace on our family—and all people of the world. Your Aunt Amina will come to help me with cooking. Tomorrow, we'll light a hundred candles, set flowers out, and decorate the house with colorful ribbons. In addition, we've hired Naziha, the famous Mullaiah in the city, to sing favorite religious songs and entertain our guests with her beautiful voice. How does all that sound to you, son?"

"It's going to be great, Mother! I love it! I remember how delightful it was last year!"

The feast festivities required exhaustive preparations from both Monira and her sister Amina. In the late afternoon, the family celebrated privately. Monira recited verses from the Qur'an, and everyone performed the prayers. The large living room sparkled with a hundred candles, colorful flowers, candies wrapped in sparkling foil, and glittering gift wrap. Aunt Amina rushed about the house, confirming that all was in order and announcing her joy with loud ululations. In the evening, the patio was clogged with guests lined around the many tables which groaned under heavy trays of rice with raisins and almonds topped by large cuts of roasted lamb. Behind the standing guests, couches and chairs were placed near the walls to provide seating for the party to come. Most guests ate traditionally with bread and hands, while a few used spoons. Salim stood with his brothers behind the dining guests, ready to carry pitchers of buttermilk and water to refill their guests' empty glasses.

After dinner, Salim's brothers quickly removed the tables and the left-over food. The patio was washed and cleaned, and two carpets were unfolded on the floor. Then the announcement: The party had started! A few minutes later, Mullaiah Naziha entered the patio, carrying her Dunbic, the traditional instrument she played to provide rhythms to her songs. The crowd greeted her with applause and cheers. Contentment shone in the young girl's face as she walked forward, her hair tied up in a red scarf, and a long black veil covering her lithe body. Taking her place on the carpet, the young Mullaiah surveyed the guests. Her eyes roamed the men's faces, settling upon a handsome man who sat on one of the couches. Ecstatic, the man responded by blowing her a kiss.

Preparing to perform, Naziha deftly examined the Dunbic's conical body—a kind of lute with an animal skin stretched over the sound chamber—and checked the skin's tightness. Then she started to play. As Naziha gently tapped the Dunbic, she was accompanied by a man on his Rubab, a small stringed instrument similar to a lute. A loud roar exploded from her audience as Naziha sang one of the most famous religious songs, praising Allah and his Prophet Mohammad:

> *Our guidance was born, lighting up the Universe*
> *To lead us, to God's mercy and grace.*
> *Let's bow down to God, the omnipotent king, for the benevolence.*

The guests were entranced, overtaken by the lovely feminine voice. An old man, who seemed possessed by the enchantment, jumped to his feet and cried, "Naziha, I'm in love with you! Please stop hurting me ..."

Without skipping a beat, an angry voice bellowed from the rooftop where the women sat watching, "Shut up, you old fool, before they throw you in the street!"

The crowd stormed with waves of laughter, and even Naziha giggled. But, the man glared up at the roof, pointing his finger to his wife, who was sitting among the other women. He shouted, "Okay, Halima, we'll see who the boss is when we get home!"

The applause swelled, and some young men shouted, supporting the old man who began singing, "I'm in love with Naziha, please, do something for me!" Laughter filled the night until the party dissolved at midnight.

Early the next morning, the circumciser showed up carrying his little bag. Salim appeared confused. Despite applause from his family, their assembled friends and neighbors, Salim whimpered in fear. As Wissam placed his son on his lap, holding Salim's legs apart, the circumciser bent down and cut off the foreskin and carefully disinfected the wound. When the circumciser wrapped up the penis with cotton gauze, Salim's cries grew more intense. Later that day, Salim sat leaning back on many pillows looking like a sick angel in his transparent white gown. He tried to smile and remember jokes his brothers tossed at him during circumcision. Even the image of a shiny new bicycle could not dull the pain between his legs.

———

Wissam and Monira continued living happily with their children, grateful to the grace of God for their loving family. They were also thankful for their spacious house and the security of a sufficient monthly income. Their brick house, about thirty years old, was one of the distinguished homes in town. It was Wissam's wedding gift to Monira. He had inherited some land from his mother. Although he had spent most of his inherited money on his own pleasure, like most men he eventually realized he must cease his reckless prolificacy, marry and have a family before it was too late. It was then that he built the house and bought the truck that he still depended on for a living. In their home, each of the four bedrooms was arranged with two iron bedsteads, two small chairs, and an old but serviceable wardrobe. In the living room, two large brown couches bracketed a round coffee table.

The house also featured a special room for Monira's fortune telling. Monira's room was somber, with walls covered by black sheets, and an anemic red lamp hung from the ceiling. Monira approached her fortune telling as seriously as her midwifery. She would shake polished stones in her hands, cast them on the table, and study them. Then, she would gaze at her client before squinting at the stones again. Finally, while penetrating the person's eyes with her own, she would begin to talk in a measured cadence about his past, present, and future.

By the time Salim was twelve, a drastic change had fallen over him. He began isolating himself, barely communicating. Whenever the family tried to start a conversation, he would blurt a brief answer, his eyes defiant and distant. Unwilling to engage in casual talk, even on normal days, Salim became a loner. After school, he usually marched directly home where he seemed to hide in his room. As his appetite decreased, he lost weight week after week. His family and classmates frequently found him talking animatedly to himself.

Often, during the pre-dawn, Salim would leap from his bed, screaming from a nightmare. The family would rush to his room. Yet within minutes, he would calm down and go back to sleep, as if nothing had happened. But in the morning, the pain and distress were etched on Salim's face. Wrinkles began to appear around his dark eyes. Every day he slumped in deeper distress than the day before. His physical and mental condition frightened his family.

Once, while Monira sat in her fortune-telling room, Salim came and sat with her. She looked at her son with affection, but he appeared unhappy. Monira's intuitions about his pitiful life upset her. Salim was not like her first five sons. He did not focus on the normal satisfactions of young men. It surprised her to see him coming to join her in the fortune telling room.

Salim, in fact, would never enter the mysterious room alone unless he had to. In the fortune telling room, he always encountered the strangest feelings. Just entering the room, he would be attacked by all kinds of bad thoughts, as if he just entered a mysterious world. When Salim was there alone, an unknown threat would abruptly take over his consciousness, leaving him completely confused. Salim told Monira that evil eyes surrounded him when he entered the room. He said that the eyes watched him and that he was sure they were ready to attack him without notice.

Sitting silently beside his mother around the small table, Salim felt awe at what his mother was able to do in her appointed place. Chills coursed through his body. He resisted the urge to leave. His bright eyes, however, studied the darkness that surrounded him there and was aware of a weird silence. It was as if an unknown mournful death attended him in that room. The odd scarlet lamp hanging from the ceiling ignited the flame of Salim's discomfort and intensified his loneliness.

Sitting before the small table covered with a plush black fabric, Salim watched as the three fortune-telling stones dropped from his mother's small transparent plastic cup and danced over the cloth. In those moments, Salim fought the urge to ask his mother how she could possibly find peace in such a weird room. He tried to understand how his religious mother always felt such serenity alone in such a bleak room. Salim struggled with the darkness and with the presence of an evil spirit that he felt surrounding him. The palpable gloom was foremost in his mind when the soft voice of his mother interrupted his thoughts.

"What are you thinking about, son ...?"

He turned toward her and made an effort to return her smile. "I wonder, mother, why it feels so strange in this room?"

Hearing the note of annoyance in her son's voice, Morina exclaimed, "Perhaps because of the room's furnishings for fortune telling? Do you feel uncomfortable in here?"

"Yes, mother, I feel uneasy." Salim whispered, and his eyes tumbled to the ground.

"Even when you are with me? I will never leave you alone in here. Could you tell me, dear, what's scaring you? I wish to know."

After some moments of silence, Salim went on, "I do not know how to explain it, Momma, but the room does not feel as safe as the rest of the house. The blackness is frightening. Every time I'm here, I feel something is watching me. It's a very terrible room, Mother."

"I'm sorry you feel it that way, Salim. It's just another room of the house, and you shouldn't feel troubled."

"I wish I could understand it, Mother. But, I hate this room."

Salim tried to avoid more talk about the fortune-telling room. His sad eyes caught a black spider on the wall. The spider was cornering a fly. Meditating upon the furious struggle between the robust spider and its desperate prey, Salim felt even more pessimistic. He was so engrossed in watching the battle on the wall that Salim completely forgot about the presence of his mother.

Just before the spider completely encircled the fly, Salim heard his mother voice, "Do you think the fly could get away?"

He winced, exclaimed, "What ... Mother ... oh ... I'm sorry. I was ...

watching"

"I noticed that. You think too much, son, please, take it easy," his mother said. "What were you thinking about?"

"I was thinking about fear, how much the fly fears the spider. The fly's fear may be no less than my own."

Before his mother replied, Salim went on, "Let me ask you, how is it that you can harbor such fondness for this terrible room?"

"This room ... my fortune telling ...is just an additional source of our livelihood, "besides ...."

"Besides what ...?"

"It's also a means to answer some people's curiosity, some assurance about the mysteries of life."

"How is that, mother? How could you—my mother—do that?"

"See son, some people feel intimidated by life. They come to this room to find certainty in their lives. I'm only trying to help by offering hints of possible future events. My words are a salve for anxieties those people suffer."

"Do you tell them the truth ... or do you just tell them what they wish to hear?"

"In most cases, I tell them the truth. Many find comfort. Sadly, some will not hear the truth even when I speak it plainly."

"Momma, how can you tell the fortunes of people you have just met?"

"I read what is written on their foreheads, son," replied Monira, pleased that Salim was trying to understand her work.

"What does my forehead say?" Salim asked.

Monira looked at him for a moment, hesitated, then tried to change the subject. When Salim persisted, his mother replied, "Why do you need to know? You won't like the answer. You don't need to hear it."

"Yes, I do! Tell me, Momma, what does the writing on my forehead say?"

"My son, I hate to tell you. I can't tell you. Just forget about it!"

"No, Momma, I want to know," he replied impatiently.

"Son, it's not as simple as you think. It's not a happy thing to tell. Besides, if I tell you, I will be very disturbed."

"Momma, please!"

"Maybe someday I will tell you, but not now."

"But Momma, haven't you said before that we should not hide anything from each other? Haven't you said we should always be truthful to each other? Haven't you, Momma?"

"Yes son, I have told you all of that, but ..."

"But? But what?" Salim was sobbing now.

After a long silence, Monira took a deep breath. In a broken voice she said, "My dear young son, pain and misery will be your closest companions. You are and always will be the prey of evil powers. They will try to control your mind and spirit. Evil will terrorize your life, take away your freedom. No sanctuary can save you. The evil ones will try to kill you. They already know that you will betray them. Nothing can change your fate, except perhaps the mercy of Allah. Only God's compassion can help you. You must follow his path, become his loyal servant."

As Monira spoke, her mind flashed to the past, remembering the afternoon when Salim was only three days old. She lay beside him, holding him gently. Suddenly a mysterious old woman materialized through the wall of his room. Her veil, long gown, and shawl were all black. Black covered her small body and hid most of her face. She stood for a few moments in silence, staring obliquely into Monira's face. A fathomless cold glaze darkened her eyes. Her wrinkled face was caked with dirt. Blotches stained her bulbous nose, high cheekbones, and cruel, thin lips. Was she a demon or was she human? The terrified Monira couldn't tell.

The old woman quickly approached Salim, picked him up, smiled maliciously, and began to breastfeed him. The stunned Monira lay motionless, frozen with fear. Watching her son suck at the breast of the old woman, she could not move. She tried to scream, but her throat would make no noise.

After the feeding, the old woman planted a kiss on Salim's tiny mouth, and returned him to Monira's numb arms. Again, she glared at Monira with a hellish hatred. She glanced at the baby once more and then disappeared through the wall. Monira had never told anyone, not even when people asked what caused her beautiful hair to fall out. A year after the old woman's appearance, Monira's hair finally re-grew, but for a long time afterward she suffered weak knees, an upset stomach, and poor breathing.

Having heard his mother's dire prediction, Salim stood in shock, hypnotized by the detached look in his mother's eyes. Suddenly, his own mother seemed a stranger. His frail body began to shake.

"Stop it, Momma … you're scaring me! Stop it!"

"I'm so sorry, son, but you insisted." She was almost moaning, seeing his tears.

Salim replied angrily, "Do you think I believe what you just told me, Mother? Do you expect me to believe you? That this terrible thing was written on my forehead, but only you could see and read it? Why can't I see it too? Make me see it so I can believe you. No, Mother, I don't accept it. My father has told me not to believe everything I hear."

Salim's words brought desperate hope to his mother. Maybe … she could be wrong. "You're right, son. I could be mistaken. Only God knows everything."

Salim snapped at her, "Why did you say it, then, if you weren't sure?"

"See, my son, human beings are weak creatures, always seeking relief against an unseen future. I'm sorry. I shouldn't have told you about things like this. But you did insist."

They stared at each other in silence.

————

Time saw Salim, unlike his brothers, continue to grow more morose and withdrawn. Thin and easily lost in a crowd, his strong face featured dark, penetrating eyes highlighted by thick eyebrows. His head was crowned with a mass of curly hair, as dark and shiny as coal. Salim's face, however, remained pale, with a sheen of misery. His poor health aggravated his naturally sour temper. He often complained about piercing headaches and a roiling stomach. Salim's chronic sadness pervaded the household. All this was exacerbated by many nights of accompanying his mother as she assisted women in giving birth. Salim hated waiting in an adjoining room, listening to the escalating moans of women in labor. He blamed those moans for his anxious nightmares.

In spite of all his troubles, Salim exhibited a facility for learning. His school grades provided a source of pleasure for his teachers and admiration from his worried parents. In the classroom, teachers and classmates often observed Salim talking to himself, as if arguing with an unseen master. When questioned, he smiled in oblique denial.

Salim's family loved their youngest son and admired his success at school. Proudly, his parents told how, despite his poor health, he studied nightly, showed respect to his teachers, and seemed to understand many of adult life's important issues. One day, his older brother Nadeem came home, happy to tell his parents that the police chief had come and thanked him. Why? His kid brother Salim's quick thinking had helped solve a hit-and-run crime.

Nadeem said, "The chief shook my hand, congratulating me because Salim had shown courage! 'Walking down the street, your brother Salim saw a car hit a woman. The driver sped away. But Salim wrote down the car's license number and gave it to us, so we were able to apprehend the driver. To us, Salim sets an example of a good, reliable citizen. Other kids in our city should follow his example.'"

The family rejoiced over Nadeem's good news.

Salim's poor health and constant unhappiness, however, continued to distress the family, particularly Monira. Time and again, she took him to the small store where a man with wrinkled hands ground and concocted remedies from roots of plants, buds of bushes, and the juices of rare berries. In a sad voice, she pleaded with the druggist, "Is there no way to cure my child? Can't you restore his health and happiness? Why can't my child be as happy and active as his brothers and other children? Why?"

Embarrassed, the old man's wrinkled eye bags flexed momentarily, then seemed to recede into his fat cheeks. Recognizing defeat, he answered, "It's really strange, the story of this boy. God knows it is! Salim's health hasn't improved since the last medicine I gave him? It is most remarkable, I can't believe it myself."

With difficulty, the old man lifted himself from his chair and hobbled into the next room. He returned with a small jar similar to others he'd given

Monira. More confidently, he said, "Fifty years in this store. Fifty years and I have made thousands of prescriptions. Never before has a person come to me twice asking for help with the same illness." His voice softened to a whisper as he stepped near the woman. "As for your son, I am afraid that his body might be inhabited by evil spirits. You know this whole town is full of them. I'm afraid I am unable to help him."

Salim looked up and saw tears forming in his mother's eyes. Could it be that his life was ebbing from him? Suddenly, Salim's fear for his own life and bitterness at the world seemed to be overcome by a deep longing to comfort her.

"Mother, I'm okay. I'm fine. Why do you cry like that? Please don't cry."

His mother received him warmly, pulling him into her soft flank as if to defend him from the druggist who stood on her other side. Her bulk comforted him. "Don't get scared like that again please, Mother. I'm just fine." Now enfolded in his mother's arms, Salim felt secure and comforted. And Monira sensed some relief.

In reality, Salim was not the only person to fear death, or to feel it always stalking nearby. In Nasiriya, everyone Salim knew suffered a similar foreboding. The shadow of death seemed to walk every street and pause near every market stall in Nasiriya—a constant presence that Salim sensed more strongly than others. Once Salim asked his mother, "What is death, Momma? Why is death so scary to everyone?"

Monira looked at her small son, and suddenly tears glistened in her eyes. She took him into her arms, and with a very tender voice replied, "We're scared of death, son, because death takes the people we love away forever."

"But why does death take them away from us?"

In her broken voice she answered, "It is Allah's will, son."

"But, where does death take people, Momma?"

Tears now covered his mother's cheeks as she explained, "Death takes them to heaven where they will become the guests of our merciful God."

In his astonishment, Salim asked her, "And my grandmother, Attia, is she also with them?"

Monira sighed before answering weakly, "Yes, son, she is with them too."

Suddenly Salim said, "Momma, I want to be with my grandmother. I want to see her, to hear her tell the old stories as in the past. Why can't I be with her, Momma?"

Monira held Salim and embraced him tightly, fearing that the power of his wish might lift him away from her at any moment.

"No, son, don't say such things. You're just an innocent child. You have not lived enough to know how precious life is. You are here with me, with your mother. I want you to have a long life, a long, long life."

Each week, Monira purchased another jar of medication. Still, anguish haunted both Monira and her son. Salim's body rejected the remedies. Sadness fill his daydreams and his nighttime dreams were just tragedy upon tragedy. Salim's moodiness tortured his entire family, especially his mother, who prayed desperately for her son to find peace and happiness. She prepared his meals with zealous care, as if her dishes were medicine. Despite his father's angry protests, Monira kept Salim in their bed at night. She longed for the boy to feel secure by sleeping next to her.

Wissam was a dutiful father, but he did not understand the malaise that distracted his youngest son. To compound his confusion, Monira—a faithful wife to this point—would chide him. "Shame on you, you selfish old crank! Don't you feel any pity toward your own son? Salim is just a scared little boy, and you want him out of the bed for the sake of your bodily pleasure!"

Salim's father roared angrily, and his face went crimson. "Damn you, woman! He is old enough to understand what goes on in a marriage bed. He is tougher and more intelligent than you think. I know my children. This boy has guts and brains. Why do you keep him sleeping with us? Why do you want to break him down?"

"Let's say that I am no longer interested in doing the things you want," she snapped back at him. "We're both getting old and have six grown children, and you've not given up your selfishness yet. Can't you see him? How can you not feel for him? You're mired in lust!"

Wissam's voice deepened. He threatened Monira, "You old hen, you're no longer worth a box of salt! Maybe I should marry a younger woman! I swear I'll do it."

"Really?! Why don't you do it then!?! I'll be the first to congratulate you. Just leave me alone to comfort our youngest son."

Angrily, Wissam struck one hand with the other and cursed his wife. Then he turned away from her and lay there like a silent bear.

Lying between his parents, Salim heard the next bouts of their fight, which they continued in their dreams. How, Salim wondered, could his headaches, stomach pains, and wobbly knees cause enmity between his parents, both of whom he loved.

But more than anything, Salim was confused. What did his parents do when they were alone in bed? What could no longer happen while he was present? Why does that make his father so angry? Why did it cause his mother to speak harshly to his father, the father of his brothers?

———

One late winter afternoon, Salim did not return home from school on time. Wissam and Monira became alarmed for their son's safety. The weather was chilly and rainy, and they worried he would catch a cold. His brothers scattered throughout the town searching for him. A neighbor went to Salim's school, but everyone had gone. The school's gate was locked. Hysterical, Monira stood in the street, crying in the rain. She darted wildly, hailing every passerby, asking if any had seen her son. No one had. As darkness fell, fear gnawed at the family, especially Monira. She recalled old stories of ghosts and Tental prowling the darkness, haunting the streets. The weather worsened, growing bone-chilling cold. She imagined her son all alone, suffering in the darkness and rain. Something terrible had happened to him.

Then, just after nightfall, Salim sauntered up to his home, lost in animated conversation with another kid. Both were soaking wet, unaware of the family's frantic search. Monira rushed to her son, took him into her arms, and cried out, "What happened to you!? Where have you been all this time, leaving us worrying to death? How could you make us worry like this, Salim?"

Salim stared blankly at his mother as if nothing had happened. "Here you are again, Mother, worrying about me over something I had to do for my

friend Nizar."

"What thing did you have to do for Nizar that would leave your family in such chaos? Where have you been?"

"Take it easy, Momma, I'll tell you everything. After school, I was on my way home, when I bumped into Nizar. He told me his father had left his coat in a company car after he got off work. The car was in the garage on the other side of the city, and Nizar was going there to get the coat for him. Nizar asked me to walk along, because he was scared to venture down the street alone after nightfall. So I went with him, and we got his father's coat. I could not let Nizar down. He is my friend. I didn't mean to upset everyone. I'm sorry, Mother."

"Do you realize what could have happened to you both while walking in these dark, empty streets in this city? Many people have been found killed in the streets at night. Don't you know that, son?"

"But, look at me mother; I'm still alive, am I not?"

Salim was smiling. Monira shook her head and hugged him.

The next morning around four, the family was roused from sleep by terrifying screams. Everyone rushed to Salim's room. They found him lying on the floor, his limbs stiff and trembling, his fists tightly closed. He appeared unconscious, as if in a trance. His whole body was soaked with perspiration. Salim's eyes, wide open, seemed to stare upward. He gasped for air, and his neck was swollen, like that of an old man with a goiter.

Monira grabbed his wrists, and with determination pulled him up toward her face, reciting verses of the Holy Qur'an. The louder she spoke, the more Salim resisted her, shaking with convulsions. But she persisted in prayer, and her words finally seemed to reach him. However, Salim's eyes remained strangely fixed upon his mother. Monira slapped his face. A few seconds later, while Monira continued reciting the verses, Salim's grotesque convulsions eased. Still, his face appeared deathlike, his body motionless. But he was alive and conscious. Monira grabbed a towel to dry his face and neck. After he had sipped some water, his brothers helped him back to bed. Soon, Salim slept, leaving the family awake in shock and astonishment.

The experience prompted his mother to take him to doctors in

Baghdad. Their diagnosis: "Salim seems to suffer from severe depression, schizophrenia, and epilepsy. We recommend sending him to Baghdad's mental health hospital for treatment."

On the train back to Nasiriya, Monira's eyes softened as she looked at her son. Speaking softly, she asked, "How did you like Baghdad?"

He replied weakly, "It was a big city. Momma. What did the doctors say about me? What exactly is wrong with me?" He turned his face toward the window.

"Nothing is wrong with you, son. They said you are a little out of mood, that's all."

"I know that, mother. That could only be part of the problem, but it's not all I'm going through. It seems no one knows why I've been ill, not even the doctors."

"What do you mean, son?" asked Monira anxiously, "Can we talk about what's bothering you? Can we talk about your dreams again? Tell me, what did you see that scared you so much?"

"I don't know exactly, Mother, I'm not sure whether they are dreams or reality."

"But, you explained it to the doctors, didn't you?"

"Yes, but the dream is never clear. A woman gets shot in the head. The blood is awful, pouring everywhere. Her eyes are wide open, staring at me. She struggles to move close to me, and I can't get away. She grabs my hand and pulls me to her. I smell the blood, the death. Her blonde hair turns red, soaked with her own blood. I want to run away, but I can't. Her eyes are evil. Her face scares me. Sometimes, I see the bullet inside her brain so clearly!"

"I know that," his mother replied softly.

"What do you mean you know? Tell me. What is going on in my life and mind? What do you know that I don't?" Salim was furious.

"I mean I realized your fears and troubles with those dreams, and I want so much to help you. What else do you see?"

After a short silence, Salim answered, again in a weak voice, "When I'm awake … I feel as if I'm always surrounded by strange people, a man or an old woman wearing black clothes. I see them sometimes. For a second, they appear before me and then very quickly they disappear."

"You see people around you?"

"Yes, just a flash, but I actually see them. The first time I was in the living room by myself. I felt someone behind me. I thought it was my imagination. One night I had the same feeling again, that someone was behind me, about to touch my shoulder. I felt terrified, tried to run, but fell down. Something grabbed my arms and shoulders and gently helped me up. I looked, but saw nothing. Then, I rushed back to my room. "One morning when I woke up, I saw a man sitting in the chair next to my bed. I was so frightened that I couldn't move. The man smiled and told me not to be afraid. He said he was a friend, that he would help and protect me. But I was afraid. I'm still afraid, Momma. I hate that man."

"What does this man look like?"

"He is short and thin. He has a massive thick beard around a small face and dirty teeth; he smiles all the time."

"Is the man here now? Can you see him?"

"Yes, he is sitting right beside you." Monira faced the spot where her son pointed. She spat into the air. "Momma, you just spat in his face," gasped Salim, "and the man ... disappeared. Did you see him too?"

Monira, with every muscle in her face drawn as taut as a sheepskin, pulled Salim to her. "Don't worry, my poor son. Just never mind. I'm here with you."

CHAPTER TWO

Salim and the Sheikh

DESPERATELY, MONIRA SEARCHED FOR A DOCTOR WHO COULD CURE HER SON. Friends advised her to take Salim back to Baghdad, this time to the holy shrines and mosques. Through their knowledge, wisdom, and piety, the holy ones had relieved the suffering of many. Their tombs were enshrined under minarets and domes, designated as holy places to worship Allah. Millions of Muslims trekked every year to commemorate the holy Imams of Baghdad, Najaf, Karbala, and Samara.

The Baghdad tombs of the Imam Al-Kathim and his grandson, Imam Al-Jawad, the seventh and ninth Shia renowned scholars, respectively, and the ancestors of the Prophet Mohammed, drew many visitors. Al-Kathim, which means the one who controls his anger, was imprisoned several times. Finally he died in prison and was buried in Baghdad. When Harun al-Rashid, the fifth Abbasid caliph threw him into prison, Al-Kathim thanked Allah, saying: "O Allah, you know that I used to ask you to give me free time to worship you. O Allah, you have done that. To you is all praise." Their elaborate mosque, with two domes and four minarets all covered with gold, was constructed more than five hundred years ago.

Worshippers crowded the shrine to pay homage to the Imams and seek help for their problems. Hundreds of men and women of all ages attended the shrine, misery and suffering etched on their faces. Surrounding the graves, they prayed loudly as if to conquer fears, hoping to be heard by the dead Imams. Some wept helplessly, while others fought the the crowd to get close to the graves. All possessed an unshakeable faith that the Imams would hear their prayers and provide relief from their suffering by God's mercy.

The tombs lay mid-shrine, in a small room covered by green silk except for four silvery windows. Although spacious, the shrine became unbearably packed with throngs of people. The high walls, beautifully ornate, sparkled with blue glazed tiles and crystal. The shrine's entrance and all roofs, the four minarets and two domes, were covered with gold. The pure gold reflected by a radiant sun dominated the scene, adding even more grandeur to the holy place.

Near the Imams' graves, inside the shrine, Salim himself was astonished to find he could not help but weep openly. Like everyone there, Monira gripped the grave's silvery window in great faith and loyalty and prayed for help. Salim could hear his mother's heartfelt petition, "Help him, please, help my son. Assist him to be healthy and happy. My son is tortured with pain, fear, and anxiety. Is it fair to leave this child in pain? My holy Imams, please, in the name of your grandfather, the Prophet Mohammed, grant my child good health and let him be happy like his brothers."

Monira led her son by the hand to the silvery window, and in a softly whispered prayer said, "Kiss your Imam's window, son. Kiss our holy Imams; kiss their hands and ask them to help you. Our holy Imams appreciate your visit. They welcome your coming to be their guest. They see you now, and they feel your pain, and they won't let you down. They will help you. I'm sure they'll help you. They are our mediators to Allah. What else do we have in this life but his mercy and forgiveness? Pray to them. I'm sure that our great Imams will supply you the power and health you need to overcome this weakness. Kiss their holy hands, son. You'll be all right soon. I'm sure."

With resurgent faith, Salim did exactly as he was told. He placed a long, deep kiss on the silvery window. His heart at that moment was filled with nothing but faith, confidence, and sincerity. He was certain what his mother told him would come to pass. The holy Imams would help him to become well.

A few minutes passed, and Salim started to feel a sort of chill up his shoulders and a slight headache, followed then quickly by a wild state of discomfort, and a disagreeable taste in his mouth. Minutes passed. Then his state of discomfort and the disagreeable taste began to ease. Suddenly, an indefinable sense of pleasure began to flow through him. A serenity and peace took over his being, making him feel happier than ever before. Salim did not understand what had happened. He was confused and scared.

"What is it?" he began whispering to himself. "What is happening to me, now, my God? Is it joy that I feel? But, where does it come from?" He kissed the window many more times. His shining, delighted eyes met the fascinating glow, the reflected mix of colorful lights, golden roofs and glistening, glazed wall tiles. It created in Salim a fantastic vision, leaving him in awe of the Imams' holiness.

The sight dizzied Salim and imbued him with a sense of peace and pleasure. His eyes beheld the magnificent arabesques and superb calligraphy. The holy place's wondrous art astonished him, giving solace to his troubled heart. At that moment, Salim's soul yielded to the grandeur of the place and the combined faith of the praying throng, filling him with ecstasy. Salim became aware of a distinct light aroma that provided yet another source of joy. What was it? Not a perfume or scent, it was some kind of breeze mixed with a mysterious fragrance. It filled the mosque and energized his being, but where did it come from? And how could it fill his being like that? How was it able to give him such happiness and tranquility? Salim looked at his mother. He saw her face shining with happiness. In extreme love, he exclaimed, "Momma, I'm so happy here! I could cry out in my happiness. I want to stay here forever!"

Then, for the first time in months, Salim felt hungry. When he told his mother of his desire to eat, she became hysterically happy. Like a little child, she danced for joy. Her voice cheered loudly, singing and telling anyone who could hear about her son's good news. "My son is cured! Our great Imams cured my child! Salim asked for something to eat. He has never asked before. Thank Allah for his mercy and thank you our great Imams!"

The people around her shouted their praise, "God is great! God is great! There is no God but Allah!"

Monira took her son in her arms, saying in great joy, "Didn't I tell you, son? Didn't I tell you that our Imams see you and feel your pain? Didn't I tell you that the Imams would award you health? That you may live happily? You've not eaten for three days, and you never asked for food before. Now that you are hungry do you know what that means? It's a sign that you're regaining your health. Thank you, Allah, for your great grace."

Salim's heart swelled with newfound contentment, as if his frail body had become one with this holy shrine. The dazzling aroma that pervaded the court seemed to Salim to infuse his very blood with new strength. In deep appreciation, Salim went to kiss the silvery window more and more, while the crowd continued chanting madly, "God is great! Our God is great! All Glory to our great Allah!"

Outside, a much larger courtyard surrounded the shrines, lined on all sides by Eiwanat, wide ornamental galleries opened on to it. The galleries were divided into small rooms used to study the holy Qur'an and traditional texts. Under a very blue May sky, the sun shone upon an afternoon of celebration. The people, exhausted after their long prayers in the shrine, sought quiet places—each family remote from others—to sit, eat, and talk quietly. Salim and his mother sat alone, happily eating shish kebabs with hot bread and drinking grape juice. After they finished, Monira performed her afternoon prayers. Salim was very pleased to hear his mother praying to Allah, thanking him and appreciating his infinite grace.

"In the Name of Allah the Most Gracious, the Most Merciful, all praise and thanks to Allah, the Lord of the Al Amlin, Mankind, Jinn and all that exists. The most Gracious, the most Merciful. The only owner and only ruling Judge of the Day of Recompense, the Day of Resurrection. You alone we worship, and you alone we ask for help for each and everything. Guide us to the straight way, the way of those on whom you have bestowed your grace, not the way of those who earned your anger, or of those who went astray." Then Monira recited from scripture,

"Say: He is Allah, the One. Allah the Self-Sufficient Master, Whom all Creatures need, He begets not, nor was he begotten. And there are none equal or comparable unto Him."

His mother's tender voice added more peace to Salim's heart. Monira and her son returned home, cheerful and grateful. Salim's health and attitude surprised his brothers. Neighbors were grateful to God's greatest grace, and for the first time, Salim's heart was filled with a sweet hope.

His life went on untroubled for weeks. By day, nothing disturbed him. However, his recurring nightmare of the blonde woman would not leave him. A frequent visitor, the nightmare was a dark companion gnawing away at his hope, like a poison in his blood.

Monira was very happy to see her son's appetite for her meals. Outwardly, Salim's spirits appeared much improved. He spoke of learning with enthusiasm, which made his mother smile. Monira wanted to express her appreciation to the holy Imams who returned her child to health. She decided to send Salim to serve in the house of the Sheikh. Monira considered it an opportunity for her son to be surrounded by the Sheikh's grace, kindness, and protection. The Sheikh was a powerful religious and political force, and he also possessed an extraordinary skill to cure the ill. People from all over the nation flooded the Sheikh's house, asking for healing, sympathy, and love. His acts of mercy endeared him to the faithful throughout Iraq. Monira had great faith in the Sheikh and was certain her son would benefit spiritually from his knowledge.

The Sheikh owned two sprawling, ornate houses on a vast tract of land near the Euphrates. They were separated by a flowing garden in the middle of a green courtyard. Each house was constructed of heavy brick and colorful glazed tiles on which were inscribed verses from the holy Qur'an. Sculptures guarded the entrance and the lofty walls were faced with veined marble.

The Sheikh, his family, and female servants occupied the larger and more attractive home. The other was located near the main road, and usually remained vacant during Friday prayers except for guests who traveled to see the Sheikh. The entire estate was contained within a high brick wall, assuring privacy for all inside. Both houses were generously furnished with new and expensive furniture. Delicate and rare hand-woven rugs, fascinating in their design and color, adorned the floors. The Sheikh possessed many charming souvenirs and special gifts coated with gold leaf. Traditional silver and copper pots, pitchers and cups of all shapes and sizes were displayed, confirming the Sheikh's wealth.

That their Sheikh made time in his demanding official schedule and room in his family's home for scores of orphans awed the townspeople. His example of hospitality and selflessness was a daily lesson, much discussed in the markets and cafes. He had become their ideal of a religious, pious, and caring man. Some parents even sent their children on their summer vacations to serve at the Sheikh's home, hoping they would obtain greater training and knowledge in the Islamic religion.

One stifling summer afternoon, Salim himself was one of thirty children in the Sheikh's house. The children were divided into teams, some swept and dusted the guest house while others watered and pruned the fragrant flowers and fruit-laden trees of the garden. Some polished the tile floors of the main residence.

Within the house a number of beautiful girls, older than Salim and the other boys and kept separate from them, moved mysteriously about. Their willowy forms showed up near the garden from time to time, their hair shining, their large brown eyes darting, and their lovely figures hidden beneath gauzy flowing robes. The girls shared responsibilities, including teaching young orphans and preparing them for the next year of school. The eldest of the mysterious girls cooked for the Sheikh and his frequent honored guests. A cadre of the most promising older girls who had earned the Sheikh's trust were blessed with special responsibilities. These girls—aged eighteen or nineteen and usually fifteen in number—trained intensively in singing and dancing for special events. After a two-month course, each girl received the title of Mullaiah. The Mullaiahs served and entertained the public by performing at special events, singing and dancing and entertaining at town ceremonies. For unhappy events, they would perform sad songs and acts. Their earnings for such duties went to the Sheikh's treasury. The Mullaiahs each served at the Sheikh's pleasure. He named their duties and obligations, and any girl who accepted this position knew she would remain in the Sheikh's house and service as long as he demanded.

Adela, a gorgeous nineteen-year-old girl, was chief of the Sheikh's Mullaiahs. Tall and slim, with brown hair flowing down to mid-back, Adela flashed hypnotic dark eyes. Charming as she swayed and sang, she stirred excitement whenever she performed. Adela seemed in perfect harmony with wild nature.

Every time Adela encountered Salim, she fixed her intense eyes upon him, leaving him trembling and confused. Adela's penetrating gaze was like no other among the Mullaiahs. Her occasional attentions excited Salim. He loved those rare feelings, but they also frightened him. Salim tossed and turned during his nights, unable to comprehend Adele's interest or intentions. Salim was a solitary boy. He worked apart from others and talked to no one. The games and play of other children held no fascination for him. He disdained the petty tricks some played, causing ringleaders to taunt him with insults and slanders.

After noticing his distress for weeks in silence, the wild creature, Adela, stepped in, using her beauty and wit to silence the ringleaders. Once, she struck two bigger boys who were fighting one another, leaving each with a bloody nose and black eye. After that, the ringleaders gave Adela a wide path. One day, about ten weeks after Salim entered the Sheikh's house, he sat alone under the big fig tree, meditating on life as was his custom after finishing his duties. Adela appeared from time to time, refilling her water can from a nearby tap. Turning toward Salim as she favored him with a glance from her bright, charming eyes, the boy could not help noticing as her deep red lips curved into an enticing smile.

Adela bent to turn the tap, her slender torso twisted from the waist, and her bare arm extended. Salim could not remove his eyes as her firm breasts slipped downward, offering a glimpse of their shape through her dress. He imagined them white as milk, each globe the size of a baby rabbit, with pointed, puffy nipples. Caught leering, Salim found himself lost in a cloud of contrition, ecstasy, and embarrassment. Desire flamed through his blood, into every inch of his trembling body. As Salim gawked, Adela's unflinching stare fed his hungry eyes. After what seemed like a long time, Salim came to his senses in an sudden acknowledgement of her desire. Then Adela stood upright quickly and walked back inside the house, her backside holding his attention until the door closed. As she disappeared, Salim floundered into a malaise of despair and uncertainty. What did her bodily display and prolonged stare portend? Salim's heart swelled one moment and deflated the next in a tumble of feelings unprecedented in his young life.

Later, Salim remembered that, before entering the house, Adela had turned back to look at him, exuding charm and mystery. She had offered him an inviting wink from her wide eyes, and then disappeared inside. Salim's throat felt dry. His heart throbbed like a scared frog. His blood slowly cooled, and he lifted a shivering hand to swipe away a cold sweat from his forehead.

From time to time, the Sheikh would come to watch the boys busily cleaning the yard, washing floors, or slicing vegetables. As usual, he found Salim alone. It seemed to Salim that the Sheikh usually gave him a shrewd look. Salim, confused by the Sheikh's demeanor, hurried to him, bowing to kiss his hands, just as the other boys did. Once, he dared a quick glance at the Sheikh, and found the Revered One carefully scrutinizing him. The Sheikh's hands patted Salim's hair, neck, and shoulders, causing the boy to shiver.

On a second occasion, Salim chanced another look at the Sheikh. This time, however, he found his master's countenance serene, full of amity and harmony. His eyes glimmering, the Sheikh continued stroking Salim's hair. A sudden cold sweat and tremor made Salim feel sick to his stomach. The Sheikh's charisma overwhelmed the boy. The master's special look dominated Salim's thoughts, intimidating and perplexing him. Filled with a flaming heart and clashing ideas, Salim wished to scream, to run far away and never come back again.

The Sheikh whispered to him. "Look at me, boy. Look at my eyes." Salim looked at him. The Sheikh smiled and said loudly, "Did you eat well, Salim? Are you satisfied?"

Feeling something inside of him shrink, Salim muttered, "Yes … yes sir, I ate. I'm satisfied."

The Sheikh, whose eyes seemed to penetrate Salim's skin and bones, as if hunting that shrinking part of the boy, then asked, "How old are you, Salim?"

The answer came quickly, "Seventeen, sir." Hardness suddenly filled the Sheikh's face, while horror engulfed Salim, his whole being bewildered by the Sheikh's expression. The Revered One quickly turned away and entered the house, leaving the boy dazed, both confused and relieved.

An old man in his seventies, the Sheikh was tall, bulky, with a large belly. His unrelenting gaze reminded Salim of a hungry wolf, yet it sprang from a distinguished face with a long white beard. The Sheikh was robed in an elegant silk cloak, princely apparel, yet he never seemed a happy man. To Salim, the Sheikh—in spite of hourly visitors—seemed friendless, even without family, unrelated to any woman or suckling child. His face, thought Salim, looked like that of a man who trusted no one.

In spite of his personal isolation, the Sheikh was admired and revered throughout Nasiriya for his religious and conservative life. To most towns-people, he symbolized the Islamic faith incarnate. They spoke of the Sheikh as a model of holiness, an undisputed leader, a tireless defender and preserver of Allah's doctrine. Fathers spoke of him in hushed tones as a teacher and interpreter of Islamic philosophy and its sacred rules.

No one in town knew about his early life, his origins or parentage. Occasionally, a story would creep forth from a mother deprived of his help or a child kicked out of his palace. Once in a great while, an elder would tell a story of the Sheikh's arrival in the town some thirty years ago. Someone said his real name was Rahman Al-Deen Gubbta and that he came from India. Someone said Afghanistan. Another Pakistan—no one was really sure. It was said that he had served during the World War as a personal guard for an English general, that following the war and the dismantling of the Ottoman Empire, that Great Britain had appointed this general to a high position in the new Baghdad government.

In the market, someone said they had heard that this Rahman Al-Deen Gubbta took advantage of his position with the general, embezzling a large sum of money from the nascent government, that he was convicted and spent seventeen months in a roach-infested cell. As the story went, the general took pity on him and, prior to leaving his post in Baghdad several years later, the general mediated the future Sheikh's release. After obtaining his freedom, it was said that Rahman Al-Deen Gubbta left Baghdad and traveled to Nasiriya where he began a new life as a wealthy young businessman. Here he bought considerable property from private citizens and the local government and built his two beautiful houses. In a short time he became a very influential man, for success is respected in most towns—and revered as a reward for honesty and devotion to Allah.

The young businessman cultivated his new-found position by proclaiming himself a conservative Muslim. A strict practitioner of the Islamic faith, he attended the Mosque for prayers five times a day. An educated man who spoke English fluently, he preached to the people about the Qur'an, interpreting its meanings with remarkable eloquence. Its rules he elucidated sternly.

In no time, the young stranger established himself in the eyes of locals as an educated man deserving of respect, even deference. Inviting the best people to feasts at his home, the young man demonstrated his charisma in moderation and wisdom when discussing pressing issues vital to Nasiriya's people. In return, the townspeople embraced their new neighbor, inviting him to attend weddings, circumcisions, and feasts, where he generously offered gifts and money. Nasiriya's residents grew to love him and found in his gifts and companionship a new hope for their lives and faith. It did not appear unseemly when, after a few years in residence, the young man proclaimed himself a Sheikh, and asserted his place as a religious leader.

Monira, like most townsfolk when seeking a favor for their daughters or sons, did not consider these old tales of the Sheikh, but rather thought only to advance their children in the eyes of this man of wisdom and generosity. Monira sought some way for Salim to benefit from the powerful one's grace and kindness, wisdom and generosity. She felt the Sheikh's spirit and wisdom would provide protection from the evil forces threatening her son's happiness. Once, as Salim was cleaning dust away in the guesthouse, a girl came to him, her eyes shining. She chirped happily, "Congratulations, Salim, the Sheikh has honored you by making you his bodyguard."

"What…What does that mean?" Salim asked with obvious astonishment.

"You'll be the most favorite one to him. You will have the honor of carrying his pitcher and towel, to pour water on his hands at times of ablution and after meals. You will take care of his library and his special needs. However, the most important thing is this: you will accompany him to the mosque."

Salim felt his mouth go dry and his lungs fill involuntarily. He seemed to momentarily lose control of his eyes, which darted from floor to wall to vase of their own impatience. He stopped the girl. "Can't someone else replace me? What if I refuse? What will happen?"

Her smile disappeared. Astonished, she glared at him and shouted angrily, "Can anyone refuse the will of the Sheikh? And you, little puppy, how can you dare deny such an honor and blessing?" She turned abruptly and stalked away.

Grief surged in Salim's heart. Strange pictures filled his head: someone shoved him back on his boyhood bed and slammed the door, seemingly never to return. He could not bear the image of suffocating in his parents' house, where so much was expected of him. He wanted to be on his own, left alone, living his own life.

The truth was that during most nights, Salim had trouble sleeping away from his family, without the sound of his mother's amulets clicking, or her sad and mournful songs. By day, the Sheikh's glances caused him great discomfort.

But becoming the bodyguard offered one compelling consolation, he would be near Adela. He went on analyzing the reasons for this honor. Why him? He convinced himself it must relate to his quiet nature. Upon receiving the news of his advancement, his mother was joyful. She said to him, "Don't you see, don't you see, my child? It has only taken a few months for you to gain the Sheikh's trust and receive his blessing. Many boys might live there for years, yet, never receive such an honor."

Salim replied, "I don't want to do it, Momma. I have no desire to carry the pitcher and wait until he slurps the last of his soup, and do many other things. And why should I do all that? I'm no one's slave."

"Listen, boy," she said reproachfully, "This honor is by the Sheikh's blessing. Besides, thanks to Allah, your body is stronger. Your being in the Sheikh's presence will make you a spiritually strong, knowledgeable, and independent man. This is your chance. How long I have waited for it. I only want to be proud of you as a man, just as I am of your brothers. Your health is getting better. You're becoming a man; this is your chance."

Salim felt sick inside. He did not like his mother's advice. Neverthe-less, Monira's serious tone obliged Salim to accept the Sheikh's honor. Salim accepted his new job, the duties of which proved less onerous than expected. Five times a day, Salim prepared the Sheikh's prayer rug. At mealtimes, Salim solemnly presented the Sheikh with his pitcher and towel. In fact, it was Salim who pushed the fragrant meal cart from the kitchen into his master's private room, where the Sheikh would eat alone, or sometimes with Adela. After morning ablutions, during which he also stood ready with the ornamented pitcher and fresh towel, Salim also helped the Sheikh dress in his gown and cloak, even fasten the Revered One's shoelaces.

At mid-afternoon, when the day's visitors had departed, the boy would bring books from the Sheikh's library to his sitting room. At dark, he would return them carefully, each to its place in the library. Salim partially commanded the house's provisions, dealing with vendors. Issuing these orders and approving deliveries, Salim realized that, in a small way, he was exercising the Sheikh's considerable temporal power.

The Sheikh was accustomed to reading. At these times, Salim kept the Revered One company by also reading until his master finished. When they read in the library room, Salim became aware of the extreme orderliness of the rug, the table, and the bookshelves. The multicolored rug smelled new, though its design was traditional. The table smelled of careful tending with olive oil and soft cloths. Oaken shelves filled the lower half of all four walls, except for a doorway and a single window opposite. Golden-lettered volumes spoke of the Sheikh's interests: philology, rhetoric, philosophy, history, poli-tics, and theology. Colorful paintings covered the polished walls above the bookshelves. In one painting, the branches of a forest bent with a burden of heavy snow. A second portrayed white pelicans standing along the coast of a faraway sea, iridescent from a distant sunset. Another featured rapacious lions chasing a flock of frightened deer. Salim was aware that he had never seen the sea or a lion, and that the last time he had seen snow was one unusu-ally cold winter day, years ago.

Hidden from public eyes, the inner rooms of the Sheikh's home failed to reflect the Sheikh's outward image of devotion to Qur'anic mysticism. Salim was shocked to see that many of the Revered One's personal habits contrasted sharply with his public image as a conservative man of the Islamic faith. During his first week as the Sheikh's bodyguard, Salim discovered that four sleeping rooms the architect provided for the Sheikh's children were unoccupied. In fact, he learned, this man was childless. Far from being an aesthete, the Sheikh lived a life of both comfort and worldly privilege. From the richness of the robes that the Sheikh donned each morning to the thick carpets that covered his floors and the jewelry on display in his large wardrobe, evidence of worldly indulgence was everywhere.

While the Sheikh had no children, he kept a young wife who was bright-eyed, intelligent, and indulged. She was also alarmingly fat. At first, Salim was chagrined by Nada's slovenly habits, feeling them an affront to his master. While Salim was not authorized to enter Nada's sleeping room, he frequently observed her loitering in bed at all hours of the day, as her door was seldom closed. She practiced no modesty, allowing anyone who passed her private room to observe her in a state of undress throughout most days, reclining indolently beside a silver platter of sweets, fruits, and juices. Her folds of belly fat competed for attention with her breasts, topped as they were with nipples that, in turn, competed for color with the red grapes Nada held above her open mouth. Surely, Salim thought indignantly, the Sheikh deserves a wife who takes care to keep herself only unto him, a wife whose habits maintain a svelte figure and preserves her modesty only for her husband's eyes.

On several such occasions, Salim considered his responsibility to inform his master of his wife's wanton disregard for the norms of a faithful Islamic household. Still, the idea of disclosing to the Sheikh that his eyes had fallen upon his wife's nakedness quelled Salim's tongue. Continuing his work in the private home, Salim often had occasion to pass Nada's open doorway, and he was not so religious that his eyes were always averted from the wanton display. While Nada was in some ways attractive, youth providing a glow even to the obesity and expensive perfumes titillating the nose of any innocent, Salim determined to avoid temptation, even while his eyes betrayed his best intentions. Nada's broad, made-up face—antimony-painted with hazel eyes and a small nose set over thick lips—spoke to parts of his body which willpower sometimes did not reach. Besides, Nada was not always alone in her lair. On several occasions, Salim saw girls of the household attending Nada in her bed, girls of perhaps nineteen years who seemed to enjoy their mistresses' attentions altogether too freely. These girls were never completely clothed, affording Salim glimpses of their small breasts, thighs, and even that forbidden tuft of hair between their legs.

Salim, spying solely to report to his master, watched Nada's thick fingers reach out to twist a girl's nipple. Surely, carrying such news to the Sheikh was beyond his duties, Salim thought as the moans of carnal release drowned out the complaints of silken pillows and the tinkling of golden bracelets and amulets.

On those rare occasions when Salim interrupted Nada in full robes, she was entertaining cloth merchants, studying their wares, fresh from the loom, selecting unusual fabrics to add to her wardrobe. Salim laughed at the thought of Nada buying more robes, given her infrequent use of those that already hung unworn in her rooms. Making a note to report her extravagant ways to his master, Salim hurried on to the kitchen, where a much-needed delivery of olive oil awaited his inspection.

When he returned from the kitchen an hour later, Salim saw that Nada had returned to her private room and, leaving the door standing open, was naked, as were the two girls in her company. The three swayed, dancing above a silver platter where fruits of several trees and wines awaited. Arms inter-twined, the young women—not more than a year or two older than Salim himself—rested their hands on each other's shoulders and smoked cigarettes.

Passing by Nada's door thirty minutes later, after inspecting his master's stable, Salim's moment at Nada's door revealed one young woman quietly and gracefully rubbing Nada's breasts, while the other used her tongue to attend to Nada's private parts, as the Sheikh's wife shivered in sensual intox-ication. When fully satiated, Nada's lustful pleasures carried her into a faint. Her attendants looked to each other then, and as they joined their bodies beside the resting form of their mistress, one girl winked at Salim. Was it an invitation? Salim realized that he had loitered at the scene longer than was necessary to report to his master, and he moved away with some regret.

Salim became accustomed to such scenes in the Sheikh's house. All the women seemed lustful, exploring one another in ways that Salim had never imagined. Demonstrating talents and techniques that his brothers had never mentioned in adolescent imaginings, the behavior of these women educated Salim to a far broader view of relationships than—he was quite sure—even his father, at his advanced age, had ever imagined. The boundaries of what he once considered reasonable and acceptable behavior had changed forever.

Every Friday morning, families poured in from the town of Nasiriya, surrounding villages, and the adjacent countryside, their donkeys and wagons loaded with precious gifts. They came to the home of the Revered One, seeking the blessings appropriate to faithful men and women. Hard-working families whose possessions in life were few, they hoped to gain God's forgiveness through the gifting of the fruits of their labor to His mediator. The open courtyard was usually packed with people leading roped sheep, cows, and goats. Some carried noisy chickens, and some shouldered wrapped fish. All of these animals were laid at the feet (or placed in the waiting sheds and storerooms) of the learned Sheikh, who appeared before them in rough robes, suitable to a humble man of wisdom and faith. A large bowl, designated for contributions, quickly filled with coins.

When not standing to greet them, the Sheikh would lounge on his large, intricately-carved chair. Whether standing among the masses or sitting to receive their holy kisses, he watched their eyes, often glistening with tears for their griefs and grievances. Some people ran to him, kissing his hands and feet and touching his cloak. To bless them, the Sheikh scooped a fingertip in a jar of henna and solemnly marked each of their foreheads as a mark of piety. Among the innocents, shouts broke out. The yard surged with passionate cries of religious ecstasy:

"God is great! God is great!"

"Cure us of our ailments!"

"Lay your hands upon us and assure us of God's forgiveness!"

"Cure our sick child!"

"Be our mediator to Allah!"

"We know you will never disappoint us! Bless us, Sheikh!"

"Mediate for us by your place with God,

and by your grandfather, Mohammed."

The Sheikh's face blossomed with delight. His eyes burned even brighter, while his cheeks warmed to a rosy glow. Arms outstretched, he beckoned to the throng, and passed his hands over their solemn, bowed heads. At these very moments, Salim would recall the vision of Nada's corpulent bulk, lying in the luxury of her private rooms, and of the attentions of her handmaidens. While Salim did not approve of the Sheikh's material indulgences, he was contrite that he had not reported Nada's indiscretions to the Revered One. Surely, no husband deserved a wife who cavorted in such a way with other women!

That night, after the stables, sheds, and storerooms brimming with the gifts of the people had been secured, Salim returned exhausted to the Sheikh's private rooms. He was overdue to present the pitcher and towel for his master's bedtime ablutions, and he rushed to perform this last duty of his long day. Quietly slipping into the Sheikh's sleeping suite through the servant's entrance into an anteroom separated from the main sleeping room by a sheer curtain, Salim was shocked at what he saw in the candlelight around his master's bed. A slim girl sat astride his master, a familiar form yet unidentified, as the hair of her bowed head hid her face. Surely this was not one of the girls who attended Nada, but some other, more desirable silhouette. As his master bucked under his bed partner, she raised her head, revealing a delicious throat and thrusting her young breasts forward. Unbelievable, thought Salim. Adela.

The old man moved with urgent thrusts followed by a period of quiet, like an old wagon horse unable to pull another mile. Salim, hardly having taken in the idea that the pure Adela was being used in this way, realized that the old man—notwithstanding his desire—was frustrated at his sexual failure. Unlike the high-pitched moans of ecstacy Salim had heard so many times in

Nada's room, here he was presented with the deep, anguished moans of an old man unable to discipline his aging body to the task at hand. And the young woman mounted atop him was herself frustrated, for the promised satisfactions of the bed had been attempted but not delivered. Observing his master's painful moaning was doubly painful for Salim, whose own nocturnal visions had placed him in the position now occupied by his master. The Revered One had dragged Salim's own Adela, the pure object of his nightly dreams and sweats, into the bed that only Nada should occupy.

Salim had watched secretly through the sheer curtain, unseen himself because the anteroom was unlit, seeing the old body of the Sheikh grasping in vain for its lost powers. No amount of perfume, no number of bedside candles, not even the beauty of the innocent Adela could bring the Sheikh's timeworn body to perform as the young woman needed. Adela smiled and started kissing the Sheikh's face and mouth. Difficult minutes passed. Adela, then, tried again to stir him. After much effort, the Sheikh would feel he had regained his manhood, while pain would overcome Adela as she forced herself to accept him. The Sheikh lay between her thighs, and in those moments lost his manhood again.

Then, in disgust at himself, the old man rolled away from Adela, facing the opposite wall, turning away in his rage, for her very beauty mocked him. Adela lay on her back in the candle light, her toned belly unsatisfied, unfilled. She lay there limp, disappointed.

But her disappointment was nothing compared to the anguish that Salim felt, coming to the realization of her loss of innocence. She was no longer the Adela of his dreams. Now some other woman occupied the familiar, lovely form of Adela, a woman incapable of looking him in the eyes. After the Sheikh slipped from the room, Salim watched Adela give her overflowing femininity to her dreams and imaginations. Her fingers playing madly with the soft hair between her sculptured thighs, she appeared to bring forth a Nirvana.

Dazed, Salim departed the Sheikh's private rooms and found himself in the courtyard. The screams of an old, stooped woman carrying the form of a limp infant abruptly returned Salim to reality. The hag presented the child to the Sheikh, who had just stepped from the shade of a doorway.

Holding the limp form at arm's length, the old woman spoke to the Sheikh, "Take him, take my grandson. He has lost his speech and all of life's senses. Bring him back to health and sensation. Bring him back to health by your place at God's right hand. Heal my grandson and make him speak and feel again."

The Sheikh straightened his backbone and his eyes shone. Slowly, he extended his upturned palms to accept the sick baby. Then he lifted the small form to his lips, kissed him, and then held the child next to his heart. Embracing the infant, the Revered One suddenly fixed his eyes on Salim, who felt captured, as if the Sheikh's eyes had turned him into a spiritless statue. Salim was unable to move or get away, like an animal finding itself caught in a hunter's trap. The Sheikh's eyes fixed on him with absolute authority. Salim's blood seemed to dry in his veins. His pulse pounded. A mad horror consumed him.

Then the Sheikh's head lowered and his eyes moved to the still baby. Salim heard a faint cry from the infant. Others heard it, faint but unmistakable. Suddenly, people started to cry as if they, too, had been awakened from a stupor. Acclamations spread. People shouted madly. Women screamed, and men kissed the Sheikh's hands. The baby's grandmother fell to her knees and kissed the Revered One's sandaled feet.

One of them—the infant's father?—cried out with a voice full of faith, "God is great! God is great, and we're all for your sake! We would die for you, Revered One! May the merciful Allah guard and protect you. You are the friend blessed by God." The people kissed the Sheikh's hands and feet, while his face melted into a smile.

The Sheikh's eyes roamed the crowd until they settled again upon Salim, whom they found astonished, marveling at what had happened. Salim's terrified heart pounded while his body began to stiffen under the Sheikh's prolonged gaze. He felt as if the old man's eyes plunged into his depths. Salim—unsure whether his master had been aware of his presence in the private rooms—was frightened by the master's eye contact. He could hear the Sheikh whispering, "Look at me, Salim. Look into my eyes. Look."

A desire to weep permeated Salim, who felt his soul encircled, and his power fading. Amid the crowd's mad screams came the Sheikh's continued whispering, "Don't be afraid, Salim. Just look at me." Salim looked. Their eyes performed a kind of solitary communion amid the throng of holy revelers. Salim felt drained, his legs shook, and his mind raced; his body even began to retreat. Re-entering a hallway adjacent to the kitchen, Salim heard the people shouting now as if their voices flooded from some remote place—from the earth's depths.

Salim began to faint, and settled on a milkmaid's stool in the unoccu-pied passageway, his whole being weak, scared, surrounded, and dominated. Some unknown force sapped his power and will. He felt that death lurked nearby. Apparitions of the dead flooded his mind. He saw his grandmother, Attia, her cheeks sunken, emaciated, stretched from bone to bone. Then came Majid, the son of the grocer, who died burning, and drowned Sabri, his cousin; and Fetehi, whose corpse was discolored by electrocution. The parade of the dead chanted as it passed, an apparent procession without end. The eyes of the Sheikh, however, still held him, piercing his depths like an emblazoned sword.

In an instant, the ordeal was over. Salim awoke to find that he was lying on his bed in the Sheikh's house, sweating profusely. His frightened eyes roamed the small room, and met Adela's. She was sitting beside him, apparently waiting for him to awake. Her beautiful face and affectionate smile made Salim's pulse surge. Yet, Salim was fearful because of the scene he had witnessed between his master and Adela. He suspected that Adela had seen his eyes behind the veil, and he did not understand how she could face him now, how she could look him in the eye. Fear filled Salim and he asked, "What happened? What happened to me?"

Her smile widened, as if in innocence. "Nothing, my dear friend. It seems you were tired and fainted among the shouting. Do not worry. The Sheikh has sent me to assure you that everything is all right."

Salim considered the events in the Sheikh's private rooms as well as the events in the courtyard. Had he dreamed either ... or both? What had happened to him, he knew not. When he recalled the Sheikh's eyes during the healing, Salim was certain that at least the courtyard scene had been real. Salim began crying, hot tears streaming over his cheeks. Embarrassed to cry in front of Adela, he turned his head toward the wall and pleaded, "I want to go home. I want to see my Momma. I'm tired and sick."

As Adela replied, Salim could not help focusing on her kissable lips. Yet her words contained no romance, "As you like, Salim. Go whenever you want, and do not forget to remember me to your dear mother." Then, she bent over him, and matching her lips with his, gave him a long kiss. His heart shook like a startled bird. Salim felt joy mixed with astonishment. She kissed and embraced him with the eagerness he had so longed for. Her flowing hair covered his face and her perfume entered his very soul. How much he had wished to live this moment. Everything else had left his heart—doubt, frustration, and uncertainty—of these nothing remained but longing, rapture, and sweet dreams. Her disarmingly feminine voice demanded, "You, dear friend, when will you grow up? Why don't you grow up quickly? Come again soon. Don't be late. Don't make me wait."

Salim went home. When he told his mother about his decision to leave the Sheikh's service, she exclaimed, "Why? Are you not happy there? All of the people in the Sheikh's house admire you and take care of you. The Sheikh himself expressed to me his happiness in your work. What is wrong with you, my child? What makes you so sad? Tell me, please."

With choked voice he answered, "Momma, I think my duty in serving the Sheikh and his house requires greater efforts than what we both had thought."

But Salim did go back, in spite of himself. He could not forget, and remained drawn to the eyes of the Sheikh, the embrace of Adela, the moans of debauchery, and the sight of naked young bodies. He could not stop thinking about the Sheikh's sexual failures and Adela's fingers playing in the soft hair between her thighs. After Friday prayers, Salim also thought that perhaps he could help in correcting the wrongdoings in that house. Salim thought Allah, who healed the sick through the Sheikh's presence, may also plan a use for his sometimes weak, sometimes willful, sometimes lustful self.

Two years had passed since Salim first came to live at the Sheikh's compound. Accordingly, his relations with his master and all others were firmly established. The Sheikh was accustomed to keeping Salim at his side, whether in sitting with guests, going to the mosque to pray, meeting people to solve their problems, or preaching sermons after prayers. Salim found that the Sheikh was educated in all fields of religion and life. He never saw the Sheikh appear awkward in answering any question or in proposing a solution. The Sheikh had a unique way of convincing others to agree with him. His calm, deep voice promoted comfort and confidence. Thus, Salim became attached to the Sheikh. But he was constantly torn between the Sheikh's public and personal lives. The public life was one to greatly admire. But the personal life, known fully only to Salim, made the young man at times lose his faith in his master and everything the Sheikh represented. This constant battle remained within Salim alone, as if his lungs were at war with his kidneys.

Salim, nineteen and no longer a child, became gradually more sexually active in the Sheikh's house. He dreamed of the Mullaiahs, those who had outgrown their childish skinniness. Those whose breasts he sometimes saw when he peered into Nada's open door. On occasion, Nada, the Sheikh's wife, invited him to her bed when the household was asleep. With her, Salim practiced the skills he had watched her Mullaiahs working with her. In spite of her corpulence, Salim found pleasure in giving Nada pleasure. Signs of passion and delight appeared in her eyes as she bade him goodnight. Also, once in a while, Nada sent one of her favorites, one of the older Mullaiahs, to his bedroom. With them, Salim pretended to be the Sheikh—but a potent, amorous Sheikh—and plunged into fantastic journeys of love-making, with different sexual experiences generously provided by each one.

Adela remained the only woman he could not bed, although her single kiss excited him more than an hour with two sweaty Mullaiahs combined. Her glance, alone, moved him so that he had to take a back stair until his excitement abated. Adele played with him: catching him alone when others were out or busy in another part of the house. At those moments, her tongue found his lips, her hands explored his body, and the occasional touch of her nipples would send him hurriedly back to his bedroom to resolve his sensations without embarrassing himself. These passionate encounters were too infrequent for Salim, and left him sorrowful and puzzled by her mysterious behavior.

One other thing occupied Salim's concerns. Every Friday, when the Sheikh met the crowds pouring into his courtyard for a blessing or cure, Salim would face the same fainting problem. He ascribed it to his physical weakness. He had come to the Sheikh's service because he was not strong in body or in spirit. That old, familiar nightmare of the blonde woman committing suicide tortured him still—almost every night. These deeply personal weaknesses, he believed, blended with the people's demanding screams, creating more sadness within his heart. All of these fears and uncertainties mixed with a new horror when the Sheikh captured Salim with his eyes and then miraculously cured the sick.

Salim blamed himself; his simultaneous state of belief and disbelief in the Sheikh seemed to contribute to his diminished physical and mental powers.

At last, Salim gathered his courage and asked the Sheikh, "Tell me, sir, by God, what is happening to me? I suddenly find myself unconscious when I'm with you and the multitude together."

A little smile was the Sheikh's only answer.

Salim, however, insisted, "Please, honorable Sheikh, let me know, guide me. Let your wisdom conduct me. I'm your obedient servant. This secret torments me. Please tell me, and ease my discomfort. Please, Sheikh."

The Sheikh turned toward Salim and his sharp eyes made Salim shiver again. The Sheikh replied in a haunting whisper, "You're my mediator, Salim. Your job is to mediate between me and the people whom I bless." Like a bird winged by a reckless shot, the reply disoriented Salim.

In all innocence and sincerity, Salim bluntly asked, "I don't understand. What do you mean I'm your mediator, Sheikh? How could I be a mediator for something when I have no idea what it is I mediate?"

A sudden wave of unpleasantness appeared on the Sheikh's face, making Salim suffer even greater fear. "I give my patients some of your power, Salim. I offer them physical and spiritual energy out of your pure soul. The youth and vigor you possess does not belong to you alone. I help my people by dispensing it, Salim. Those for whom I care cannot be cured without your help. And naturally, as I strip power out of your soul, you're unable to stay strong, and so you temporarily lose consciousness."

Salim shuddered. A great hatred toward the Sheikh overwhelmed him. "How is that, Sheikh? How are you able to do this? How can you transfer power out of my body?"

The Sheikh laughed. While his face again became stern, the Sheikh continued in a more conciliatory voice, "It is not easy, Salim, to comprehend such peculiar work. It takes a long time to learn. First you have to overcome all your weaknesses and fears. Someday, I will teach you. Someday, you will know my secrets and eventually, you will replace me. On the day when I die, Salim, you will become Sheikh of these people." As he finished this statement, the Sheikh let out a sudden laugh as though he, himself, could not believe it.

Salim gathered his strength to reply firmly, "I do not want to be Sheikh! I have no desire to replace you—not now, not ever! It is *my life* that you have been sucking out, *my life* you have been destroying. I came to you to become strong, but you have been trying to kill me! Why would you do such an evil thing?" Salim's panicked eyes met the Sheikh's angry eyes for an eternal moment. An eerie silence took possession of the room.

Then the Sheikh exhibited a strange robustness and breathed deeply, as if summoning the strength to reveal his innermost secret to Salim. In obvious revulsion, the Sheikh replied very quietly, "Why, dear boy, because I can. Those innocent people you're always meeting, they have faith in me. They deify me. To them, I am the prudence and wisdom that reassures them. Their faith in me has been imprinted in their blood. They trust me so that I've become the secret to their happiness and hope.

"And for everyone entrusted in me, I must provide protection. I must harness all possible means to allow them to live in serenity and peace. This path comforts the people, who are frightened by death, by sickness, even by the weather. This is also my path, so that I can continue to rule over them. I get to help them feel God's serenity. I heal them and their infants. Joy is mine when they happily obey me and bring treasure to my house. My tools to provide strength include you, my dear Salim. Your strength goes through me to the people, providing happiness and health."

In bewilderment and despair, Salim cried out, "But that is an iniquity, Sheikh! I believed in you, I trusted you. You knowingly took the power of my youth and health. Instead of helping me, you've been using me; you've been draining me of my life force!"

In a saturnine voice, the Sheikh commented, "Oh, Salim! Save your superfluous words for another time. You can't deceive me with your pretend innocence. You've no faith in me anymore, Salim. You and I both know that. Or let's say your faith in me is not real, at any rate. I know that too, but I'm still keeping you in this house because I need you. You see, Salim, we share a number of mutual interests. But talking about my people is a completely different story. Don't you ever dare to compare yourself with any of them!

"You already know some of my weaknesses, Salim, but my people are completely ignorant of my problems. To them, I'm a celestial being. Do you know what that means to me, Salim? Do you know what it feels like to be worshipped? Well, you'll be mediating between us whether you like it or not. Besides, I've cherished you and paid lavishly for all your physical satisfactions. I think you know what I'm talking about, don't you?"

Salim backed away, realizing he had come to the Sheikh's service to nurture his body and spirit, yet had sold his soul for gratifications of the flesh. Sex. Salim, who was no longer a boy, knew in his heart that he had partaken of the same unholy pastimes of which, only a few months before, he had schemed to reveal to the Sheikh. Salim knew that he had made an exchange for the pleasures of the bed and for the greed of living close to worldly power.

———

One afternoon while Salim was in the guest house, he happened to notice—through the window—a stranger standing in the front yard, looking around. The stranger stepped deliberately, peering into windows, observing the elegant garden, as if inspecting the compound for possible purchase.

Salim entered the courtyard and addressed the stranger, "Peace is upon you, friend." Salim waited patiently to determine the nature of the visitor's business.

"And peace is upon you, too. It's a very nice place you've got here."

"Thank you, yes, I appreciate it as well," Salim hedged.

"I'm here to see the Sheikh. Is he at home?" the stranger continued.

"What's your business with him?" Salim questioned.

"Oh, I'm an old friend, but we haven't seen each other for a very long time. Life is strange sometimes. Anyway, my name is Omer Mahdi. Just let him know I'm here."

"Welcome, Omer, to you and all friends of the Sheikh. My name is Salim. Please, come inside and be comfortable." The man followed Salim into the guest house.

"Look at that!" the man cried out in disbelief. "Everything is so neatly arranged and so expensive. How is it that some people are so lucky to have such wealth? How is it that some afford to live like this, Salim? Do you have any idea?"

Salim just looked at the man and did not answer. He, too, wondered how one acquires such wealth in life. "I'll get you some tea," Salim said calmly. "Have you eaten lunch yet? I can bring a meal if you're hungry."

"No, tea will be perfect," the man said as he himself seemed lost in thought.

"Are you his son or a relative of the Sheikh, Salim?"

"No, I'm just ... just his assistant. Look, if you would like to wash up, the bathroom is over there. I'll get your tea and see about notifying the Sheikh of your arrival," Salim said as he hurried to leave the room.

The Sheikh had just finished his prayers when Salim stepped into his room. "There's a man in the guest house who wishes to see you," Salim reported excitedly.

"A man? What does he want?"

"I have no idea, but he said he was an old friend and that you and he haven't seen each other for a long time," Salim responded, short of breath.

"What's his name?"

"Omer Mahdi."

Suddenly, the Sheikh's eyes twitched and glowed strangely, and his face took on a dark expression. He stood up, looked around thoughtfully, and then demanded nervously, "Describe this man."

"He's maybe in his fifties, of medium height, dark skinned, black eyes, thin and gray haired," Salim replied quickly, noticing an unusual concern in the Sheikh's voice.

The Sheikh brooded while Salim went on talking, "There is something unusual about the man. He sounds mean, or perhaps it is certainty about something, like a man who knows the answers to his own questions."

"Send him to me," the Sheikh commanded, in a tone that Salim had not heard before.

The man followed Salim through the big garden and into the main house. Salim opened the library door and introduced the stranger to the Sheikh. When he saw Mahdi, the Sheikh smiled and exclaimed, "Omer Mahdi, the troubled man! So you finally got out? How long have you been free?"

"Last month." Without invitation, the man threw himself into the largest chair in the room and continued, "The first thing I did was look you up. But, surprisingly, I didn't have to search very hard to find you. You've become well known with your little empire in Nasiriya. I hear you've even earned the title of Sheikh. What a ridiculous life," Omer huffed, emitting a sarcastic laugh.

The Sheikh's face flushed as he waved to Salim to leave them alone. Salim left but, troubled and curious, hid himself in the adjoining room where he could hear them talk and watch their shadows on a wall.

"So, what has brought you here, Omer?"

"A smart person like you shouldn't have to ask such a stupid question. However, you know very well why I'm here, Rahman Al-Deen, or should I say Sheikh, or whoever it is you are now. You know very well why I'm here."

"You better be careful of what you're saying here. I'm warning you. Don't mess with me, Omer. I'm a completely different person now." The Sheikh's tone was threatening. He paused, took a deep breath, and said, "Anyway, tell me what you want from me?"

For several moments, the man looked the Sheikh in the eyes, sighed and then turned his eyes to roam the sumptuous room with its elegant furniture.

At last he replied, "What do you think? What can you do to make up for the twenty years of my life that I have wasted due to your treachery? Meanwhile, you end up living in such luxury? The twenty very long years of my youth wasted, my health and my future lost over trash like you. I could have taken the reduced sentence. Instead, I'm the one who was sent to prison for the money you've used to build your little empire. This all belongs to me. I was the man who robbed the government of its money, not you. You stole it from me. Everything you've got rightfully belongs to me. Do you understand what I'm saying, Rahman Al-Deen?"

The Sheikh remained silent. Omer went on, "You remember your job in that robbery, don't you? You were just to pick me up after I stole the money, right? I was the man who risked his life. It was me out there who got the money, not you. I left the money with you before I went to prison. Why? Because you persuaded me that it would be safer with you since that general whom you'd been working for could assist you if the government found the stolen money with you. Well, I believed you. I thought we were friends and partners, so I left the money with you. I trusted you. Was I right or wrong?"

The Sheikh did not reply, but sat in silent thought. Finally, he looked at his unwelcome guest and asked, "And what do you want now?"

"Half of everything you've got. Isn't that fair enough? I'm not asking for it all. That's fair isn't it?"

The Sheikh let out a hysterical laugh and said, "You must be dreaming, Omer."

"Dreaming? Why would I be dreaming about something that rightfully belongs to me, you son of a bitch? You have enjoyed the fruits of my efforts. You have enjoyed everything I earned and meanwhile I rotted in prison."

The Sheikh and his visitor glared at one another. Finally, the Sheikh smiled and responded in a low voice, "Come on, Omer, I was just kidding you. We're friends. You're my *only* friend. Don't worry; you'll get what you deserve. I want you to be happy as well. Stay here for a few days until I've figured out how I can do it. Don't worry about anything. I'll see you get what you rightfully deserve. *Friends?*" the Sheikh asked offering his hand.

"Friends," Omer replied as they shook hands.

"Great. Right now," the Sheikh continued. "I am sure you need rest for a few days. I understand what you've been going through. Don't worry; I'm going to make it up to you. Tonight we will celebrate our being reunited and have a private party—just you and me. We will talk about our days together and about our future. Everything will be fine. Tell me, Omer, do you still like Scotch Whiskey the way you used to? For our friendship, I'll let you drink in my house and have a good time. Of course, I've never done that before. But, you're different. You're my old friend."

Salim, in his hidden place, was terrified as he listened. He hurried to his room to lie down and ponder the revelations he had overheard.

That night after the feast of the Sheikh and his guest, the two men who had shared a common past sat talking for a long while, Omer sipping a favorite Scotch Whiskey while the Sheikh drank pineapple juice. By midnight, Omer—drunk—excused himself, and lumbered to the guest house where his bed was prepared. The light in his window was promptly extinguished and no noises were heard from his room.

During the night, Salim was awakened by heavy steps in the courtyard. Slipping quietly from bed, Salim peeked through a finger-width crack in the curtains. The Sheikh was carrying an ungainly burden. He walked toward the garden. *What was the Sheikh carrying?* When his master was backlit by a security light behind the trees of the house garden, Salim saw feet … and fingers. Returning to his bed in a cold sweat, Salim listened to the sounds of a shovel striking dirt under the trees. Salim's horror kept him awake.

In the morning, Omer was not in his bed. The Sheikh, in a dry-throated voice, asked Salim if he had seen his guest leave.

"No, sir, I've not seen him since the last evening," Salim responded cautiously.

"Well, Omer must have been in a hurry to leave, but I thought he would have said goodbye, at least left a note," the Sheikh said as he shrugged his shoulders in mock disbelief. "Anyway, Salim, I hope you've had a good night's rest."

"Yes." Salim replied in a low voice, avoiding the Sheikh eyes.

"Good for you," the Sheikh said, glancing at Salim's very tired face and smiling.

Days passed with no news of the Sheikh's old friend. Then one night, while Salim sat studying his homework, the Sheikh came to him. "Salim, I think it is time for you to get married."

The sudden, strange remark confused Salim. His heart pounded heavily, while his limbs seemed transfixed. "Get married? Me? Why? You're not serious?"

In sort of painful radiance, the Sheikh sighed, then looked into Salim's eyes. "Yes, I'm very serious, Salim."

"Why? I'm too young to get married. I'm still a student, Sheikh."

"It doesn't matter. I think that you ought to get married, Salim," the Sheikh said.

"But whom will I marry?"

"Adela. You will marry Adela, Salim," the Sheikh said as though it should have been obvious.

Salim was utterly baffled. He lost contact with everything in the room—including the Sheikh, who went on talking. A few minutes passed before Salim was able to comprehend the Sheikh's intent. In his stupefaction, Salim repeated in disbelief, "To Adela, Sheikh? Adela is the woman you want me to marry?"

"Yes, Adela," the Sheikh replied firmly. "Adela will be your wife."

"But, can you tell me why Adela, herself? Why have you chosen her in particular to be my wife?" Salim asked. "Why would you want to honor me with her as my bride?"

"She is young and the most suitable woman for you," answered the Sheikh. "Besides, I know you've been crazy over her. Don't you love her, Salim?"

Ignoring the Sheikh's embarrassing question was the most difficult thing Salim could remember having to do in his life. When he regained his place in the conversation, Salim protested, "But Adela is your woman, Sheikh. She is your mistress!"

"That's true, Salim, but it does not matter anymore. Appearances are important and I must avoid gossip. Thus, I believe you should be her husband."

"But, Sheikh, please, how could that be? How could I be husband of the woman you love?"

"Love, you said? What do you know of love, Salim? Do you understand what love is? Do you, Salim? Answer me! Do you?"

Salim was mute.

"Nothing is important anymore," continued the Sheikh sadly, "not even love. Love has always been just a game for failures. Failures need love to make up for their defeats, since there's nothing else left for them. Yes, Salim, love is just a game for losers. Sinners never appreciate love, because they cannot understand it, nor can they feel it or relate to it. Sinners have no hearts, Salim, and you and I, we are sinners. Besides, a man will often lose things much more precious than love. So do not tell me about things you neither appreciate nor understand. I love nothing."

"I don't believe it, Sheikh. I can't imagine myself the husband of your woman, Adela. I just cannot."

The Sheikh abruptly stood up, looked deeply into Salim's eyes, smiled maliciously, and then left the room. Salim heard the Sheikh's fading voice, "The wedding will be next week. Get ready for it. Congratulations, Salim."

Salim sank into his thoughts. *How can this son of a bitch hate me so much? How will this pretend marriage to Adela hurt me even more?* His mind ventured back to the near past, the unforgettable visions of the Sheikh and Adela together in bed. Naked. *How many times have I seen them making love?* How happy it made him to remember seeing the Sheikh powerless and impotent. *Adela needs a young, strong man to satisfy her. The master will try again and again, but all his attempts will fail.* The Sheikh was just a wretched, impotent old man, a wounded beast.

Salim could never forget the obstinate expression on the Sheikh's face at those painful moments. Neither could he forget the agony on Adela's angelic face when the Sheikh was torturing her femininity—when she was forced to create undeserved illusions.

Now Adela is going to be my wife. How can I accept that? Why have others always made my decisions for me? What could I do to stop this marriage? Yes, Salim had been crazy over Adela, but he wanted her as a lover, not a wife in name only. He never dreamed she would be his wife. She belonged to the Sheikh and everybody in the house knew that. What could he do? Salim spent all night agonizing over how to stop this wedding, but he could not find a solution. If he ran away, the Sheikh would surely send somebody to kill him. The Sheikh was a killer. He wanted Salim to do everything for him. The Sheikh dominated his life. His weakness toward the Sheikh pained him like an obstinate illness, a fear that couldn't be conquered.

The idea came at midnight. Salim went to Nada's bed and told the Sheikh's wife about her husband's decision. He begged Nada to help him stop this marriage. The rotund woman's eyes gleamed. As she started stripping her underwear off, Nada asked, "What do you care? Why are you so upset, Salim? Aren't you the real man of the house anyway?" If the Sheikh's wife was bothered by this turn of events, or if she felt any compassion for Salim's situation, her voice didn't reveal it.

The Sheikh spent a great deal of money to make the wedding ceremony an exceptional event. Townspeople crammed the Sheikh's house and garden, sniffing the twenty sheep the Sheikh had ordered to be grilled over hot coals, and simmering cauldrons of spicy side dishes that would prove more than enough for the guests. The Mullaiahs' lovely voices offered beautiful songs, adding more anguish to Salim's heart.

Salim's mother proved the happiest person present. She sang and danced joyfully, impervious to Salim's pain. People came to congratulate Monira. Many obviously envied her for the Sheikh's recognition of and care for her son.

At midnight, as the great party ended, the people left for home full of joy. The Sheikh, Salim, and his bride sat in the living room in total silence. Salim and Adela appeared sad, but the Sheikh seemed blissful. Suddenly, the Sheikh got up, took Adela by her hand, led her to his bedroom and closed the door behind them. Salim was in shock.

How dare the Sheikh take my own bride from me? How can he be so insolent? Adela is my wife! How dare the old dirty man insult me before the entire household? Salim burned with anger and choked with hatred. He so abhorred the Sheikh that he found himself ready to murder him. Then shame pierced his heart like a jagged knife.

A week passed. Nothing changed. To the outside world all appeared quite normal, but Adela remained Salim's wife in name only. Salim continued to receive wedding gifts, but he had no access to his bride. She lived with the Sheikh, just as before their marriage.

Despondent, Salim lost his appetite and suffered disabling headaches every day. Salim had no confidant to hear his heart's bitterness—except for the Sheikh's neglected wife. Nada sent him herbs from the garden, and ordered the kitchen to prepare healing teas for Salim's headaches. However, she had no authority or influence over the Sheikh. Having swallowed her self-esteem by accepting her ineffectual life (not to mention the compensations of sensual indulgence, which were no secret from her husband), Nada had acquiesced in the immoral charade that was the Sheikh's household.

But Nada did lend Salim a badly needed ear. Even a flawed listener can be a solace for the brokenhearted. Salim told her everything he had seen while serving in the Sheikh's private rooms. Nada listened, but she could do nothing to help him. In fact, Nada's chief reward for listening patiently to Salim was a deepening of her despair for her own broken marriage. When Salim complained to her that his presence at this house was for the sake of his health, but instead he was suffering, Nada could relate. He explained that he only stayed so he could help correct the wrongdoing and falsehood festering there. Nada listened, but nothing more.

Then one night, Salim told Nada that he had decided to kill the Sheikh. Nada's eyes glittered as she relished sharing in the fruits of his retribution. On second thought, she stared him in the eye, and asked, "Are you able to do that for sure, Salim?"

Without hesitation, Salim replied, "Yes, Nada, I can. You would be surprised at what I can do."

"How could you do it? I mean what's your plan?"

"I'll wait until he starts his prayers. Then, I will attack him with a knife."

"Be careful," she warned. "I have wished for you to come to such a conclusion for months, Salim. I knew you had the strength, but so far I've only seen you use it in bed." Then Nada threw her head back and laughed.

Salim thought it was an ugly, bitter noise, but made no comment to his new co-conspirator.

———

The next day, Salim found the kitchen empty, selected a ten-inch butcher knife with a sturdy blade, and took it to his room where he hid it carefully. The effort to appear normal around the Sheikh was difficult throughout the day. Salim hoped the Sheikh would not notice his unusually rapid breath and flushed neck. After he and the Sheikh returned from afternoon prayers at the Mosque, Salim joined his master in the library for afternoon reading as usual. All this time, Salim's mind swirled in worry, fearing his strength might prove insufficient. However, he found that his fears of the consequences were overpowered by his hatred. Under the law, Salim knew that he would pay with his own life, if he was discovered as the murderer. Yet, the silent fury that consumed him—and his shame of being denied the attentions of his wife—continued stinging him. *I must kill the ursurper, even if he is a Sheikh.*

At evening prayer time, the Sheikh stood in his room on his prayer rug. Salim took his usual position behind the bowing cleric, pretending to pray as well. His heart pounded as his trembling fist gripped the knife concealed in his coat pocket. Then he drew the butcher knife, grasped it with both hands, and lunged toward the Sheikh's back.

At that moment, as if sensing Salim's movement, the Sheikh wheeled to avoid the knife, gripping Salim's left wrist. But Salim's momentum and two-fisted hold on the knife propelled the blade into the Sheikh's right shoulder. Seeing him staggering and shouting out from pain, Salim struck again. But this time the Sheikh deflected the knife with a flailing arm. With his other hand, the wounded Sheikh punched Salim in the face, causing him to drop the knife. Stunned, Salim saw the knife twirl toward the prayer rug. Then, Salim fled from the room and out of the house.

His attempt at retribution having failed, Salim ran through winding streets, avoiding imagined pursuers. Within minutes, Salim found himself closing the door of his parents' home. Would it be the first place that authorities would look for him? Unsure of anything but the desire to seek a familiar haven, Salim decided to lock himself inside his bedroom, the room of his tormented childhood, and never come out.

Salim need not have worried about the authorities, because the guilty Sheikh gathered his entire household as soon as his wound was bandaged. His nurse was Adela, who felt herself torn between the two men who claimed her. Wincing with pain, the Sheikh addressed his household sternly, ordering each to remain mute about the attack, under pain of severe lashings.

Another youth was promoted to be the Sheikh's bodyguard and, except for new security over the kitchen knives, life in the Sheikh's compound continued its same routines. The Sheikh continued to advise visitors from his spiritual wisdom, crowds arrived offering goats, cows, and chickens. Distraught parents brought frail children in need of healing. Nada returned to her habits with the vulnerable Mullaiahs. And in the Sheikh's private rooms, Adela's best efforts continued to frustrate the old Sheikh.

But Salim's life among his family dealt with nothing but anxiety. Salim had to confess everything to his mother and brothers. And he had to face his amazed father, when he returned from a lucrative trip to Kirkuk. How Salim winced at the shame of his revelations. His mother at first refused to believe his tales of immorality in the Sheikh's household. His brothers struggled to overcome their masculine titillation when hearing of Nada's habits, and those of the Sheikh's ways with Adela. Salim persevered, describing all he had endured in the Sheikh's house, even the disappearance of the Sheikh's old friend underneath the garden fruit trees. Salim was certain that the Sheikh would send either the authorities or a private assassin to kill him, probably during the night. However, Monira and her older sons were determined to provide Salim protection from the Sheikh's revenge. Whenever Salim ventured from the sanctuary of his childhood room, two musclebound brothers escorted him. Even when he returned for his final year at the neighborhood school, his brotherly escort accompanied him at Monira's insistence.

———

Seven months later, the early morning stillness was pierced by horrible screams from the Sheikh's house. Driven by fear, servants tore through the hallways and stately rooms, fleeing the terrifying sounds. Gathering in the courtyard, they looked into each other's terror-stricken eyes, before realizing that the Sheikh was not among them. Nor was Adela.

In trepidation, townspeople rushed to the compound and encountered the frightened souls who had begun to comfort one another in the courtyard. Shaken servants, Mullaiahs, and serving boys joined cautiously with strong men from the town to begin a room-by-room search. Sensing tragedy, Nada and her servants refused to re-enter the house until all was known.

In the Sheikh's lavish bedroom, two bodies were found slaughtered like animals, their naked bodies covered with blood. Their heads had been hacked off and placed together on silk pillows: the Sheikh and Adela. Women's screams issued from the gruesome scene. As the curious filed in, it sounded as if the very windows of the house poured forth a river of terror. Townspeople tripped from the compound, heads bowed, unable to make any sense of the crime scene. If there was one house in Nasiriya in which something so terrible should surely never happen, the Sheikh's compound should be that safe house.

The police arrived and interrogated everyone in the Sheikh's household, but they departed without accusing anyone. They investigated thoroughly, but could discover no evidence. Nothing was left behind by whomever might have fled the scene, not even a fingerprint.

"The crime seems to have been performed by professionals. It is an unbelievably savage crime, just unbelievable," the Chief of Police tried to explain to the Sheikh's widow. "But, I promise you that we will pursue the criminals until we bring them to justice."

Two young Mullaiahs were arrested and questioned about aiding professional bandits from Baghdad, but after two days they were released due to insufficient evidence. The case remains unsolved to this day. On first hearing of the murders, the townspeople had been shocked. Of the hundreds who had swarmed through the Sheikh's house, many spoke loudly, demanding revenge. But as months passed, the police compelled them to focus on their own affairs. Rumors continued to circulate for a year or more. Gradually, the entire crime just became a wearisome story to everyone.

After the incident, Salim's nightmares of a dismembered Adela caused chronic night sweats and vomiting. He grew more depressed and appeared almost cadaverous. Every night he suffered from horrible illusions and nightmares. Some dreams featured an angry Sheikh or visions of the beautiful but disfigured Adela. Eventurally, figures from the Sheikh's compound faded and his dreams of the blonde woman returned to haunt him nightly.

CHAPTER THREE
Spring's Fragrance

Spring's few short weeks brought Nasiriya relief after Iraq's harsh winter. In this gentle season, people visited in their neighborhoods, relaxed in coffee shops, and ambled along the riverside, listening to boating fishermen singing traditional melodies. Farmers from surrounding villages brought vegetables, fruits, sheep and chickens to sell.

In the afternoon, young women went to wash in the Euphrates, balancing clothes baskets on their heads as they walked home. Some practiced an ancient ritual at the river, wishing for a distant lover's return or the appearance of a future husband by fixing several candles upright on a piece of wood. Then they closed their eyes, made their wish, and sent their candles floating downriver. Women of the Euphrates valley have practiced this tradition for scores of generations, believing that it worked for grandma, so it must bring her offspring luck in love.

Salim and his mother always enjoyed seeing fishermen gathered in groups at the river. A few men stood on the bank smoking, while others cast their nets from dinghies. Their nets in the water, the fishermen would pull one side to the riverbank, where helpers waited. Together, they then would lift the nets up from the rolling tide, usually hauling in ten to twenty fish. Meanwhile, shoppers gathered to spend their coins for the best of the fresh catch.

Monira's diversion worked to distract Salim from looming adult responsibilities and harsh memories of humiliation and loss. "Salim, it's time to go to school, dear." His mother's words interrupted Salim's trance. Memories of his painful past life at the Sheikh's house had isolated him. Monira believed that her son desperately needed to forget the past. She sensed that Salim longed for a new path in life, a new direction that might be motivated by the right young woman.

"There are only a few more weeks left, and it's your last year of high school," said his mother, still talking as he went to brush his teeth. "It's a beautiful day outside, darling. I know how you love spring, and this will be a special spring for you. You are almost twenty years old, and women in the neighborhood will begin to whisper about you." She winked at him jokingly.

Salim forced a smile. On his way to school, Salim shivered, still obsessed with last evening's nightmare. He murmured to himself, "How can I feel any pleasure when I suffer almost every night with awful dreams? How can I feel content with this surrounding beauty when I am the only one in my family—or in the world—living this horror every night? How can I be happy? How can spring find its way to my aching heart? And why is my anguish always stronger than both my pleasure and my will?"

His pace slowed as his mood changed. Salim realized how he had come to enjoy being alone. *Perhaps,* he thought, *it would help my mood if I tried to focus on the natural beauty of the season.* Spring *was* his favorite season. He did feel stirrings of a new optimism, attributing the swelling in his heart to the seasonal promise of new life, the birdsongs, colorful blossoms, and the gentle breeze on his cheek. The fragrance of jasmine suddenly seemed to flow through his every pore. He inhaled deeply. In the past, Salim realized that he had found the essence of jasmine, mixed with the soft breeze, a soothing medication for his tortured soul. So it seemed on this day.

The variety of colorful birds, bulbuls, sparrows, and pigeons singing happily fascinated him anew as he walked among the spring greenery, creating a long-lost enthusiasm in his chest. For a moment, Salim felt as if he were flying away among the clouds. Then, his daydream receded.

Why are these little creatures so happy? What is their secret? They are just weak little things! They lack security. They don't know how to protect themselves from bad weather or cruel men or animals. These creatures live a year—two at the most, if they are lucky. Yet, they sing happily and continue regenerating, taking care of their young so optimistically and confidently. Why? How much I wish Allah had created me as one of them, instead of being the miserable human being I am.

A profound sense of wonder and inquiry engulfed his soul. His questions about the secret behind those little birds' enviable happiness and their apparently joyous existence stayed in Salim's mind, urgent and adamant. Suddenly, he reached an epiphany, a relief. *It's the freedom! That is their secret. Their lives are devoted to joy and happiness, and mine only to confusion and remorse. They are free, and I am not. They are loose, and I am chained. Where could I find happiness? Where is my peace? I wish I had never been born.*

Salim slowly wound his way toward school. And then again, a burst of hope seemed to suddenly engulf him. This gorgeous day breathed new life, life potent enough to nurture every plant, animal, and person. The giant date palms and eucalyptus lining the street nearly embraced each other as a soft north wind caressed their leaves, carrying the sweet smell of roses and carnations. Red, yellow, purple, and white flowers decorated the grounds. Cornice River Street ran less than fifty yards from the river, with no houses to block the view. Choirs of birds sang in harmony among the trees. This morning, Salim could imagine the birds celebrating a wedding ceremony. The sun shone through a small space in the tree branches, flirting with his dark eyes and warming his face. Satisfaction and enjoyment of the moment filled his entire body. What a marvelous day!

As he entered the school gate, a beautiful aroma swept over him. He closed his eyes for a moment and whispered to himself, "Maybe I'll never know why I am alive, but I do know one thing. Spring surrounds and enters me, and I am reborn like any plant or flower on this earth."

That afternoon after school, Salim and his mother walked to the Euphrates. Townspeople huddled to watch the fishermen working with their nets. Women washing their clothes or dishes whispered among themselves as they glimpsed a handsome man nearby. Several men shed shirts and jumped in the river despite the cool weather—perhaps to earn the women's attention. One fisherman called out, urging the jumpers to get out immediately, but the young men refused. The fisherman grabbed their clothes and threatened to throw them into the river.

"Why?" one swimmer objected strongly.

"Why? Because you're scaring the fish away!" the fisherman replied.

"I'm not getting out until you promise us a big, fresh carp!"

"Okay, I will ... just get out, now!" The fisherman implored. Observers in the crowd laughed, including Salim and his mother. As the day drew to a close, people began returning home. The shore crowd had thinned to just a few groups by the time that the sun's forehead bowed to the tree line. Orange gave way to red in the sky as the sun reflected in the river, slowly penetrating the dense date palms, falling on the people's faces before finally disappearing behind the trees.

Salim heard a man's faint singing as he rowed his small boat from mid-river.
The closer he rowed to shore, the clearer his deep, lilting voice became: You
don't love me anymore.
You don't care for my tears or being hurt or sore.
You've told everyone but me, I'm sure.
After all those years you want to leave.
Oh my faithful heart you deceive.
I wish I knew your game before
So there won't be any sorrow for
I can read the answer in your eye
And can tell when you love or you lie.
What had changed you and me, tell me, why?
If I could forget, I would be wise.

The man in the boat passed them by, but Salim followed him with sad eyes.

CHAPTER FOUR

Stranger in Town

ONE FRIDAY MORNING, JUST AS SALIM'S FAMILY FINISHED BREAKFAST, a large truck stopped at a house across the street. The motor's roar brought Monira and her sons to the window, peering out curiously.

A short, elderly man emerged from the cab. Dressed in a white shirt, brown pants, and black sandals, he carried a round belly out of proportion to his body. His chubby face framed brown eyes, a big nose, and a large mouth. The man's thick hair, bushy eyebrows, mustache, and closely cropped beard were mostly gray. Monira suspected that the man's gray hair made him appear older than his actual age. His determined face portrayed seriousness, concentration, and vitality.

Walking to the passenger side, the man extended a hand to help an aged woman descend the high steps. The woman never took her eyes off her new house, but cupped her hands around her face, marveling at the home's appearance. The newly built house, freshly painted white, was obviously a marvel to her. A black gown and veil covered most of the woman's face and body, giving her a widow's appearance. The pair walked a few steps toward their new residence, and then the man saw Salim's family, still gazing through their window. The man smiled slightly and waved. Monira waved back, calling, "Good morning!"

"My name is Abdul Karim and this is my wife, Majid," he responded as he moved toward the window-framed family. "We are your new neighbors. We have just moved from Baghdad."

"Peace be upon you, brother. How was your trip?" Monira asked.

The short man smiled and put his arm around his wife. "Thank God, sister, our trip was fine, but as you know, the road was rough. We had to make many stops. My wife is a bit tired, but other than that, a good trip."

"I think you might need some help unloading your truck. My sons can assist you."

The boys shot toward the door before the man could reply, and Abdul chuckled at their eagerness.

"Yes, thank you. I need help and really appreciate it. Thank you all very much."

"You're very welcome!" Monira's voice became more excited. "And welcome to our street. We and all our neighbors are like one big family. We hope you will enjoy our friendship."

The new neighbors had much to unload: valuable antique furniture, large steel and wooden boxes heavy with household wares and a library of books, some new and others in ancient leather bindings. Many books displayed titles in foreign languages, which fascinated Monira, as did boxes of framed posters and large pictures. Some posters revealed diagrams of the human body. Others showed tiny people, their strange faces—almost tangible—laughing in madness.

For a moment, the elder of the brothers, Nadeem, imagined the poster people moving about, lively and full of spirit. He became frightened, clearly envisioning laughter in some faces and tears falling from reddened eyes of other faces. Nadeem quickly turned away, and then suddenly felt nauseous and hot, with a burning in his neck and limbs. Feeling that he was about to get sick, Nadeem turned to look again, found the tiny people still laughing … He rubbed his eyes, sighing, "I must be tired." Nadeem stepped outside to fill his lungs with fresh air. A few minutes later, feeling restored, he returned to see Majida sitting in a chair. Her eyes searched the room apprehensively. Nadeem smiled and spoke, attempting to comfort her. She just sat in silence.

Her husband, seeing this, explained, "My wife can't speak—the result of an accident a long time ago. However, Majida is a fine lady. She is just a little tired."

"I am sorry," Nadeem replied sympathetically as he lifted a heavy box to carry to the next room. Salim watched as his brothers helped unload the truck. "Come on, brother, you need some exercise," Nadeem prodded him. "Let us see your big muscles."

Salim replied with a smile and rolled up his sleeve, pretending to show big muscles, then turned, retreating to his room. The short man followed Salim with his sharp eyes until the boy disappeared into the house.

That evening, Salim's mother fixed dinner for their new neighbors, part of their welcoming tradition. The families talked about life in town and what Abdul could expect from the people and the new environment. As Abdul and Majida retired to their home, they expressed warmth and gratitude to Monira and her family. Salim, however, had stayed in his room until the guests left.

A few days later, a sign appeared on their new neighbor's door:

Mr. Abdul Karim Hasson Jarrallah,
Diploma from Egypt
Specialist in Mental and Spiritual Health
and Expert in Interpreting
the Secret Laws of Nature

Observing this, a marveling Monira noted softly to Salim, "Ah! The name of Jarrallah means 'God's neighbor.'" Abdul's sign caused much curiosity and talk among the townspeople, since Nasiriya boasted only two physicians and no private clinic. The pair of physicians were seldom available to see patients, usually staffing their offices with only inexperienced nurses who heard complaints and wrote prescriptions. Anyone who fell seriously ill would be taken by family to Baghdad, where doctors kept regular hours. Now that Nasiriya was home to an expert, as the sign proclaimed, naive locals thought that he should know everything. Families rushed to his clinic in large numbers: those suffering with mental and emotional problems, elderly residents wanting to get married and needing vitamins, the insecure who craved to gain or lose weight, and women waiting for husbands who had deserted them. Every problem imaginable flooded in, seeking Abdul Karim's care. The clinic offered services from seven in the morning until seven in the evening. For the first time in the town's history, at least one street seemed always crowded.

Abdul made a waiting room of in the large room next to the clinic's main door. Couches occupied one wall, with a small seat on the opposite. A table with six chairs stood mid-room, featuring a large vase of ancient origin between smaller vessels in which incense smoldered. A large floor-length mirror hung on the third wall, across from the main entrance. The fourth wall housed the door through which patients were escorted to the doctor's examination room. It was decorated with two framed oil paintings of odd hues and one poster depicting two skeletons shaking hands. Through the door leading to the examination room, more posters depicted the human body's skeletal, gastrointestinal, and reproductive systems. Nadeem's old nemesis— the poster of tiny people laughing hysterically—hung in the examination room itself, where an eye chart with lines of bold letters hung, ready to test clients' eyesight and patience. In another exam room, art displayed images of dead people lying in coffins surrounded by strange creatures—human from the neck up, fish from the waist down. Over the doctor's high examination chair hung a glistening chandelier, larger than the one in the waiting room.

Abdul seemed to know a great deal about the aches of stomachs of all sizes, pains of every part of the back, causes of limps, coughs, blurry eyes, and ears that refused to function as they once had. With extraordinary expertise to handle nearly all conditions, Abdul's treatments relieved many complaints almost immediately.

The specialist would sit very close in front of the patient, speaking empathetically in a language no one could understand. His large eyes fixed upon the patient with a piercing, hypnotic stare. Applying both hands, he would touch the patient's problem area, increasing the pressure gradually until the sick one showed signs of discomfort. After repeating this procedure numerous times, Abdul then blew on the patient's face, as if washing away dust. Extracting a finger of saliva from his mouth, he placed a dollop of it on the patient's forehead, then offered a sip of a fermented potion from a jar, which each patient seemed to wish to repeat. Instead, Abdul clapped his hands together one time, signaling treatment's end for that day. Some patients came back many times, even after forgetting the ailment that had caused them to seek the doctor's services in the first place.

Abdul treated mentally ill people in a different manner. First, he tied a scarlet scarf around the patient's head, just above the eyes. Then he placed both hands on the temples and moved his fingers in a circular, massaging motion, all the while speaking his unintelligible language. Suddenly, his eyebrows would arch and his face would assume an an evil expression. At this time, the doctor's eyes seemed about to pop from their sockets. In a very deep voice, he would begin calling out names, before suddenly grabbing the patient's head tightly with both hands, as if trying to pry open the skull. Next, Abdul would yell, as if shouting orders to an invisible orderly standing in the room. As the procedure progressed, the patient would sweat, shake with fear, and usually faint. Abdul himself would appear exhausted, with eyes wide open and unblinking. Hearing the proceeding from the waiting room, others were unsure whether they should applaud or run from the clinic. Few ran, because the client who had been treated always appeared from the examination room in a dazed state, which seemed preferable to that in which they had entered.

Because treating the mentally ill was the most exhausting, the doctor scheduled those treatments last each day. Each patient received a sip of the fermented potion from a jar, which seemed always to instill a serene calm prior to departure. Abdul's successful treatments brought him recognition and respect. He never charged the poor for his services, asked very little money from artisans and shopkeepers, and surprised his wealthiest patients with fees of startling modesty. Thus, due to Abdul's skill and generosity, Nasiriya became the refuge for sick people from all over Iraq. Most of them returned home feeling blessed relief from his cure, often bearing magical remedies which they promised never to divulge, and always with coins remaining in their purses.

CHAPTER FIVE

A Meeting with the Stranger

WHILE ABDUL CONTINUED TO HEAL MANY IN HIS CLINIC, across the street Salim's condition was deteriorating. Salim's vivid nightmares plagued him more frequently. He was quite certain that the blonde woman of his nightmares had taken up residence in Monira's room, and now he spat at, cursed, and tried to bite anyone who approached his bed to offer help. During seizures, his body shook the mattress until he rolled on the floor like a hooked fish. At those times, his limbs became rigid and his face pale. His eyes rolled back, his body soaked with sweat, and his tongue filled his mouth. Salim's seizures often stunned his family and shocked any guest who happened to be in the home at the time.

Monira somehow seemed to accept Salim's erratic and frightening behavior with patience and a grace that other midwives found remarkable. Much more than a mother's acceptance, her ministrations seemed almost understanding. When a seizure hit, Monira would order his brothers to grab his arms and legs so that he could not injure himself, while she sat on his stomach as Salim bucked in resistance. In her unknown language, Monira would shout at him louder and louder. Then, she would raise both hands and slap each side of his face. Salim's fighting would increase. Then his mother's face would distort, forming an image of evil. She would slap Salim again, growling in her mysterious language, as if ordering some force to desist. Then Salim's flailing would lessen, and within minutes he would be calm.

Salim's pale face and half-opened eyes would slowly return to normal.

His mother would bring cold water for him to drink, and proceed to dry his sweat. She would patiently rub his forehead, hands and feet. Salim finally would regain his senses, and fall into an exhausted sleep almost immediately. Each of his brothers would slump back to his own room and fall asleep for hours. But there was no sleeping for Monira. She closed herself off in her fortune-telling room, crying and talking with someone, her tones steeped in muffled anger.

One morning following Salim's latest seizure, after his brothers left for work, Monira entered Salim's room in her usual cheerful way. "Would you like to sit with me in the front yard? The weather is nice today. I brought you a special treat: watermelon."

They lounged on comfortable chairs in the corner of the porch where the sun shone through the apple tree. Spring was waning as summer approached, yet still embraced the town. Light breezes blew from the north, carrying a perfume from the seeds of the date palm trees. The red and yellow flowers in Monira's garden delighted the senses. Salim and his mother were facing different directions, but she could clearly feel his sadness. Salim's thoughts touched his very soul as he watched the sun glisten through the tree branches.

"What are you thinking about, son?"

"Just thinking," Salim replied without turning toward her.

"Abdul is still looking forward to meeting with you," Monira confided. "I know he might be able to help us, and he likes you. He thinks you are a special person."

"No, Momma, listen to me, I don't need any help from anybody. I just need to be left alone. The Sheikh's bitter memory still tortures me; I can't forget it," Salim answered sorrowfully. "I don't want anyone to complicate my life anymore."

"Son, I know you suffered a very bad experience, but you need to get on your feet again. Forget what happened; start a new life. You know this very well: nobody in this world loves and cares for you like your mother. You have the right to enjoy a happy life. Don't withdraw from the world because of one unfortunate experience." His mother's voice was kind and confident.

"No, mother, no, just forget the idea. I hate people now. The only people

I can trust are my family."

"Salim, listen to me, son. The Sheikh fooled everyone, not only you. He deceived the entire city by claiming piety and religious reverence, but he finally paid for his lies. We saw the kind of death that deceivers get. So who is the winner and who is the loser?"

"I am scared, okay? I fear I'll suffer more pain. Even more!"

"Trust me, son. Just trust your mother and let me walk with you on the right path. You're my beloved son, and I'll search any means to make you happy. Just trust me, and you won't regret it. Accept this opportunity. Accept Abdul as a friend. You won't have to stay in his house. He is our neighbor. Try him … please, for me?"

"How can he help?" Salim turned and faced his mother.

"I don't know exactly how, but I know he can."

"How can you be so sure about him or other people? It's a terrible world filled with terrible people, Mother," snapped Salim, glaring into his mother's eyes.

"I wouldn't say it if it weren't true. Don't worry, my dearest son. This time I will be near you. I will not allow anybody to harm you," she said firmly.

Salim gazed at her. Then he sighed and softened. He spoke reluctantly.

"All right, I'll do it for you. When do you want us to meet him?" Salim saw his mother's face shining with excitement.

"Tonight, after he finishes work."

Monira stood up and threw her arms around Salim. He returned her kiss before she crossed the street to make the appointment. That evening, Abdul opened his door to greet Salim and his mother. He shook hands with Salim, welcoming him warmly. This was Salim's first time to see Abdul face to face, and enter his house. Abdul led them to a large space in the family rooms, not the examination room. There were two sofas and a rectangular table with three chairs. Salim and his mother sat down on one sofa, and Abdul pulled up a chair to face them.

"Salim, your mother explained everything about your troubles. I'll try to help you," said Abdul with confidence. "I've noticed how lonely you are. Life is not so bad, Salim. Most people are burdened with some kind of trouble, but most rise on their feet and resume life. This is our nature. Every person you see at the market carries a secret burden, yet they find the strength to do a day's work, find someone to love, and live in peace. It will please me so much if you accept me as a friend."

Salim studied Abdul, then asked, "Tell me, sir, why bother to help me? What's your purpose, and what would you achieve?"

Abdul smiled broadly, and exchanged glances with Monira. "Salim, I can relate to the distrust you feel toward everyone. It's natural for anybody to withdraw, and even hate all people after a calamity like you went through. I won't answer your question with a lot of details, but let me tell you this, in our world, there are good and bad people, with good and bad intentions. To me, the good people with good intentions fear God, and anticipate meeting Him in the hereafter. They only achieve such a great goal by doing good things for others. I consider myself one of these good people. It makes me extremely happy to help people like you become happy. Is my answer enough to satisfy you?"

Salim thought that Abdul sounded sincere.

The healer went on, "All I'll ask you is this, trust me. Believe in me and learn everything about me, the same way I am going to trust you, believe in you, and learn everything about you. Now, I want you to discard your fear of me this minute. This is the first step," Abdul said firmly.

"I like that," Salim said, "but, how did you know what I was feeling? Can you see through me?"

"I can read your mind, Salim. I can feel your weakness and your strength. I can tell you how many times your heart beats a minute without touching your chest."

Abdul stood up and walked upstairs. He came back holding a necklace with three stones: two black, with a white one in the middle. Abdul held the necklace close to his chest. Then, he raised it in front of Salim's face and said in a very soft voice, "Salim, let's all stand up to pray."

Salim's mother stood beside her son. Abdul closed his eyes and began speaking in a strange tongue. Then Abdul and Monira both began reciting in a low tone the verses of the holy Qur'an. Salim was pleased to hear his mother recite the long verses.

The three remained standing until the prayer was finished. Afterwards, Abdul kissed the necklace, and Monira did the same. Salim kissed it only after instructed to do so. Abdul placed the necklace around Salim's neck. The boy felt an electric charge streak throughout his body. Then, suddenly, his intense fear and fatigue vanished. The depression that had been so constant seemed to fade, giving rise to a new feeling that Salim decided must be hope.

"I do feel good!" Salim felt tears as he smiled. "Momma, I feel better already. Tell me, what happened? Is this temporary? Why is this happening to me? Who am I now? Something great happened to me. Please, someone must explain." Salim reached out and hugged his mother.

"I am asking you to be patient—everything in time," replied Abdul, putting his arm around Salim's shoulders. "You will learn what you want to know, but be patient. That necklace is your exorcist, your protection from all evil spirits."

That night Salim went to bed free of any disturbing thoughts. He did not talk in his sleep or jump out of bed screaming deliriously, as he had so frequently for the past year. His brothers enjoyed a good night's sleep without fears for their brother. Even Monira rested peacefully.

Salim was happy to have finally found someone other than his mother to depend on, someone who surrounded him with kindness, provided security and protection—a mature person to talk with anytime and about anything in his life. He could learn from Abdul's deep thoughts and remarkable experience. At the same time, Abdul had found what he had always been looking for: a young man who looked on him with respect, seeing him as a mentor, even as a father figure.

Abdul admired Salim, an exceptional spirit coping with so much misery and pain. Salim proved to be a willing, cooperative patient. Abdul was surprised to watch Salim demonstrate openness to his treatments and advice, as well as outstanding ability to learn the art of healing. Never before had Abdul experienced a young man who sought to learn without any objection, to listen without the filter of pride, and to practice healing arts with exceptional patience.

One afternoon while returning from school, Salim bumped into Nejat, who had been a Mullaiah he had known at the Sheikh's house. Nejat had been the first of the Mullaiahs sent to his bed there, and Salim remembered her feminine charms with relish. Salim could hardly recognize Nejat, for she had lost her youthful glow and girlish allure. In fact, Salim thought, she did not appear very healthy. Nejat stood unevenly as if one leg was injured, and she wore black mourning clothes.

Deciding to overlook anything distasteful, Salim greeted his former friend brightly, "Hey, Nejat, how've you been? What has happened to you? You look different. Are you all right?"

"Hi, Salim, how are you doing? I was ill for some time. I'm doing better now. My brother Aziz was killed about three months ago, and my family is ruined." Salim thought the girl was holding back tears, and he noticed her eyes shifting from street vendors to passersby. Salim wondered what or whom Nejat feared.

"I'm sorry to hear that. I was familiar with your brother; he used to frequent the Sheikh's house. What happened?"

"I can't tell you. I'm afraid that if I say, I might get killed myself."

Salim wanted to learn more, but decided to ease Nejat's tension, and changed the subject. "Well, what are you doing these days? Are you still in the Sheikh's house?"

"No, I'm working on my own as a Mullaiah. Things changed entirely after the Sheikh's death, and most of the Mullaiahs quit their careers. They moved back to their homes, regained their place in their families. I went back home, also, but I like entertaining people with dancing and singing. I have been blessed with a good voice and townspeople frequently ask me to do services for them."

Salim looked with a slight smile into her sad eyes, and asked, "Are you married now?"

Nejat grinned broadly and replied, "To your relief, I'm engaged. But, I bet you still remember those great nights in bed at the Sheikh's house, don't you?"

"I loved them, and you did too, Nejat," he laughed.

"What are you doing these days—still going to school?" Nejat asked, studying his handsome features.

"Yeah, I have less than a year to finish high school."

"Good for you. Listen, I also have another job. I own a little grocery store on the north side, near the General Health Clinic. You should come to see me, and we'll talk more."

"Wonderful, I'll be seeing you, girl."

The sight of Nejat upset Salim. She reminded him of his painful past. But he decided to visit her anyway, hoping to learn more about the Sheikh's mysterious death, and his strange life, since Nejat had lived longer than Salim at the Sheikh's house. Salim also reminisced about those wanton nights with Nejat, hopeful that he could resume a relationship with her. But Salim's fantasies were not destined to happen.

Nejat refused to speak about the Sheikh's murder, and she declined his advances, talking fondly of her engagement. Nejat seemed proud of how she had matured and made it clear that she now regretted her past. Nejat also encouraged Salim to repent, insisting he should join a group called the Dervishes, which she described as devout. She stressed the importance of affiliating himself with those who revered Islam, to learn about the depth of his faith, and become a scholar like the Sheikh had been.

"I don't wish for you to be like the Sheikh, okay?

"I'm talking about his fantastic knowledge," she explained.

"But, I don't need such great knowledge. Why do I need it?"

"Salim, on this point you're totally wrong. Just forget about becoming the most respected Muslim in the whole town. Forget about giving your family an honorable title by being a scholar and revered among your brothers. Only think about the horrible day when every creature will be put to a severe account in the hereafter. Imagine yourself among the pious believers sent to live eternally in paradise. Wouldn't that be an honorable life—something worth doing?"

A week later, when Salim's next visited Nejat's store, she introduced him to an old, white-bearded man with handsome features, Hajj Ajil. The Hajj was wearing a plain religious cloak and appeared to be in his early sixties. His soft voice and polite demeanor did not impress Salim much. It was all too easy for Salim to envision the Hajj as the hateful Sheikh.

Surprisingly, the old man didn't talk about religion. He only asked Salim about his school, the educational system, and whether the teachers were still as qualified as when the Hajj was young. Then, the man asked Salim about his family and said how everyone in the city appreciated his mother for helping women deliver their children. The man wanted to know whether Salim intended to go to college after finishing high school. The Hajj asked other questions, but nothing too personal. Then Salim listened as the Hajj recalled memories about Nasiriya fifty years earlier.

"There were not many houses built then, and I still remember the day when your father and mother got married. Actually, I'm older than your father," the Hajj remarked jokingly. "It was about thirty years ago, when your father, after proposing to your mother, built the house for her wedding gift. Everyone in the city knew about it; we were a small community. We all knew what was going on in each other's lives. He bought his truck after building the house. I still remember that beautiful yellow truck, brand new, the first truck ever to arrive in the city. At the time, only a few cars ran on the streets of Nasiriya, and townspeople often poked heads out their windows to look at the passing miracle on the street. It was something astonishing for many people to see the cars drive by."

"Do you really know my father?" asked the pleased Salim.

"What? Are you kidding? And who didn't know your father then? Who doesn't know Wissam, that tall, handsome guy with broad shoulders who had everything then that anyone could wish to have! He was young, tough, and coins filled his pockets. Your father was one of the city team's best soccer players. He was recruited to play with the English officers' team at their camp, making friends among them. And, yes, he was tough. At one match where I was a spectator, he was fouled by a dirty player, an officer who injured Wissam's leg. Wissam sprang to his feet and hit the officer, knocking him flat on his back. He was given the red card and had to leave the match.

His friend, the English colonel, sitting in the stand, liked what your father did to that officer; and was sorry to see him leaving the game. Did you know that your father was such a good soccer player in his youth?"

"Yes, and we still have some of his trophies."

"I bet he would still have them! Your father was a popular man in town, and before his marriage to your mother, he was fun-loving. He loved to go to Basra, where he was often seen in the nightclubs, sitting among a bunch of artists, drinking and conversing. Some people swore they saw him light up one of the artist's cigarettes with a 1,000 dinar bill. He was something, your father!"

Back at home, an excited Salim related Hajj Ajil's stories.

Monira looked at her son and said, "Yeah, your father was all that and more! Thank God he finally settled down with one woman, me." Salim and his mother both laughed.

Salim became a frequent visitor to Nejat's store, where he listened ardently to Hajj Ajil, who kept telling him anecdotes about the city before his birth. "One time in the late fifties, after King Faisal was crowned, he toured Iraqi cities and visited Nasiriya. The king spoke with the townspeople through microphones from the balcony of the 'Sarai,' the Governors Palace, surrounded by local authorities. The citizens cheered the king fanatically. Then he left the palace and went on a little city tour. His car had to pass over the old wooden bridge while Wissam and some friends were swimming, and diving from the bridge into the river. As they saw the motor cavalcade, your father and the other boys got out of the water and stood in the middle of the bridge, cheering the King. They clustered around his car, and accidently, the King's car ran over Wissam's foot. No bones were broken, but the king ordered his driver to stop. The king got out seeing if the boy, your father, was injured. But Wissam politely bent his head down and kissed the King's hand. The king hugged your father, and gave him his personal card, inviting him to visit at the palace in Baghdad. I don't know whether your father made that trip or not, do you?"

"I really have no idea."

"If he had made that visit, there would have been a picture taken with the King. Have you ever seen a picture like that at home?"

"No, I haven't."

"Anyway, Wissam was a lucky man, and if I were him, I would have gone to see the King!"

Among the talks with the Hajj, Salim sometimes heard interesting facts about the history of Islam. The Hajj told how the Prophet Mohammad, alone, and by Almighty Allah's will, established such a powerful religion that Muslims count in the billions nowadays. He told about the Prophet emerging from Mecca to Al-Medina after his followers were subjected to sanctions and torture by unbelievers. The Hajj gradually introduced Salim to life's wonders within Islam. He told Salim how, if he joined the Dervishes, he would receive great peace of mind and live happily among his brother Muslims. Salim felt a genuine affection for this decent man and listened intently. He also began reading books the Hajj brought him—texts about Islam's principles and virtues, and interpretation of the Qur'an.

Eventually, Salim brought the Hajj Ajil to meet his family. The old man assured them Salim would be in good hands, and the religious group would be greatly blessed by Allah for raising this talented boy to become a pious believer. During the meeting, Salim's older brother Nadeem expressed concern about rumors of the Dervishes' excesses. Nadeem said, "I hear that some of the Dervishes are dealing in usury. And in Islam, usury is considered a great sin."

The Hajj responded politely, "Frankly, I have no knowledge of those people. Do you know their names? Do you know who are they? If I could get their names, we could investigate."

"I really don't know their names. People just say they are the Dervishes. If so, then the Dervishes have shown hard-heartedness towards the city's impoverished people. Some say the Dervishes have lent them money, but they could not pay off on time. I saw the lenders knocking on doors, demanding payment in public. The lenders rejected their requests for a little more time to pay. Instead, they barged inside the house, taking their personal belongings by force. I was left wondering about the kind of faith practiced by these supposed Muslim brothers."

"If anything like that had ever happened, I'm very sure that those people were not among our group," the Hajj responded. "We have donated thousands of dinars to help impoverished people. We frequently buy food, clothes, shoes, and toys for the poor. Each Thursday night we provide a bounty of food for the hungry at the Mosque. We do much better than taking poor people's belongings. Usury is a sin, and we don't wish to anger Almighty Allah by committing the great sin, and to be punished in the fires of Hell."

"I hope that I am wrong" Nadeem replied.

"I must introduce Salim to other brother Dervishes," the Hajj explained. "Will you give your permission? We want to see your younger brother Salim getting on with his duties among the Dervishes."

"It's all right, if it suits Salim," his mother said.

Salim nodded his head agreeably.

The following week, Salim told Abdul that he had joined the Dervishes to further his religious education. Abdul was devastated. In extreme fury, he sprang to his feet and began upbraiding him. "Why would you join the Dervishes without consulting with me? Why would you take the advice of a man you met on the street without asking advice from the doctor who has taken you into his personal care? How could an intelligent person like you be so stupid, Salim? Why? Why did you do such bad things to hurt yourself and your family while we have desperately tried to relieve your misery? What happened to you? Tell me? What have they told you?

"What drew you to them? Was it their atrocities to Allah's religion and to Nasiriya's people? Or are you just so reckless, so careless or maybe heartless—and I didn't know? How could you be so naïve ... so weak ... to let these evil men laugh at you like that? My God, you've hurt me, Salim—deeply. You backed off on our pledge and you hurt my pride, your family's pride, and the pride of every honest person in the city! What happened to our promise? Hadn't we vowed to be truthful to each other? No, Salim, you have hurt us all. Why? How could you do such things to yourself? How can you face our neighbors after you join those roaches?"

Salim took a step back and stood in shock. He'd known Abdul to be a wise, calm, and mature man. Now—witnessing him so distraught—so burning in rage, Salim slumped motionless, eyes downcast.

"I didn't know all that, Abdul," he uttered weakly. "I didn't know I was wrong to listen to the Hajj. I'm sorry. I apologize for not letting you know. Hajj Ajil was my father's friend, who beautified the Qur'an and Islam. I believed him. He knew my father, and I trusted him for that. I thought I could become a knowledgeable believer. I thought it might please you. I wanted to … surprise you."

"Ajil is your example of piety?" Abdul snarled. "You don't know Ajil. Do you know that when Ajil went to Mecca for Hajj, he bought merchandise—electronic tools and fine rugs—to sell at a profit when he returned to Nasiriya? That is Ajil's faith."

Salim stood in shamed silence. Then he asked Abdul, "What should I do to get out?"

The healer sadly shook his head. "There is no getting out; don't you know that, Salim? Once in, you are a Dervish for life."

"What will happen if I leave?" Salim asked fearfully.

"You cannot leave. The Dervishes consider leaving an insult to their faith. They will hurt you. But, having acted so foolishly, you deserve all that, Salim. Why would a loving person like you want to be among those thieves? They are deceivers, usurers, and killers."

Tears formed in Salim's eyes. "I'm so sorry. Please forgive me. I'm in terrible trouble now."

"Just blame yourself for your trouble," Abdul said soberly. "And, if you end up dead, no one can change that, Salim. You failed me. We had promised each other to be truthful, hadn't we? How could you not discuss such a decision with me before stepping into the abyss? I still can't believe that you could do that to yourself—and to me. Now, it is too late to turn back. Let's see where this road takes you, Salim. I will be near you, though I'm not sure what I can do for you. We'll see."

Abdul sighed, his eyes still burning with sadness and chagrin. He and Salim stood, separated by generations and years of study in the ways of God and man. The walls of the room were stained with desperate silence.

CHAPTER SIX

Abdul's Misery

IN HIS PSYCHOLOGICAL TREATMENT OF SALIM, Abdul now turned to teaching him an esoteric language that few could speak. "This ancient tongue will hone your potential, your gifts from Allah," Abdul told him. The healer's home library contained many large books, so heavy that Salim had to hold them in both hands, and so old that the original rich colors of their bindings had faded. Abdul taught Salim to turn their once-sturdy pages, now fragile and easily torn, with loving care. Salim was astonished to comprehend that he was beginning to learn ancient Sumerian. Once the doctor's anger subsided, his joy at sharing the old tongue with an eager student was apparent in his eyes and his voice.

"I studied Sumerian history in school, Abdul!" Salim brimmed with enthusiasm. "If you remember, two months ago, our history teacher took our class to Ur. He explained the Sumerian culture and their progress from scattered single-family farms to an urban society."

"Yes, I remember your trip to Ur. What else do you know about the Sumerian empire?"

"I know the irrigation network of the plain with its dams and canals was a remarkable achievement! Greater than any contemporary system."

"Yes! Tell me more, Salim. What does history say about the ancient civilization?" Abdul was smiling with pride.

"Our teacher said the Sumerians wrote and kept historical records, and their scholars studied man's history from approximately 3200 B.C. Do you know those ancient people invented the four-wheel chariot or cart, and new forms of water transport such as the sailboat? Abdul, why don't you let me read what the history book says?"

Salim carefully opened the book and began to read how the Sumerians pioneered political institutions, how they drew up the first laws to regulate and protect society. The civilization's greatness lay not only in its incomparable literary achievements, but also its system of philosophy and metaphysics. He read of the Lyre of Ur, dating from 2450 B.C., how the world's museums exhibit Sumerian sculptures, engravings, precious stone inlays, and jewelry.

"Some of those precious stones hang around your neck right now," interrupted Abdul.

"Are you telling me the truth!?!" Salim's eyes opened wide.

"What else did you learn about ancient Sumeria?" Abdul asked.

Salim reported how architecture flourished as the Sumerians built cities. They invented the arch, the vault, and the dome. Their skillfully designed towns were surrounded by strong ramparts, and dotted with towers and temples decorated with paintings and mosaics.

"Each city had its own ziggurats and temples with towers forming gigantic staircases." Salim spoke with excitement, his arms stretching to support his descriptions. "They were solidly constructed with glazed bricks and often designed to appear as spirals. Ur's ziggurat consisted of three flights of stairs with the top level a small but very beautiful temple dedicated to Sin, the moon god, the city's chief deity. The first towers were built at Erode, Ur, and Uric. They symbolized how Sumer, from the beginning of the fifth millennium B.C., stood as the scene of man's greatest power and progress." Salim put the book aside and looked at Abdul. "Where did you learn the Sumerian language?" the boy asked with wonder in his voice and eyes.

"You will soon know everything, I promise you." Abdul said softly. "Are you ready to begin?"

"I am ready." Salim was captivated by the written words, even the sculpture of the letters, their large, thickly curved lines. Some wound together like a bow; others reached out like domes or like many umbrellas in different positions. The lines and curves melded in an aesthetically-appealing arrangement. However, Salim struggled to understand and memorize the shapes and sounds, in spite of his great desire to learn. He spent many hours studying every day. On Fridays, the weekly holiday, Abdul usually tested him to measure his progress.

Salim relished the challenge of the new language, and welcomed his teacher's enthusiasm. Abdul's efforts gradually made it easier to learn. He also told Salim more about Sumerian life, customs, and traditions and how they differed from those practiced in Iraq today.

Salim began to realize that his life held more meaning than he had previously grasped. Almost nothing disturbed him now, except for the recurring nightmare of the blonde woman shooting herself. Although this violent dream persisted, he no longer suffered from trances, seizures, or the awful fits of shaking.

One Friday evening at Abdul's house, Salim and Abdul were relaxing after a quiet dinner. Abdul, wearing a long white gown, sat with eyes closed, as if meditating. He had entered earlier with a slide projector, which remained unused on the corner of the table. The hot weather invited a lazy mood. The winds blew and ebbed from the north, carrying the river's smells of fish and mud, mingled with the aroma of a neighbor grilling lamb. "Tonight, I'll tell you everything you want to know about me and my life," Abdul spoke quietly, almost secretly.

"All right," Salim replied, watching the healer and sipping his iced tea.

Abdul's clear eyes studied Salim, and he began his story. "I'm a scientist, an archaeologist, and I'm happy to show you some memories of my personal life through slides I kept from the work I loved and used to do." Abdul clicked on the slide projector, its light reflecting on a screen set up across the room.

"At the beginning of my career, I was very successful. My loving wife is my cousin and our beautiful only son, Mirath, made our life overwhelming with joy and satisfaction. After his birth, I took them both to England when I went to study archaeology, and received my M.S. degree. Soon, the University hired me to travel on several missions, searching the world's ancient cultures. I would often leave my wife and son in England, since he was going to school. Then, Mirath was enrolled in the College of Medicine and graduated in the top ten in his class. In some pictures you see me with my family in different places around the world. Others show my team where we searched for old civilizations in southwestern Asia, Africa, India, and a few areas of the Americas. Most of the pictures were taken in Ur.

"The Sumerian life, culture and civilization were my indisputable passion. I had to dwell in Ur for many years, only two miles from Nasiriya, so I could study the Sumerian language. My team and I dug day and night trying to recover evidence of the early Sumerian civilization who built the city of Ur. We were able to recover priceless treasures and valuable historical items. We discovered evidence dating back to the Gilgamesh era. We also realized past Sumerian behavior through examining material remains of their ancient culture. We recovered bones of humans, ruins of buildings, and human artifacts—items such as jewelry, pottery, and tools. We studied written records: the ancient Sumerian government archives, personal correspondence, and business records.

"Our discoveries catapulted Iraq to the highest cultural plateau, higher than other nations bragging about owning priceless archaeological masterpieces. With my devoted and hard-working team, we brought the ancient Iraqi civilization back to life. We enabled our nation to preserve the greatest remaining artifacts with the richest evidence. We outlined the daily lives from our ancient history.

"Then, after my return from my missions to India, Africa and Egypt, I decided to return to Iraq. We discovered more ruins in every city in the country. It was something really amazing."

Abdul grew quiet, studying the final slide: the broken lower half of a bronze sculpture, a nude human figure on a round pedestal—the famous Basset Ki statue. Then he turned off the machine, sat down on the chair, and sighed.

Salim studied his blessed mentor, waiting patiently for him to continue.

"In my research of the Gilgamesh era, I discovered many intriguing stories that seemed to have taken place in Ur. They related and confirmed a curse that seems to have afflicted each successive generation. It might explain why Nasiriya has seen so many calamities, such as floods, fires, and

Dervishes who have now taken over town life. History indicates that each generation has a curse. And very likely, my ancestors were among the families who had moved to Nasiriya from Ur. We have been cursed ever since. "I'm saying this because my cousin and wife Majida, our only son Mirath, and I have all been afflicted by disaster. Majida had always been ill and depressed, requiring medical attention. Once, she was in a fire that nearly killed her. Since then, Majida has suffered three miscarriages. Our greatest catastrophe was when our only son, Mirath, was unjustly sentenced to death. Majida has been unable to speak ever since.

"I searched the folklore of Sumerians who had moved from Ur to Nasiriya, and I was amazed to find similar curses that had fallen on my people. An ancient Sumerian text told of Soberian, a man who suffered a sad, tormented love affair with his wife, Morisona. I don't know if you would like to hear the story. Perhaps some other time, Salim? It might be true, no one is sure."

Salim edged closer on his seat. "Sure, please, by all means."

Abdul breathed deeply, and then continued in a sad voice, "After our son Mirath's graduation, he finished his residency and became a specialist in internal medicine. My wife, though, wanted the family to return to Baghdad, where her dear folks lived. We so did in 1960. During our first week there, the prime minister received me at his office. In no time, I was nominated for the job of General Manager of Iraqi Archaeology and Museums. A hospital in Baghdad hired our son as a physician shortly thereafter. Life was good for several years." Abdul paused again, seeming lost in his memories. Then his face hardened, and he continued his story. "In 1963, the Ba'athist coup overtook Iraq, and the political troubles started devastating the society, making people struggle toward an unknown future. One day, a hypertensive woman was admitted to the VIP hospital under Dr. Mirath's treatment. The woman was a close kin to the new Ba'athist prime minister—a wife or sister, I don't remember exactly. My son treated her and her blood pressure, which soon receded to normal. Every evening, before getting off work, he checked on her to see how the treatment was going. He found that she was recovering.

"But when Dr. Mirath checked on her each morning, her blood pressure registered alarmingly high. He wondered, *how could sleep be causing her blood pressure to spike?* Nurses confided in him, saying the woman loved pickles. At night, she would send her bodyguard to buy food that the hospital would not serve her. She desired salted roasted hazelnuts, peanuts and pistachios. Upon hearing this, Dr. Mirath became infuriated, knowing that the unauthorized salt was dangerous to her health. He complained to his supervisor, but, the supervisor turned a deaf ear, ignoring this irregular behavior because he feared the prime minister. This enraged Dr. Mirath even more. He tore off his lab coat and stethoscope, threw them in his supervisor's face, and stormed out. He told him he could not accept such unprofessional practices.

"That night, the woman died. When the hospital supervisor told the authorities that Mirath had been her doctor, the prime minister held Mirath responsible for her death. Security men of the Ba'ath regime banged on our door, arrested our son, and threw him in prison. The authorities pretended to investigate, subjected Mirath to a hasty trial and executed him. They also arrested my wife and me. I was subjected to heinous torture that left me with fractures in both of my legs. They also knocked out my wife's teeth. Ever since then, she has suffered from psychological trauma. My wife has never uttered a word since. I resigned from work. Then we moved from Baghdad to Nasiriya.

"Licensing my clinic here took only a week. The steady work relieved my anxiety and restored my sense of purpose. My previous scientific background included training in psychology and health, as well as archaeology. Years of correspondence courses with an Egyptian health institute had resulted in a diploma in psychology and physiology, so opening the clinic here seemed natural. The daily flow of patients has helped ... take away my pain."

Abdul turned and studied Salim. "I wanted to tell you all of this so you will truly know me and trust me. I won't hide anything from you, Salim. You're like the son I lost. I also want you to realize that you are not the only human being who has faced troubles. Troubles are a part of life. Others may experience worse trials than you and me. We can accept our own trials, help each other, and not only fight to survive, but stand on our feet again."

The two friends studied each other. Nothing else was said. There was only a brief silence, followed by a determined nod of Salim's head.

A few evenings later, Abdul led Salim to a locked room on the second floor of the doctor's house. Inside stood two antique kingly chairs of black wood. They were upholstered with soft, expensive-looking leather. Each featured a sponge-like pillow for resting the back and head. In the center of the room, beneath a chandelier, was a round table of the same black wood, covered with a red cloth. Another table in one corner held numerous small statues and ancient precious stones, chalcedony, and emeralds. On one side of the room many red pillows sat on fur rugs. A floor lamp stood in each corner. Hundreds of books, old and new, large and small, lined shelves against three of the room's walls. A black-framed mirror about three feet long hung on the fourth wall. Mid-mirror was a portrait: a man's profile and an attractive woman with black eyes, narrow nose, and small mouth and lips. They both gazed unhappily to one side.

Salim was still examining everything when Abdul began to speak. "This is my special room, or, if you like, my special world. In here are my life and history. Besides Majida, my wife, you are the first person to have the privilege of entering."

Abdul turned the chandelier off, and switched on a little light bulb in the room's furthest corner. He pulled up two chairs, placing them side by side in front of a screen on the wall. He clicked on a slide projector, and then said, "The old Sumerian story told of a married couple, Soberian and Morisona, who were slaves in the Ur temple. The temple was their home. They had devoted themselves to serve the temple and share its religious ceremonies day and night. The couple loved each other heartily. One day, feeling great passion, they sneaked away from their chores and made love in a temple closet.

When the god, Sin, discovered their offense, he became infuriated. He considered their lovemaking a profanity that desecrated the temple, for which he cursed them forever. Separating them, he banished them from the kingdom, forcing them to live apart for thousands of years, despite their unforgettable love for each other. He cursed their hearts to burn with flames of love and lust.

All of that time, Soberian could not have sex with another woman. Morisona was cursed to live in the sea, forever alone. They could never meet again despite the flame of love and the tortured longing in their hearts. I'm going to read some parts of their story written in the Sumerian language:

"Soberian felt the unbearable flame of love burning in his heart for his wife, Morisona. He went praying and begging to Sin, their god. With tears in his eyes, Soberian fell to his knees, and pleaded, 'my great god Sin, I am your slave Soberian. Please god, forgive me for my transgressions. Grant me your power and strength again. Let me regain my dignity and pride to continue the struggle against my failures. Fill me up with your eternal pardon and absolve my soul. Renew my spirit and let your blessings light up my life's darkness and fortify my weakness. Award me your wisdom and relieve my heart's burning lust. God, take my body as a humble sacrifice for the great Sumer kingdom. My great god Sin, I am your slave Soberian, begging you with eyes full of tears and a heart full of love. Let me see her again. Let me see my wife again. Give me the strength to conquer the void in which my soul is living. I have been dead a long time. I am dead despite the blood running in my veins. Bless me, god, resurrect me, and send me as a living human again. Let me see Morisona one more time.'"

Abdul paused and studied Salim, who stared intently at the screen. Then the master again spoke, "The story says, in that moment a cold wind rose from nowhere. The wind sounded like a woman's deep wailing, calling from far away. The wall around Soberian began vibrating. Then the woman's voice became clearer and clearer until Soberian recognized who possessed its desperate call.

"'Soberian, my husband, can you still recognize my face after all these years?'

"'Morisona, my wife, you are in my heart,' Soberian whispered. 'You will live within me forever.'

"His eyes fixed upon the wall. He trembled. The woman's image began to appear: beautiful, nude, her graceful dark body covered to her knees with long shining, ebony hair. She stood on the shore of a great, mysterious sea. She turned her eyes to her husband. In spite of her smile at seeing him, her stunning eyes revealed deep pain.

"She stood, staring in silence at her husband for a long time. Then she waved, with an expression of blame. Soberian froze in his place, his face forlorn and bloodless, his lips parched, quivering. He waved back, tears streaming down his face. The woman waved again, then descended, disappearing into the sea.

"Soberian jumped up, sobbing, wanting to follow her.

"'Don't leave me again, Morisona. Don't leave me in pain and torment. I have had enough. Take me with you. Don't leave me in this prison. It has been thousands of years, and I am still waiting for the god Sin's mercy to absolve me or destroy me. I have been punished enough. Don't leave me Morisona, please, don't.'"

Abdul stopped speaking. Salim gazed at him. They sat in sad silence. Then Salim spoke. "It's a sad and painful story, Abdul. I assume the pictures on the mirror are theirs?"

"That's right. I drew them to bring their story to life. To portray their curse. I believe the Dervishes could be among those who carry the curse." Abdul gazed longer, then added: "I believe they carry the curse to you."

CHAPTER SEVEN
The Dervishes

DAYS LATER, AROUND MIDNIGHT, SALIM AND HAJJ AJIL WERE WALKING along the dark empty streets. Hidden drums grew louder and louder as the two walkers approached the forest. To Salim, the hypnotic drumbeats felt as if they entered his very soul.

The two found their way with flashlights and the bright moon, as the forest began to close in. Salim breathed faster. He remembered old, terrifying stories about the forest. Anxiety gripped him as his heart pounded. An owl hoot startled him, and he gasped.

Ajil sensed that Salim was troubled, "There is absolutely nothing to worry about, Salim. Our fears are created by our own imaginations. When we are terrified by our absurd thoughts, they can destroy our perception of reality. Fear is man's natural and ultimate enemy. It can destroy our power. Yet, our fears are vital to our existence. They motivate us to find protection, to keep searching for hope and truth. Defy your fears, Salim. Don't ever let them defeat you."

Ajil's confident words calmed Salim. The drums pounded fiercely as the two reached the forest's center. Salim could now see a group of men sitting in a circle around a huge campfire, drumming passionately. Nearly all had small faces, beards, and mustaches. They wore ankle-length white pants, white long-sleeved shirts, with black cloths covering their heads.

Another group, both young and old men, sat in a long line outside the circle, swaying their bodies from right to left with the drums' captivating rhythms. They too wore black over their heads, but only small vests over their bare chests. Their white pants flowed from their waists to their feet, which were covered with light slippers.

The scene frightened Salim. Yet he found himself seated beside the Hajj, a part of the outside circle. An old, wrinkle-faced man brought them a jar of watery liquid. His mouth was almost completely hidden under a thick, gray mustache and beard, his small, luminous eyes bracketing a bulbous nose. He offered Salim a drink, mumbling words Salim couldn't understand. Sipping it, Salim winced from its bitter taste, and then passed the jar to Ajil, who drank and handed the jar back to the old man. He too drank some and then returned to sit in his place.

"That was Chief Omran, and the rest are my friends, the Dervishes," Ajil whispered, studying Salim. "You're not scared, are you?"

"Yes, I am, and this is ridiculous," Salim snapped, his eyes downcast.

Ajil spoke softly to reassure him, "They are kindred souls, and you'll be safe. You will love them." The drums grew even louder and the fire swelled as a man shook the jar, splashing some of the potion. Suddenly, all the Dervishes stood up. Each approached Salim, hugging him and kissing both of his shoulders; then each returned to sit.

Chief Omran jumped inside the swaying circle, holding up a sharp skewer. Bright-eyed, agile, he danced perilously close to the fire, peering at nothing and no one. He swirled the skewer around, up and down. He threw his head back, bending his body at the waist with his feet apart, as if in a trance. Suddenly he raised his arm, slipped the skewer into his open mouth, and eased it smoothly, penetrating his cheek, showing no signs of pain. The skewer's end appeared inside his mouth. One more push sent it through his tongue. Salim trembled as he watched. He saw no blood, no sign of pain. The old man then pulled the skewer from his cheek and danced happily back, sitting in his place. The circle continued swaying, the drums pounding.

A young man sitting beside Salim became agitated, stood up and pulled a large skewer from under his vest. He jumped inside the circle, dancing about with great agility and strength. He lifted his left arm and began pushing the skewer slowly, skillfully through the arm's muscle and out to the other side.

Again no blood, no pain. After a few seconds, he pulled the skewer from his arm, only to dance around, bend backward with his legs apart, and push the skewer's sharp end into his stomach. Using both hands, he painlessly, bloodlessly cut from his abdomen to his belly button.

Salim's entire body vibrated with fear. He turned pale with nausea.

"Hajj, I'm so scared," Salim gasped. "I want to go home. This is too much for me. I must go home."

"Be quiet, Salim!" Ajil insisted in a hushed voice.

The young man removed the skewer from his stomach and placed it between his teeth. He pranced around the circle for a few minutes before taking his seat, and continued swaying from left to right in sync with the drums. A third Dervish removed his vest and jumped into the circle. He carried a pin about twelve inches long and one-half inch in diameter. Shaking trancelike, he pushed the sharp pin into his neck. There was no sign of harm. He swayed and swayed, removed the pin, then sat down in his place.

Omran rose and came over, sitting in front of Salim. The drummers abruptly stopped playing. The old man's eyes became even smaller as he looked into Salim's eyes. Both Omran and Ajil closed their eyes and began mumbling indiscernible phrases. Salim paled even more, and felt faint. Every muscle grew rigid. When their mumbling finished, Omran took some potion and washed Salim's face and hands, and then offered him some drink. Salim sipped the bitter liquid again. The old man moved back to his place. Ajil stood up, looked at Salim, and cried in a loud voice, "Welcome to the Dervishes! Welcome, Salim! You are one of us!"

The drums again rumbled and everyone rose. Ajil led Salim to the middle of the circle. The men wearing vests all began dancing inside the circle, including Ajil. Everyone pulled out a sharp skewer. Salim was surprised to find that Ajil also carried one. In time with the drums' hypnotic rhythm, each dancer pushed his skewer into his body, some in the chest, and others in the shoulder, and a few in the jaw. Salim watched the Hajj insert his skewer under his lower jaw, up through the inside of his open mouth until it penetrated his tongue. The Dervishes continued to dance until they collapsed with exhaustion. Ajil left Salim at his home around four o'clock the next morning.

Salim slept until afternoon.

After waking, Salim contemplated his experience with the Dervishes. He was unable to explain the sharp skewers penetrating their flesh, the chest, neck, and stomach, without any bleeding, pain, or fear. He remained amazed by their ritual piercings, but understood that the Dervishes considered their unusual acts as evidence of faith. Salim thought, *they are either insane or very sacred, and I must know what the heck is going on.*

Salim accompanied Ajil every Thursday night to experience the Dervishes. Now, he watched their dancing and piercings with a new fearlessness. In fact, he began to enjoy the rituals, especially when the Hajj took him to the middle of the circle, inviting him to dance with them.

At first Salim had hesitated, but Ajil commanded, "Dance, my good Salim; dance and be one of us. Just dance to the drums." After only a few minutes, Salim was astonished, overcome with ecstasy as he danced among the Dervishes.

From the other side of the circle, the old man began to sing, and in a few seconds, the other Dervishes joined him:

> *Tossing as a small boat on a stormy sea*
> *My heart was lonely before*
> *We met, both you and me.*
> *You led me to the shore and awarded me the key*
> *To wisdom; to all happiness, you gave me the key.*

After nearly three years, Salim had become one of the Dervishes. He let his beard grow and shaped his mustache like theirs. He followed their diet, mainly of vegetables, fruits, dairy products, and barley bread. Meat was prohibited. The Dervishes' philosophy emphasized asceticism and celibacy. A person must neglect his body, restrain his passions and overcome his lusts to become spiritually powerful. "Our vision is to create a good generation of Muslims," the Hajj had explained, "by inculcating values of faith and principles of ethics through Islamic educational lectures."

Ritualistic ceremonies and tests for beginners were held on different weekdays. Omran lectured prior to the Thursday night dancing ceremonies.

Salim listened intently and memorized the old man's words, "Only with a pure spirit can man become guiltless. Only with unity of mind and body can man conquer wickedness. Oneness is the first basic step on the path of wisdom. Fortitude gives him power beyond mortal limitations. Always remember that your soul is your essential source, the center of your wellbeing. The soul is your pride and source of glory. Your soul will never forsake or betray you."

Salim immersed himself in this new life. The lectures captivated his mind and dancing to the hypnotic drums embraced his emotions. Sitting in his appointed place, his body swaying with the other Dervishes to the drums, he would grow more and more excited. His stomach would vibrate and tickle; his body jerked involuntarily, and he gradually surrendered control of his immediate surroundings. Vitality ran through his body, and he began to feel happy and content. Salim surrendered ordinary reality and felt himself flying away, sensing only his heart keeping time with the drums. He was entering another world—a world of ultimate peace, contentment, and freedom. Salim found himself dancing and holding his own skewer. Each time he danced, Salim's skewer cut himself without drawing blood or bringing pain.

For the first time in his life, Salim felt free from his childhood illness, from the anxiety that had controlled him as long as he could remember. Now he adored the rituals that he shared with his brothers. He felt deep bonding with the Dervishes, who loved and respected him. Omran's teaching and philosophical lessons fortified his self-confidence and brought security to his soul. And for a while, Salim was content and free of agitation.

Yet, during these years, negatives also began to creep in and surround him. Salim awakened to a contradiction. On the one hand, he found satisfaction in the theoretical, disciplined Islamic education he was receiving. On the other hand, he witnessed reckless behavior among the Dervishes. Though honored leaders regularly outlined the divine faith prescribed for all through philosophical lectures, members were sinning. While lessons emphasized soul purification through Islamic principles, the failures to apply such virtues were not limited to new converts. Salim was becoming confused and disillusioned.

Behaviors and perversions grew more and more grotesque. Salim could

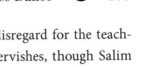

not feel empathy with any of the brothers because disregard for the teachings permeated every level of the fellowship. The Dervishes, though Salim fought to perceive them as pure, came to resemble caricatures of the faith. As they sensed Salim seeing through the veneer of their faithfulness, brother after brother became estranged, unfriendly, sulky, arrogant, distrustful, and finally, silent.

Then they began repeating to him a shocking oath: They assured him that, as he belonged to them, no one would ever threaten or harm him, not even his own brothers or father. Anyone who threatened him, no matter who he was, would be killed.

This brought Salim to a fateful question: How could a true Muslim kill people? How could killing to be acceptable among them?

Salim often heard his family saying bad things about some of the Dervishes, for some were money-lenders and usurers, forbidden as one of the great sins of Islam. Salim himself had witnessed incidents which revealed their hardened hearts.

An impoverished family had borrowed money from the Dervishes, but could not repay the loans on time. One day, Salim saw two Dervishes knocking on the family's door, demanding payment. The debtors pleaded for a little more time to pay, but the lenders rejected their plea. The Dervishes bullied their way inside the house and confiscated the family's belongings by force. Such events lingered in Salim's blood like a poison, and although he became increasingly frightened of the Dervishes, he could find no way out. "No one gets out after becoming a brother. Remember that, Salim." Omran had told him that from the very beginning.

When Salim joined them, he soon found out how ruthless and extreme they could be. To qualify as a member, he had to pass a rigorous test for a whole week—fasting for days without water or food, and walking barefoot through a path of snakes and scorpions. Salim had passed these trials, but their demands left him devastated and ill for days. It had been the most terrifying experience of his life.

Ajil explained that the process was part of every member's rite of entry. It assured his loyalty and readiness for anything he was asked to do.

"Do you mean ... including sacrificing one's own self?"

"Yes, in fact, sacrificing oneself is the final objective," Ajil responded solemnly. The answer horrified Salim. He wished he had never joined them.

"Why should I sacrifice myself for them? I thought that you brought me here to find happiness and to heal, not to sacrifice myself for such evil, Hajj?"

"Don't worry Salim, I'm here with you. I won't let anything do you any harm."

"I want out!" Salim was angry.

"It's not a good idea to do that, Salim. No one can get out after joining. They can be ruthless."

"Why did you throw me in with such troubled souls, Hajj?"

"Don't worry, Salim. Trust me."

The Dervishes' real goals gradually became apparent to Salim. As time passed, he could even discern their falsehood when they simulated piety and wisdom, or when they emphasized asceticism and celibacy only to trap people. They wanted to look like good Muslims but hid behind Islam's name to deceive innocent people into joining them. The lectures emphasized purity of man's spirit as the only certain way to enter paradise. Members, teachers insisted, must deny every passion and bury their own desires. Only then would they transcend pettiness and merge their souls into one. In the lectures, Omran insisted that a member must persevere with them, that there was no way out. Each man must work sincerely for the faith's fulfillment, even to the point of martyrdom. An honorable death would send a person to *Janna*, paradise.

"How can people comply with such outrageous rules?" Salim scoffed. "Do they really expect me to die for them?"

"At the present stage, no, they don't expect you to die for them," Ajil said simply. "But, if you complete the process, then someday you might be asked to give your life for Allah."

"Are you serious? What are you talking about? Do you really think that one day I will change my mind and consider dying for such bastards? Tell me, Hajj: Are you ready to sacrifice your own life for them?"

"See, Salim, there is a big difference between dying for them and dying for Allah's cause. If you ask me whether I could die for them, the answer is definitely no. But, if it is for Allah's cause, my answer would be yes. And it will be a great honor. Our perspectives are different. The difference in our ages, experience, and understanding all have much to do with answering a question like yours. However, within time, your opinion will change toward many things. No perspective will remain unchanged forever. At the present, you should learn how to survive in places you might hate or where people might dislike you. Try that and see if it deepens your soul."

"I don't understand some of your opinions, Ajil. How can they be sure that members are not cheating on the rules anyway? Do they have someone watching over them to see how they behave?"

"It's a good question, but, as far as I know, most people who join do not need to cheat. The group can be divided into three categories. First, the honest and pious believers who actually wish to die martyrs. In this category, people's sincerity of faith derives by fearing Almighty Allah and extreme love for Him. To them, life is what Allah has explained in the Qur'an, a period of time for testing people's intentions, so Allah may distinguish between those who hold fast and obey His commands, and those who go astray.

"The second category involves those who survive like blind men. They joined the group to follow Islam's faith, hoping for Allah's forgiveness. Most used to be either thieves or killers. Others experienced lives filled with atrocities, but sought repentance. These people are easy victims who can be exploited readily by their leaders. They can kill and perform other atrocities, thinking it's in the name of Islam.

"The third group is the masters, the politicians and strategists. They hide behind Islam's name to cover up falsehood. They plan and initiate financial campaigns, and might be connected with international fanatics. These are the really destructive and evils ones."

"So, where I do I stand? I don't see myself in any of the three categories, Hajj."

"That's right; you're not in any of them."

"Why am I congregating with them, then? I don't see myself assimilating in philosophy or behavior."

"Well, maybe to learn more about life and people, to benefit from lectures concerning the knowledge of Allah's creations, so you can appreciate and venerate the Disposer of all affairs for his creatures. Perhaps to grow in knowledge of Islam's precepts, its doctrines of love, tolerance, forgiveness, and redemption."

Ajil watched him, then continued, "I know they were only lectures uttered by a bunch of liars, twisting facts to trap people, but they are still the holy words of Allah. You'll learn that their lectures, regardless of the purpose, elucidate our religion's most complicated issues. And finally, you might learn much about the true Muslim's commitment to Islam, the happiness that people can find in their devotion to Allah.

"See, Salim, here's the problem for these fanatics: They put their own interests over their beliefs. They subvert Islam's principals to their own agendas, but, when it comes to the knowledge they possess, it is still venerable scholarship. They are like the Muslim who can pray the five daily prayers, go to Mecca for Hajj, help others, but still drink alcohol and commit other sins. After all, you don't have to do the despicble things they do. As long as you're with them, they respect you, as you deserve. What are you losing? Just look at the bright side and learn more, Salim."

Ajil's strategy proved successful with Salim. He stayed with the group, listening to Islamic lectures teaching adoration of Almighty God and obedience to His rules. He considered and appreciated what he heard about Islam's philosophy. Salim's life in the Sheikh's house had left too many wounds deep in his soul. Some were forgotten, others were about to heal, but many still festered. In time—after attending scores of lectures—guilt crept back into his soul, like a tiger in the night.

The lecturers introduced Salim to a new meaning of Islam. Like architects with unlimited budgets, they painted visions of an intricate construction in which the philosophy of the Qur'an was both doctrine and constitution. Lavishing phases of the Prophet Mohammad's message and prophecy, the lecturers also glorified the happiness Muslims found in martyrdom and the rewards of the hereafter. Despite Salim's ever-present guilt, he found himself wondering about the happiness he could achieve through practicing the faith as Omran described it. Could a new relationship with God save him from evil? Could it reinvigorate him in holiness and subdue his fears?

"What can I lose if I try?" Salim asked himself.

The Dervishes held ritual ceremonies and tests on different days of the week. Omran lectured before each Thursday dance ceremony. Salim always listened to the old man's lectures and often memorized them:

"Death is only the beginning of life, a life of rewards for believers. This life we're living is nothing but torment, affliction, and tests. It's for pagans obsessed with lust and sins. No pious believer should be fooled by life's adornments and lewd or vain desires. It is the eternal life in the hereafter that we should prepare for. It is the *Janna* we should be striving to fulfill. The promise from the Almighty is our triumph. We shall see the Lord in all his majesty—the Lord of heaven and earth and between! Eternal life has been promised to all the repentant, so be patient in joy as you bow down and prostrate yourselves before Allah, the Omnipotent King."

One Friday morning, Salim went to see Nejat at her store. She sat alone, sad and thoughtful, her eyes downcast.

"Hi, girl, what's happening? Why are you looking so gloomy?"

"Hello Salim, how are you?"

"Good, good. What's bothering you?"

"Well, I'm having trouble with Omran: He's begun taking all the money I earn as a Mullaiah. He's adamant that the store brings in more than enough for my needs. He also wants to force all the Mullaiahs to return to work, just like we did for the Sheikh, only this time, to work for him. If we refuse, he threatens to have us killed."

"What? Chief Omran? What happened to his faith and his commitment to kindness and morals? What happened to all that? Do you want me to plead your case before him?"

Nejat smiled, responding with a sarcastic twist of her nose. "Do you imagine he will listen to you, poor fellow? You don't understand Omran's true nature yet. Omran—and the rest of the Dervish leadership—is heartless. He talks faith okay, but really only worships money. He is a sadistic killer, and you'd better pretend you don't know about his secrets."

Then Nejat lifted her sad gaze to Salim. "I so regret having concealed the true nature of the Dervishes from you, Salim. I'm *really* sorry. It was Omran who killed my brother, Aziz. My brother was a leader among the Dervishes. He was also Omran's best friend. You know that they both had shares in the Sheikh's business. But, when they got into trouble with the Sheikh, our Sheikh embezzled their shares, banished them from his palace, and told them he never wanted to see them again.

"However, it seems that the troubles mounted between the Sheikh and his wife over Adela, the Sheikh's mistress. Nada hired Aziz and Omran to kill the Sheikh. After they murdered him, Omran became the Chief of the Dervishes, while my brother remained his working partner. Their business prospered, but Omran discovered that Aziz was having an affair with his American wife. So Omran killed Aziz. He sent the wife back to her country and … and … I've become his mistress. That was the reason I didn't want to have an affair with you. I know Omran. He would kill you."

Salim glared at her, growling, "Why did you get me involved with killers, Nejat, why? You thought that my troubles were not enough? You wanted to add to my grief? How Nejat, how can you be so cheap? How can I suffer your deception? Does everyone feel happy when they hurt me?"

"I'm sorry, Salim. I had to; they threatened me. The Hajj was determined to recruit you. If I failed to convince you to affiliate with them, they would have killed me. You don't know these people. They kill for joy."

That night at home, many questions burned in Salim's mind. He tossed and turned in his bed on the roof, looking at the sky, boiling in rage. He determined then to get out of the Dervishes. His conscience was inflamed; he would not return to them. Nejat and Ajil both had lied to him. He had been tricked twice, once by the Sheikh and now by these two devils. Ashamed because he had walked willingly to his misery, Salim knew he had to get out of this trap. To be honorable, Salim knew he must face Ajil about Omran's treachery, then give them a goodbye kiss. That's exactly what he would do tomorrow.

The temperature dropped that night, and a light breeze carried a fresh scent from the river. The clear sky shone with too many stars to count. Salim lay watching them flash as they gazed down at the earth. A star fell from the south and faded. When evil spirits were trying to reach heaven, Salim had heard it said, a star would intercede, sacrificing itself to consume the bad spirits.

Two hours had passed, and Salim still could not sleep. He shifted positions restlessly as his mind shuffled from worry to fear. Why was his life always only pain and suffering? Why could he not be strong and defeat his enemy? Why was he compelled to a dark fate? Why are humans too weak to conquer evil?

Salim remembered that his mother had once told him the Islamic faith emphasized that Allah, before creating every human being, already knew each one's destiny, whether it would turn out good or bad. Because he loved justice, Allah had also commanded that the Islamic faith should never be a compulsory religion. Allah had absolved and created people free of sin at birth and had given them freedom to choose their own paths. Also Allah, in his great mercy, had awarded man enough logic and wisdom to discern the right path from the wrong one.

In the meantime, as the creator of all things, Allah had commanded all creatures to worship him, glorify his greatness, acknowledge his authority in heaven and on earth, and obey his will entirely. On the Day of Judgment, everyone would account for themselves and be rewarded accordingly. On that day, as Allah said, the righteous people will be sent to Paradise to live forever, while the evil people will be thrown into hellfire, there to suffer eternally.

More restless than ever, Salim obsessed about Allah, the ultimate judge. Salim's own suffering had to do with his own intention and will. Allah never oppressed anyone. A person's faith, deeds and will determine their fate. Therefore, since his own faith was so insincere, his troubles must have been related to his own decisions.

Salim began mumbling to himself. "But what makes people choose an evil path while they know what extreme punishment awaits? Does Satan trick humans to commit sins? Aren't other people afraid of the hellfire that I am so scared of? The Judgment Day terrifies me. So why don't I try to be good and live up to Allah's commandments? Shouldn't I give up the Dervishes first and obey God?"

Salim still couldn't understand why even good people had to go through hardship and pain, no matter how righteous they are. He remembered his mother saying that Allah, the most merciful God who loves all his servants, puts each through tests to see how much of true faith is in their hearts. Salim guessed Abdul had been put to that test too, although he was behaving like an honorable person, and had helped everyone in town. *How long will an honorable man be made to suffer for one mistake?*

Salim tossed in his bed, changing positions, now lying on his back and again facing the sky. He reasoned in wonder, *Only Allah could create that beautiful sky and shape those gorgeous stars. Only Allah has created all of these magnificent things around us. No one could do such marvelous things but Him.*

As Salim shifted on his bed, he accidentally touched his necklace and wondered, *Is it true that these Sumerian stones are protecting me from evil? Have these three stones made a difference in my spirit? How could stones bestow happiness and security? How could they be so powerful and invincible? What are their secrets? Who blessed them and gave them the power to heal? Where did their holiness arise?*

I do not believe these stones could perform any healing or contain any curse without God's blessing. It is only by Allah's will that people benefit or suffer. If these stones could really help anyone, they might just as well have helped Abdul when he needed it. Who is going to answer these questions? Who is going to save my life from agony?"

Their glowing rhythms dancing in his eyes, the stars continued to fascinate Salim.

In the morning, Salim ached from the restless night. Exhausted, he stayed in bed and didn't go help in Abdul's clinic. Salim had learned a great deal observing Abdul treat people who suffered emotional and physiological distress. He had helped elderly people to lie down in the examining room, helped as needed to remove their shoes or shirts. Salim operated an unusual light that Abdul used when treating mentally ill patients. He even washed some patients' faces and hands, taking care to be gentle though thorough. Taking out the trash and refilling swab dispensers were not beneath Salim and Abdul always offered payment for his help.

Later that day, Salim went to meet Ajil. Sitting quietly with the Hajj, Salim spoke, "Ajil, I don't know how to begin. However, I want you to know this, I'm fed up with the Dervishes. Since I joined you over three years ago, I've been extremely unhappy. Besides, I was trapped in the first place. The ways you presented the faith never felt right, not the way to true happiness for me. When I look at what I've accomplished working with you, I resent having lost time and having tainted my family's reputation in the city.

"Your life and the way you seek happiness, whether for yourself or for other people, have not worked for me—or for others I've observed. Dervish leaders assume reverence and love for people, but their followers take advantage of people's weaknesses and neediness, plundering their money and property, and behaving like unbelievers. In conclusion, I am out, and this is final. I do not want to see you or to be near you. As I said, it's final."

Ajil smiled broadly, sighing sarcastically, "Oh, you scare me Salim, you're making me terrified."

Then Ajil's face distorted. He glared and snapped harshly, "And who do you think you are, you little rascal, to decide whether the Dervishes are good or not? Who are you in the community to judge us? Don't you know we can stomp you like an insect? Don't you know yet who we are? And what we Dervishes could do to you or your family? Why don't you just shut up so we might keep honoring you among us? Listen, you go home and reconsider this as seriously as you can, before we put you through hell."

"I don't need to rethink anything!" Salim shot back. "Moreover, I do not care about your threats. If you're a true believer, then you know that I only could die by Almighty Allah's leave. Meanwhile, old man, your death is likely to be sooner than mine. Just think of that, Ajil." Salim rose abruptly and walked away.

That day, Salim stayed home studying the Sumerian language, and mentally replaying his confrontation with Ajil. Salim prayed a humble supplication to Allah, asking God to protect him and his family from Ajil and the Dervishes.

Time passed. Salim noticed that his mother's mood had improved.

Perhaps, it was because he was rejuvinated, or perhaps because Nadeem was going to marry his cousin in a couple of weeks, according to the old tradition.

Salim busied himself helping Abdul, which seemed to bury fears about the Dervishes. The days passed quickly, and Nadeem's wedding day arrived. Salim's oldest brother shared vows with a young woman whom he had seen only a couple of times, and had never touched. In fact, they had spoken to each other only twice.

After the wedding ceremonies, Nadeem and his new bride walked to the car waiting outside. Neighbors and townspeople crowded about them. Many of the women were singing and dancing, their vocal ululations swirling joyously through the air. The harmonies seemed to release hidden anguish as they waved jeweled arms above their breasts.

CHAPTER EIGHT

The Surprise Journey

ONE MORNING SALIM RUSHED TO ABDUL ANGRILY AND CHALLENGED HIM, "Tell me, Abdul, why the nightmares are still assailing me and leaving me hopeless? What is the meaning of the blonde woman shooting herself? The sight and smell of blood covering her hair are so realistic. I panic and try to run away, but I can't. She grasps my hand and pulls me closer."

Salim stopped to wipe the sweat from his face, and continued, "Last night I dreamed so clearly I saw a birthmark on her neck. Always everything happens exactly the same way, but last night the birthmark became vividly clear, making the nightmare more frightening than ever before. It was as if I was experiencing it for the first time." Salim's voice grew weaker. "Abdul, please, tell me what it means. Who is the blonde woman and why do I still dream of her?"

Abdul looked at Salim with a sorrowful scowl. His voice breaking as he tried to comfort his friend, Abdul said, "Salim, I'm not sure, but all the signs indicate that you saw your fate, your future. My experience tells me that everything you saw in your nightmare will happen again in reality. Every detail will be part of your life one day. You will meet the blonde woman, and the bad dream will come true. I think soon after that dream becomes reality, your life will end."

Salim froze, staring in shock.

Abdul continued, "While I speak from long experience, I'm just guessing. Events are unpredictable, and only God knows what may happen.

Only Almighty Allah has power over everything. But I have been thinking about you and your distress since the day I met you. And I've concluded that your misery someday must stop. After observing thousands of lives as a doctor, I've seldom seen a case of a constant, repeated nightmare that did not end in misery. I'm sorry, my friend, to say all that, but it's my honest perspective on your case."

"How can you predict a fate so wretched, Abdul, tell me?"

"Salim, you're a very smart person, and I don't think you will stay with these Dervishes forever. Ajil brought you to them through deception. He did you no favor. He just confused you ... and scared you. Those villains will be after you, making your life a living hell until you die. The Dervishes will make you so miserable and hopeless, you will decide your life is not worth living. Of course, I hope I'm wrong, but my judgment is based on long analysis of their natures. For years, I have watched them twist young men to their service."

The New Year came. Salim was now almost twenty-one. In two months he would graduate from high school. Still, Abdul's prediction stabbed at his heart like a jagged knife. Now more pessimistic than ever, he saw no hope for his life.

One uncommonly cold February night, a small wagon stopped in front of Salim's house. A short young man, his round face almost concealed by a black beard, climbed down from the wagon. The man's skin matched his dark eyes. His clothes were different from any Salim had ever seen. He wore a thick leather vest laced up the front with a rope. A piece of brown cambric cloth covered him from his waist to his knees. His leather shoes were tied up to his shin, and a long brown cape hung around his neck and down over his shoulders.

He walked up to Salim's house and knocked. When Salim opened the door, the stranger began talking in the Sumerian language. Salim asked his mother to interpret. The man needed a midwife's help for a woman who had been in labor for twelve hours. She was only two miles from Nasiriya, and he asked if Monira could go to help immediately to deliver the baby. Monira prepared her small bag and asked Salim to accompany her.

They rode with the stranger, sitting silently as the two strong horses pulled the small wagon rhythmically along the dark road. Soon, a heavy rain covered Salim's face and his mother's. Lifting his coat collar, Salim sat close to his mother, hoping to warm them both.

In less than an hour, the wagon stopped suddenly. They sat before the old holy temple of the Sumerian Kingdom at Ur, a building that Salim knew had been in ruins for centuries. Salim was astonished to see that the city was occupied and thriving. *It can't be. It's impossible,* Salim thought. *I was here not long ago with my history class and everything I see here was in ruins, just like the pictures in the history books!*

Salim was even more surprised to see guards standing before the temple, ancient-style swords by their sides. They wore clothes similar to the short man. Salim glanced at his mother to find her gazing upon the busy temple in awe.

The man leaped off the wagon and led them up the ziggurat. They reached the temple's center by way of a large stairway built of rocks and bricks. A throng of people sitting inside stood when they saw Salim's mother. Then, all eyes turned toward a man sitting in a large chair surrounded by guards. His chair reminded Salim of the pair of carved chairs in Abdul's special room. The man was perhaps fifty years old, with a massive beard and thick eyebrows shading his bright, black eyes. Monira walked steadily toward him, and then knelt in respect and loyalty. Lifting her face to look at the man, she spoke carefully, "Your Majesty, I am ready to serve you," she said humbly. "Please, order me and let me be honored."

The king looked at her with regard, and said gently, "Thank you for coming over. You are welcome here with us."

He motioned for her to stand up. She stood, bowed, and was led through a passageway illuminated by torches mounted on the walls.

Looking around, Salim saw that the temple consisted of a large courtyard surrounded with many tall windows, arched at their tops. The stone walls were illustrated with carvings depicting hunting scenes, battles, and prayer ceremonies. The scenes portrayed men dressed in military armor and carrying swords, ready to fight. An intricate stone arch built above the king's throne boasted splendid designs of precious stones, lined all around with alabaster and gold. Larger-than-life sculptures of Sumerian gods occupied each corner.

Behind the king's throne was a semi-circular area for prayer and sacrifices with many torches lining the walls. A small iron pot produced a blue flame and an aroma of holiness which diffused throughout the hall. Near the middle of one wall stood a monolithic statue of a man sitting in his war uniform, one arm resting on the jeweled handle of a long sword, the point of which rested next to the statue's feet.

Salim, seated on a chair behind a large table, pondered the greatness of this scene and these people. He listened to a beautiful woman playing on a large instrument like a guitar and several other small instruments. She struck them with little sticks, producing a pleasing, calming sound.

The king clapped his hands as a signal, and a young female dancer entered the room. With sparkling brown eyes, long black hair, she wore a long, two-piece red gown that showed her slim, graceful legs. Salim was transfixed. She danced to several melodies before kneeling in front of the king, who waved a finger to dismiss her.

Salim noticed that nobody paid any attention to him, which was something of a relief. When Salim spoke to a guard, the guard walked away as if he had not heard. Two hours passed before Salim's mother appeared holding a baby wrapped in a bright white cloth. Smiling, Monira announced to the king, "You have a boy—a beautiful, healthy boy."

The king smiled. Monira brought the baby to a raised area behind the king and placed the infant on a large table covered with a scarlet sheet. She then bathed him, rubbing his small body with a liquid from her bag. The king rose and went over to the boy. He studied the child with a tender smile, then bowed to the huge statue and began reciting a prayer.

After praying, the king bent down to kiss the baby, and placed a golden chain around his neck. He then turned to Salim's mother, laying his hand on her head as if to thank her by offering her a blessing.

The bearded man who had fetched Salim and Monira reappeared and returned them to his wagon. They arrived at their home early the next morning. Without speaking a word, they both went to bed. Salim could not sleep, thinking about what he had witnessed in the thriving temple of Ur, in the city of ruins. It was difficult to accept what his eyes had seen. Yet, Salim knew that the experience was real.

How could things like that be? he whispered to himself. *Am I mad?*

Many hours passed and Salim still lay restlessly in his bed. Around seven in the morning, he finally fell asleep.

Midday, Salim woke up to someone knocking on the front door. It was Abdul, who had waited for Salim to show up as usual. When he did not appear, Abdul decided to come next door and find out why.

CHAPTER NINE
The Angel of Death

SALIM, STILL IN HIS BEDCLOTHES AND HALF ASLEEP, OPENED THE DOOR FOR ABDUL. "Peace upon you, Salim. I've been waiting for you," Abdul said softly. "Are you sick or something?"

"I'm fine. I just didn't get to sleep until early this morning, and for some reason, my mother did not wake me as usual." Salim covered his eyes with his hand to avoid the glare of the sun. "Please come in."

Abdul sat on the couch while Salim went to check on his mother. He was surprised to find her still in bed. She was lying on her back, eyes open and a half-smile on her sallow face.

"Momma?"

She did not respond. Salim shook her, but she would not move. He shook harder, and then raised her arm, but it dropped when released. Salim panicked. "Abdul, come quickly!" Salim cried, trembling.

"What is it?" Abdul called as he came running.

"My mother won't move. Do something!" Salim cried hysterically. Abdul grabbed her wrist, felt for her pulse, then bent and laid an ear on her chest to check for a heartbeat. Salim's eyes were glued to his mother's face in disbelief. "What is wrong with her, Abdul?"

Monira's empathetic heart, always full of love and kindness, was now still. Abdul, removing his ear from her chest, had heard only the silence of death. He looked at Monira's face, then turned to Salim. "I am sorry, Salim, your mother is dead. It seems that she had a heart attack while she slept."

Before Abdul could finish his sentence, Salim felt suddenly weakened at every joint, and his throat was dry. The room and everything around him was spinning. His tongue was dry and he fell to the ground, unconscious.

He did not open his eyes again for four days. When he finally awoke, he found Abdul sitting near his bed, rubbing his forehead with a cold, damp towel. Abdul smiled. "You are coming back to us."

Tears flooded Salim's face and he turned his head away.

Abdul told him his brother, Nadeem, had thrown himself into the grave and demanded to be buried with his mother. A few of the many respectful mourners had helped him back out when his grief was spent. "We are proud your mother had a large funeral. The entire town has been in mourning for her death," Abdul said with deep sorrow. "I lost a great friend. Nothing can replace her in my heart. Your mother's death was a great loss to us all."

Salim didn't speak. He only turned and stared at Abdul with sadness and gratitude.

A few days later, when Salim had regained strength, he took halawa, an Iraqi pastry, to the cemetery. Standing in front of the grave, he imagined his mother's face. What a caring, loving woman she was. Except for his friend Abdul, she was the only person who had truly loved him. He pictured her smiling at him, no matter what her own troubles or mood and recalled how wisely she handled others' problems, in her great desire to help all people. Remembering the extraordinary love and devotion she had for him through all of his miserable life, Salim cried. Thinking of how she had fought unfailingly for his safety and happiness, he wiped the tears from his eyes before lying down on her grave and placed his offering of halawa upon it.

"Momma, can you hear me?" he prayed in a weak voice. "Please, wake up and let me see your beautiful face once more. Let me hug you, kiss you, and hear your lovely voice lighting up my dark nights once again. What happened to your power, Mother? Aren't you the woman who defeated evil spirits? Aren't you the one who always protected me with your prayers and fortified my weak soul against the devil? How can you be dead? Aren't you the one who promised me you would never abandon me? Why have you left me alone? I need you today, just as I needed you before. Rise up again and sweep my pain and darkness away, please, Momma."

Salim wept over his mother's grave for hours. Finally, he stood up, brushed dirt from his pants, and returned to Abdul's house. Salim's trembling legs barely carried him down the road.

Abdul tried to cheer Salim up. As they sat at the supper table, where Salim hardly ate, Abdul said, "I know it hasn't been easy for you, Salim. Your mother was more than a sister to me. She came knocking on my door, asking me to help her with you. I was happy to grant her request with the best of what I had. As a midwife, your mother had helped hundreds of women give birth. She is remembered for gracious kindness in almost every household in Nasiriya. Neighbors won't forget such a generous woman."

Salim, who had no hunger, was sobbing into his napkin. Abdul advised him, "You can be proud of the well-attended funeral and burial that people prepared for your mother. May she rest in peace."

After a long silence, Salim said, "I am thinking about going to Baghdad to attend college. Maybe by living in a metropolis like Baghdad, I might find something to help me forget … before I lose my mind. My mother was everything to me, and now that she is gone I have nothing to keep me here. In this place, I become more miserable with each passing day."

"Do you think you will be happy in Baghdad?"

"Perhaps, if there is anything in this life that can make me happy, but I want to get away from here."

"What will you study, Salim?"

"Foreign languages, English and French, I guess. I want to read the literature of the world and learn about other cultures."

"If that's what you want to do, very well. I wish you luck." Bowing his head, Abdul said, "I will be lonely here without you. As you know, much of the pleasure I feel is because of you. Teaching you and telling you of my past have brightened my days."

Salim graduated from high school with high marks. In Iraq, a graduate usually writes down his first three college preferences. The Ministry of Higher Education and Scientific Research then assigns students according to their aptitude and grade-point average. Those with the highest scores are usually accepted into a college for medicine, engineering, pharmacy or dentistry. Graduates with lesser averages are directed into different majors according to the competitive results.

Salim's name appeared in the newspaper. As one of the top graduates, he had been accepted to the college of medicine and pharmacy, a high honor. He would also be considered for the college of foreign languages, the final decision was his. Soon Salim was pleased to receive an acceptance letter welcoming him to Baghdad University, and wishing him luck in studying foreign languages.

Salim's oldest brother planned to stay with him in Baghdad until he settled in and learned his way around. Within a few days, Salim would leave Nasiriya, the town that now held nothing for him, except for his strong relationship with Abdul. Salim was anxious to depart. The longer his family wore black clothes, the more depressed he became. Neighbors reminded him of how he missed his mother. Every time a woman was in labor, it reminded him of her absence, and he longed desperately to be with her again.

CHAPTER TEN

Life and Death in Baghdad

ON THE EVENING OF SALIM'S DEPARTURE FOR BAGHDAD, he waited with his brother at the railway station, filled with anxiety. He was leaving the people he loved. Salim now dreaded the thought of living in Baghdad, Iraq's largest city, surrounded by strangers. While they were waiting, Abdul appeared. He wanted to talk to his student privately. It was as if he could read Salim's mind.

"Salim, don't forget your gift of power and uniqueness, and don't let things worry you. You will be just fine in Baghdad. You will love it. But be wary, for a city that big can corrupt your soul. I will be your constant friend. Whenever you need me, I will be there to help you."

Abdul hugged Salim gently, trying not to cry in front of the few friends who had come to say goodbye. For the first time in Salim's memory, this man who was now his spiritual father wept as he held him in his arms. Abdul told him, "Son, in Baghdad, life will be full of excitement. I want you to enjoy life, but please use good judgment and take care of yourself."

Salim nodded, struggling to hold tears back.

The old train moved slowly through the desert. Stopping frequently to take on passengers at villages and crossings, the train lumbered ten hours to reach Baghdad. Salim and Nadeem hailed a taxi at the railway station and were soon at their hotel. At the hotel, Nadeem bought a city map to help them locate the college. Salim studied the map, trying to learn about the city. Nadeem watched him, smiling, pleased to see his brother's calm demeanor. Nadeem stayed ten days, making sure his brother was well settled both in his

college and the dorm. Salim shared a room with one other student on the top floor of the new three-story dormitory. Their window offered a lovely view of a spacious court and beautiful garden.

A ten-minute walk from the dorm to the classroom buildings traced through the Waziriah neighborhood, which was green most of the year. Lined with big eucalyptus trees and tall palms flourishing with dates, the streets were thronged with pedestrians, cars, and buses. In the green squares, flowers of yellow, white, and red bloomed profusely. Wide sidewalks welcomed conversation, with large brick seats every few meters. Cafes invited relaxation under the broad shade trees. Waziriah's streets and impressive, beautiful houses offered a sense of sophistication to the area. The quiet green avenues reminded Salim of the Cornice in his hometown. Life in this wealthy section of Baghdad proved carefree and peaceful. Salim felt secure in its serene atmosphere. He noticed that most house doors were left open all day long. The brick houses all appeared clean and nicely painted, with neatly tended gardens often surrounded by shoulder-high walls.

Fashion in Baghdad was European in flavor. Women wore pants and jeans, which surprised Salim. Women here did not cover their faces with the black veil called abaya, as they did in Nasiriya. Men and women freely walked hand-in-hand along the streets. In class, Salim was introduced to his first experience with co-education. Girls glanced shyly at him, with an evident willingness to make eye contact. However, as the young man, it was Salim who had to initiate that smile.

He enjoyed the college's new facilities and easy-going milieu. Large classrooms, a theater, and several basketball courts promised both study and relaxation. A casual cafeteria provided tempting and inexpensive foods and pastries. Nearby, the library, one of the country's largest, offered tens of thousands of books—many in foreign languages. Salim's schedule was much more flexible than in high school. There were about thirty students in his class, mostly young women with eyes that shone. Their Western hairstyles and makeup excited Salim. Around campus and on the streets of Baghdad, young men and women talked to each other without the hesitation—if not outright fear—that characterized young life in Nasiriya.

Relaxed in his dorm room after four days at the college, Salim reclined in a chair next to a small table, gazing across the room at a wall poster entitled "Baghdad at Night." The photo had been taken from an airplane above the city illuminated by streetlights and neon, as though swallowing the darkness. Clean white curtains hung at the windows, matching the white walls. Salim looked at the two steel lockers, one on each side of the room. He wondered about his roommate, who had not yet arrived, though his clothes and books had.

Later, in the middle of the night, a knock at the door awakened Salim. He opened to a handsome young man who smiled and shook his hand. "My name is Ekram, I'm your roommate. Sorry to bother you at this hour."

"Don't worry about that. I am Salim."

Ekram's dark eyes glistened of dreams and ambitions, but also hinted of sadness. His nose was large, and a thick mustache almost hid his lips. His dark hair was longer than most men's, and he wore a neck chain with the large letters E and F. Sitting down on his bed, he looked at Salim with interest. "Where are you from, Salim? What are you studying?"

"I'm from Nasiriya," Salim replied quietly. "I am studying American Literature."

"Have you been in Baghdad before?" Ekram asked, slipping off his shoes.

"Once, but I didn't see much of it," Salim answered.

"You will now, and you'll like it, too. I can guarantee that!" Ekram replied with a smile as he undressed for bed. "Good night, Salim, and have pleasant dreams." Ekram's voice sounded sincere, which pleased his roommate.

Salim savored his new life in Baghdad, a city of many contrasts with the conservative Nasiriya. Baghdad's pace was relaxed and friendly. At first, college life consisted of eating, sleeping, classes, and homework, repeated day after day. Salim began to realize that one only lives life once. *When it is time to die, no matter how young or old, how smart or dull, we each must go. Nothing, absolutely nothing, can change destiny. We must walk those unavoidable steps on our path at a certain time, whether we like it or not. Every one of us must walk their own last steps. It is the same end for everyone. That sounds fair enough,* Salim thought. *Yet, it is still terrifying and extremely sad.*

Still, most of the time we find that life is good, he decided. *We learn how to cope with life's uncertainty. People live as happily as they can, regardless of their troubles. Why do they try their very best to accomplish their goals and dreams, to fulfill their wishes and obligations, in spite of their burdens? Why do people still take chances again and again after suffering defeat? It's the nature of life—the will to survive—and the instinct for living.*

Salim kept these musings to himself as he walked quickly back to his dorm after a hectic day of classes. He was hoping to see Ekram, who had not been to their room for three days. Salim and Ekram had grown close, sharing their expressive spirits and tender hearts. They understood each other and related despite their different lifestyles.

Ekram lived as a free spirit. He drank alcohol and chased women, yet he balanced that with enough self-discipline to fulfill his responsibilities, both in school and to the people he cared for. He was a self-made man. He had put himself through high school and enrolled in the college of foreign languages. Ekram's parents had both died when he was still a boy, leaving him heavy debts plus the responsibility of caring for two brothers and three sisters. He took a job at age twelve to pay his parents' debts. Two of his sisters finally married and the third one lived with their uncle in the northern part of the country. Ekram had learned how to enjoy living and he knew how to stand up for himself. His early life had crushed him enough. Ekram told Salim that, at home, he and his siblings had to sleep many nights on empty stomachs. Ekram also told Salim that he had never before had a friend in whom he could confide. Ekram described how people took advantage of him by making him work overtime without pay, and how he had to carry heavy bags and boxes on his back when he was just a little boy.

"I have had much hurt and humiliation in my life," Ekram said as he sat with Salim in their room one night. "I will never forget it. I saw my own mother burned to death when I was just a boy. The fire was all over her and she cried desperately for help. My brothers and sisters trembled with me, all powerless. We were all too young to do anything.

"The fire ate away her dress and soon ate her too. She ran about screaming until she finally collapsed. She burned like a piece of coal. It happened so quickly. The neighbors rushed to help when they heard her screaming, but it was too late. She died on the way to the hospital. Dinner was left on the stove; she had been removing a dish from the stove when her clothes caught on fire."

Ekram stopped for a moment, and then continued in a weak voice, "I couldn't sleep after I saw it, and I was sick in bed for a long time." He dried the tears from his eyes.

Salim shared Ekram's sorrow as he asked himself many questions. *"Why can't I meet a friend who is happy? Why have all the people I have met been sad? Where can I find someone to tell me of joy instead of adding to my pain? But maybe if I met a happy person, I wouldn't understand him. Maybe I wouldn't be able to like him. Maybe I couldn't relate to him. Perhaps I would envy him and not get along with him. Could it be that people of quality are only those tested through bitterness, pain, and torment? No, that can't be."*

When Salim reached his room, he found Ekram waiting. "Peace upon you, Salim. How is school going?"

"Peace upon you, Ekram. School is just fine. Where have you been, Ekram? I was worried about you."

"I am okay. Thanks anyway," Ekram replied, smiling while trimming his mustache with small scissors. "Listen, tonight is Thursday, so we don't have classes tomorrow. How about coming with me tonight to have some fun? Manal wants to meet you. I've told her everything I know about you."

"I don't know, Ekram," Salim replied hesitatingly, but with obvious interest.

"Come on, Salim! You need a break. Give yourself some time to relax. Besides, you need to see Baghdad at night," Ekram said, winking and smiling.

"I don't know, Ekram."

"Come on my friend; let's have some fun."

"I guess we'll go, then," Salim replied in a quiet voice. Soon he and Ekram were riding down Al-Rashid Street. An ancient city, Baghdad always had struggled to maintain its reputation and customs. The very old civilizations passed from the Syrian Umayyad's hands to those of Abbasids who, in taking over the Caliphates, enriched both the Islamic and other civilizations beginning with their reign in 750 A.D. The second Caliph, Abu Afar Al-Mansur, founded what would become Baghdad, which became his empire's capital and a symbol of advanced knowledge and learning to all mankind. Under the powerful caliphate of Heron Al-Rashid, the empire established its boundaries and strengthened its government, and wealth and prosperity spread throughout. Al-Rashid's son, Caliph Al-Mammon, was a scholar in his own right, bringing translators to Baghdad from every continent of the world. They translated the most important academic works from their own countries into Arabic. It was one of Baghdad's greatest times ever.

However, this great civilization was destroyed on February 20, 1258, when Haulage, grandson of Genghis Khan, conquered Baghdad at the head of his Tartars, and killed so many that the Tigris River ran red with blood, and then black from the ink of countless books thrown into it. The Tartars burned hundreds of libraries and slaughtered thousands of scholars. After the great civilization's destruction and systematic genocide, Mesopotamia plunged into dark ages of ignorance, poverty, and corruption. Salim recalled studying the history in high school as he and Ekram rode the slow-moving bus down the busy Al-Rashid Street.

"How long is this street?" Salim asked, looking at the lighted stores, shops and buildings they passed.

"About a mile. The end of it merges with another famous street called Abu-Nua'as. That's about two miles long, and follows the Tigris. All the nightclubs and bars are on that street," Ekram explained. He propped up his feet on the seat in front of him.

Salim was impressed with the variety of commerce on Al-Rashid Street: department stores, restaurants, supermarkets, banks, libraries, condominiums, hotels, coffeehouses, movie houses, large and small companies, and entertainments. New and old houses stood in long lines on side streets, displaying signs of the old life and the struggling to cope with demands of the new. "All life is here," observed an impressed Salim.

Ekram nodded. "Everything a person needs. Despite the new malls built in the suburbs, this street is still as crowded as ever."

After forty minutes of crawling progress, the bus reached the end of Al-Rashid and merged with Abu-Nua'as. This wide street was decorated with flowers, shrubs, and date palms. A glow from the nightclubs, bars, restaurants, casinos, and first-class hotels flooded out onto the Tigris River, pushing darkness onto side streets.

Salim and Ekram stood on the sidewalk and looked at the quiet river. It nuzzled the colorful lights, reflecting them back on the date palms lining the opposite shore.

"I have never seen such a fantastic sight in my entire life!" Salim exclaimed.

"It's wonderful isn't it?" Ekram replied, staring at the dazzling view. They walked slowly down the crowded street, as rhythms of music and the aromas wafting from bars filled Salim with excitement and apprehension.

After several blocks, they entered a place with a big sign in front announcing "Paradise." A waiter led them to one of many round tables covered with red tablecloths. Each table's soft candlelight produced a romantic mood. Most customers were male and chatted with each other in low voices. Ekram ordered two amber bottles of beer and poured a glass for each of them. Salim was apprehensive. Ekram noticed his friend's nervousness and reassured him. "There is nothing to worry about. It is just beer made from barley and will not harm you. People in the West drink beer daily with their meals instead of water. It is soft, tasty, and light. Drink it slowly, you'll see." Ekram patted Salim on his shoulder as he picked up his glass. "Cheers, Salim. This is to you and to our friendship, and to the new life of a good person who will soon know how to live."

At Ekram's insistence and spurred by his own curiosity, Salim raised the glass to his lips. The cold beer had a soft, bitter flavor, different from anything he had ever tasted. It went down smoothly, warming his stomach. He drank a little more, this time not so slowly. He did the same again and again, each time discovering something enjoyable about the drink.

After less than an hour, Salim's glass was empty and his face felt warm. His lips and cheeks began numbing, his forehead was sweating, his eyelids began to relax, and heat coursed through his veins. He took off his jacket.

As Ekram refilled their glasses and Salim continued to drink, he felt more relaxed. Everything around him seemed much prettier, drifting him into a romantic mood. He began to remember his hometown, his old friend Abdul, and his life with the Dervishes. Every memory came back to him suddenly, and a marvelous joy filled his heart. Then, Salim recalled Abdul's parting words that he would like Baghdad, but that it would corrupt his spirit.

Under the beer's influence, he somehow sensed that same ambivalence as when he was ready to jump into the circle among the Dervishes, ready to stab his body with a skewer. Salim decided to cut himself to see whether he could feel anything. First he pinched himself, and the usual pain changed his mind. He took another drink instead.

"I feel sublime. I'm Sublime Salim! I'm so relaxed and all warm inside."

"Good, I'm glad. Enjoy yourself." Ekram picked a Greek olive from the plate and popped it into his mouth. "I'm going to take you somewhere else tonight … where you will have more fun."

"Really, what is on your mind, my dear friend?"

"*You* are going to have sex with a woman tonight," Ekram replied.

"You don't mean that!"

"Yes, I do. She is a prostitute, but she's a friend of my girlfriend. She is pretty and you won't have to pay."

"Prostitute! Really?" Salim asked with a rising voice.

"Yes, she and my girlfriend, Manal, are in the same house. I thought I told you my girlfriend is a prostitute! She is the sexiest girl in the world, and she truly loves me."

"You are such a great friend!"

"Yeah, I know," Ekram replied, and they shared a long laugh. After they finished their beers, the roommates left the bar and strolled to a big house with large windows. Ekram climbed the few steps to push the doorbell, with Salim following behind. An attractive woman in her early twenties opened the door. Her black hair covered most of her forehead and fell down around the sides of her face. She was wearing a dress that exposed half of her thighs. When she saw Ekram, she smiled in delight and hugged him.

"I've been waiting for you, darling."

"This is my best friend, Salim," Ekram said, turning back to face his companion. Manal smiled and extended her hand to Salim. Salim moved slowly up the steps and shook her hand without speaking.

"Please, come in," Manal said as she stepped inside the house, her arm still around Ekram. They entered a brightly furnished living room, with two overstuffed red couches. Colorful flowers in a large brass urn decorated a table in the center of the room. A dimly-lit, elaborate chandelier hung from the ceiling, and lamps offered havens of soft light. A plush red carpet covered the floor from wall to wall. Soft music flowed from nearby rooms, promising romance. Salim noticed an expensive Persian rug, like the one in Abdul's house, covering one wall.

He sat on one of the couches facing Ekram and Manal, who were kissing and talking. Manal's long fingernails tapped Ekram's chest.

An attractive woman, perhaps in her late thirties, entered the living room and smiled at Ekram. "Hello, Ekram. How are you doing?" the woman asked softly.

"Hello. How are you doing? You look wonderful."

"Thank you," the woman said, before turning her eyes to Salim and smiling.

"This is my friend, Salim. The friend I told you about," said Ekram while his fingers gently caressed Manal's hair.

"How are you, good looking?"

"I am at peace, and how are you doing?" Salim replied pleasantly.

The woman moved to sit down beside him. Salim studied her attractive brown eyes, enhanced by her high cheekbones and carefully plucked eyebrows. Her nose was small and her nicely shaped lips posed above a sculptured chin. Salim's eyes roamed over her body. She was wearing a blue slip that exposed her thighs, and he noticed tattoos on both of them. The sight aroused him. In only a few moments she put her arms around his shoulders, and whispered warmly, "Are you ready to go to my room so we'll have some privacy?"

Before Salim could reply, she stood up. He found himself rising with her. Her arms found his waist, pulling him to her. Her perfume excited him.

His heart was pounding. He raised his hand to dry the sweat from his fore-head as she led him to one of the bedrooms.

A poster of a western movie star hung on the newly-painted wall. A lounging sofa, with red covers and golden pillows on each end, sat on one side of the room. A large dresser with a big mirror held many small bottles of perfume and makeup, neatly arranged.

Salim noticed a big sign on the wall that read

"Enjoy Yourself Today, For You Never

Know What Tomorrow May Bring."

That's true. She and I apparently have something in common, Salim thought to himself as he sat on the bed. She turned on a lamp, started soft music, and then pulled her slip slowly over her head. Even though she left her black underwear on, Salim's heartbeat increased as he looked at her bare shoulders and stomach. Her small shoulders seemed graceful, and the mystery of her still-veiled breasts was almost too much for Salim. Her soft belly was decorated with a tattoo. Gracefully, the woman moved to Salim, took off his coat and unbuttoned his shirt. She began kissing his lips, then his chest, tickling him pleasurably. Salim was happy to show her all the skills he had learned in the Sheikh's house.

The next morning he offered her money, but she refused it. "Thank you anyway. Next time I'll charge you, but this time, it was a favor for your friend, Ekram. Besides, I enjoyed it. But, where did one so young learn those things?"

Salim smiled broadly and said, "Oh, at the Sheikh's house."

"What?"

"Nothing, never mind," Salim replied, smiling. "Thank you."

"Are you coming back again?" asked the woman.

"Sure, and very soon," Salim replied. "What is your name?"

"Wafa'a," said the woman, kissing his lips tenderly.

"Are you as sincere as the meaning of your name?" he teased her.

"Try me." Waffa'a replied, smiling.

Salim took the bus home after expressing his appreciation to Ekram, who stayed behind with Manal.

Back at the dorm, Salim washed clothes, then read his homework, a story about a horseman with no head by a fellow named Washington Irving. Salim thought it odd that the story was apparently authored by a relative of the first American president. Later, he watched television, and exhausted, went to bed early, carrying with him memories of the night before. In spite of his exhaustion, he soon began to toss and turn. After a couple of hours of fitfulness, he woke up shivering from another nightmare, the blonde woman shooting herself in the head. Her face and entire body were covered with a grotesque cape of blood. This time she was naked, and he himself was clad only in his underwear. An instinct to flee was, as in all the other bad dreams, impossible. He could not move. Terrified, Salim wanted to cry out, but he could not. The bloody figure grabbed his wrist, and with the last of her strength, pulled him close.

Salim awoke in horror. He looked over to find Ekram's bed still empty. An hour later, Salim was able to fall back to sleep, only to another nightmare. In the dream, he stood among the Dervishes, inside the circle near the huge fire. Loud drums propelled the Dervishes rhythmically. As they passed him, they stared menacingly into his eyes. Their merciless faces, which somehow also seemed sad, scared him. *There must be something wrong, something bad has happened, but what?* Salim thought. Suddenly, the drums stopped.

Omran moved close to him and spoke angrily, "Salim, you are no longer one of us. You've betrayed us, and you have become an infidel. You have committed the two sins we cannot forgive. We will never tolerate your brazenness or forget your sin. You drank alcohol, and you've had sexual intercourse with a woman. You've disrespected our faith and violated the rules we taught you. You followed an evil path. Your soul is infected with sin. You have estranged yourself from God and become a disgrace to us. You must pay for your iniquity. You will die *now!*"

The drums began to pound again. Shuddering, Salim realized he was about to faint. The Dervishes danced around him while his body rattled. One of the Dervishes grabbed the stone necklace, Abdul's gift, jerking it from his neck. Salim cried out. Everyone raised skewers to strike him. Suddenly Abdul appeared, shoving himself into Salim to protect him.

At that moment Salim awoke screaming. Glancing around in fear, he found himself still alone in his dorm room. In extreme shock, sinking in horror and sweat, he lay in bed suffering incredible physical pain in his chest, arms, and neck. When Salim felt his neck, there were scratches. He looked next to his pillow. His stone necklace lay there, broken.

His mind raced. *What was all that about? Merely another nightmare? Was it reality or insanity?*

Weary and distraught, Salim tried to calm down. Still confused about what had actually happened, Salim arose and peered out of the window. Baghdad slept. Returning to his bed, Salim feared the return of sleep. He grasped the broken necklace in a sweaty palm.Was it an hour later when he heard a key in the door? He was unsure of the passage of time, but relieved to hear Ekram enter, and he pretended to be asleep. Within a few minutes, he was. Salim slept until the alarm clock woke him to bright sunshine. All day long, Salim tried desperately to rid himself of last night's shadowed dreams, especially of the Dervishes. He still could not quite believe it was merely a nightmare, even a brutal one. His shoulders and back hurt where Abdul, in the dream, had shoved in to protect him from the skewers.

For more than a week, Salim avoided his classes, brooding in his room. In that safe place, he focused on his life's direction. Surely, his dreams, like those of so many others, must melt into the fog of yesterdays, no matter how terrible and painful. Eventually he found the courage to venture out, making his way back to Waffa'a. Within a day, Salim was lying on his back, reaching out to Waffa'a in her comfortable bed. He thought, *How quickly a person forgets—how an event seems critically important one day, yet is vaguely remembered the next.*

Waffa'a was relaxing her head on his stomach, playing with the few hairs on his chest. Salim's eyes stared dreamily at the ceiling. As he ran his fingers through Waffa'a's shining hair, he spoke softly. "Tell me, Waffa'a, do you know why some of our dreams seem so real, as if they actually were happening in life?"

"What do you mean, darling?"

"I mean, have you ever had a dream that frightened and tortured you for days? You felt as if it really happened?"

"I don't know. I've had a recurring dream, but it's sort of a happy one, not scary. It gives me relief and pleasure for a few minutes, but when I wake up, it's all gone. When I dream it again, I realize even during the dream that it's only the same dream, and will vanish when I wake up. I figured everyone must be aware of their dreams in the same way."

"Tell me your dream, Waffa'a."

"It's about my childhood, when I was a little girl surrounded by my parents' love and respect. I loved them more than anything." As Waffa'a continued, her mouth became dry. "I enjoy it so much, but even within the dream I realize the few minutes of contentment are false, and won't stay long. It's just my fantasy, soon to end."

"I don't know what to say. You could make a good philosopher, Waffa'a," Salim replied.

"Why do you ask? Do you always have bad dreams?"

Waffa'a kissed his lips tenderly.

Trying to avoid the question, Salim inquired, "Tell me more. What do you dream about?"

"I see myself as a decent girl, the way I used to be, living with my parents and my younger brother before they were killed in a car accident. My father was an elementary school teacher, and my mother a seamstress. She would use her sewing machine to make women's clothes, and brought in good money. We lived here in Baghdad in a large house with many nicely furnished rooms. I loved that house. In all my dreams I am in our house or in our yard. I used to climb up our date palm. I would stay up there for hours listening to the birds singing happily above me. At other times I would play with my younger brother, fighting over our toys. I used to love watching my mother sew. I'd help her wash dishes or just stand near her while she cooked meals or washed clothes. Life was wonderful then. I was happy.

"Then, suddenly, I was all alone with no one to care for me. The government took me to live in an orphanage. I was abused and repeatedly raped by an officer who worked there. When I was sixteen, I ran away, and met this woman who owned a whorehouse. That's what I've done ever since—having had nothing to live on except my body. I sacrificed my pride just to survive."

Tears from her pretty eyes ran like little rivers through the makeup on her face. Salim hugged her and wiped away her tears with his handkerchief.

"I have daydreams, too," Waffa'a continued. "I dream that someday someone will overlook my humiliation and marry me." Waffa'a cried for a long moment. Salim held her in silence. Then she continued in a broken voice. "But who can forgive a woman for selling her body? Who can understand that most of the time a woman alone, among men hungry for sex, has no choice? Who can believe that I am tired of living like this? That I am starving for a decent life with a man who comes home each evening with bread in one hand and love in the other? I might be dead before it comes true."

Salim choked back tears as he listened to her. He held her tighter, not speaking but thinking to himself, *I would marry you and make you happy, but I will be dead soon, and dead people can't make anyone happy. You would be miserable again and your sadness would only increase. I wish I could marry you, Waffa'a.*

Waffa'a saw tears falling on his cheeks. "I am sorry, Salim. I don't mean to make you unhappy." She seemed surprised to see him weeping. As if to make their troubles vanish, they began kissing each other, and in a few seconds they were wrestling under the bed sheet, tickling and giggling.

The following night Salim was crushed by another bestial nightmare. He saw himself face to face with a woman. She was in a rage, charging at him, bellowing, reprimanding him about something he could not understand. As she gripped his hair, Salim faltered and quivered, powerless, as her grip dug past skin and skull into his brain. The pain was incredible. Petrified, he felt some force had disarmed his willpower. The woman dragged him off by his hair into a dark cave, and bound him with chains to a stake in the ground. As his eyes adjusted to the dark, he realized he was surrounded by dead bodies, shrouded with white sheets and placed in a single file.

Most terrifying of all, he seemed not to experience it as a nightmare, but reality.

Growing more and more confused, and in more and more pain, Salim saw the woman approaching with a whip in her hand. She started lashing him savagely. Then Salim's dreadful realization came: *She was the ruler of his nightmares, the one always shot in the head. The same woman, who had been terrorizing his life, was now whipping him severely;* and under the relentless scourging, Salim could only scream for help.

The woman, then, seemed to tire, and threw the whip away only to attack him with her hands, which were around his throat in an instant. Chained, he was unable to pry her hands from his windpipe. Her powerful grip was cutting off his air. Shaking, Salim weakened more with each passing second.

Suddenly, another young woman appeared, shoving his attacker away while shouting, "No ... No ... Stop it, what are you doing? Stop it ... or else."

In her madness, his attacker turned, glared at the younger woman, and yelled,

"Don't you know who he is?" Her insane eyes burned into Salim, she scornfully spit in his face, and then she limped away into the darkness. Salim awoke to find himself out of his bed, drenched in sweat, and screaming. After a few minutes, he calmed down. He tried to pull himself together, whispering how this was only another episode of his terrifying old dream. But it all seemed mystifyingly real.

As days passed, his nightmares grew more intense, and his waking hours found him more despondent. In school, he performed well despite his constant misery. He had noticed that one classmate, a lovely girl called Salwa, was showing an interest in him. Every time she saw him, she hastened to sit with him to chat. Looking into his eyes smiling, she seemed to grow glamorous while near him. The dark-skinned girl was short, a bit overweight and had never been a regular attendee of classes. When she did show up at school, she appeared preoccupied and heavy-hearted. Salim offered her his class notes for the lectures she had missed. Salwa was grateful.

For some reason, Salim felt uncomfortable around her. Every time their eyes met during a chat, he noticed she would sometimes stare at him, unblinking. At the same time, he had the sense that she was not listening to him. Then, suddenly, her face would distort, seeming to ripple with unpleasant expressions. If he raised his eyebrows, she would insist that nothing was wrong.

Salwa pressed him for details about his own business and personal life. But when *he* questioned *her* about herself and her folks, she would equivocate. She told him once that her father owned a small fast-food restaurant in a popular Baghdad neighborhood, and her mother helped him in the business. She said that she had two brothers and one sister. That was all Salim really knew about Salwa. He saw her two brothers dropping her off and picking her up from school. The brothers looked much alike, and Salim assumed that they were twins.

Religion seemed to preoccupy Salwa. She frequently asked Salim whether he prayed the five daily prayers. She asked if he drank alcohol or did other bad things, and warned him about the blazing fires of the hereafter. One time, Salim could not help getting mad, and spoke shraply to his friend. "Salwa, I have respect for you as my classmate, but you're asking some very personal questions. Don't you think you're being a little inappropriate?"

"No! How could my curiosity be inappropriate? I don't see anything sinister in my questions," Salwa answered boldly. "Why is helpful advice from a kind classmate something to get mad over? I am doing it for your own sake, Salim."

"I hardly know you, Salwa," he retorted. "In fact, I don't want to know you more than I already do, which is very little. However, my practices and habits are my prerogative. It's my life, and no one has the right to judge or instruct friends about their own business."

"If you hardly know me, why don't you try to give me a chance so you could understand me better? Let's be friends. Surely, in friendship you could know me better?"

"I'm not interested, besides I don't have a time for going out?"

"I would like to invite you for dinner. Choose any place you want."

"Why, what for?"

"You can't understand others because you're so scared of people! I just want to be your friend!"

"I'm not so sure! Maybe I don't trust people, but I fear no one. I'm not scared of people."

"Then prove it by accepting my invitation."

"Why is it so important to accept your invitation?"

"Because, we could be acquainted better."

"Who said I want to be acquainted with you?"

"And why not? Do you think you're better than others?"

"No, not necessarily."

"Then prove it to me, prove it that you're not arrogant."

"I'm not arrogant. I'm just a simple man minding my own business."

"I'm thirsty; let's go the cafeteria to get something to drink. Please …?"

Salim sighed, and he looked at her as he stood, saying, "You won't give up, will you?"

"No … never."

In the cafeteria, which was almost cleared out for the afternoon, only a few others remained, engaged in their own animated conversations. Salim and Salwa chose a table, and she asked him, "What would you like to drink, my treat."

"Okay, a tea, but we can both go to get the drink."

"No, I'll do it."

She walked to the counter, and Salim sat brooding, wondering about her terrible manners. She returned with a small tray, arranged his tea, spoon, and napkin before him, then sat to drink her own Pepsi.

Salim sipped his tea, remaining quiet. He was feeling confused and upset. It appeared to him that Salwa either had a mental problem or—for some unknown reason—she was trying to provoke him. Before Salim could decide, he heard her saying, "Never mind what I said. Am I silly, just to want to chat with you?"

Salwa leaned forward and seized his hand in hers. Salim felt the coolness of her hand seep into his skin. She seemed to scrutinize him closely. Instantly, Salim's mind was jolted with flashbacks. He began to feel that his ability to think was blocked, and his vision was peculiarly distorted. A force began to surge through his head. Salim felt as if he was in a trance that stole his manly power.

As his strength left him, fear replaced it. Not knowing what was happening, Salim felt himself trapped in an illusion. Shapes resolved themselves into hideous faces. The heads of corpses that had been pushed up from their graves shrieked at him, but he was the only one who could hear them. Salim felt himself running as fast as he could to get away until he reached a big river, but the river was dark red in color. He heard a woman screaming, "Blood … I want your blood … draw nearer Salim, let us sacrifice your sinful blood." Petrified that the woman called his name, and frightened by her demand, Salim tried to shout in protest, but his voice died in his throat. The woman kept calling him. Salim gasped for air and opened his eyes, finding that he was still in the cafeteria with Salwa. He felt shaken, and terror held him in its grasp.

"What the heck just happened?" Salim shouted, causing everyone in the cafeteria to turn and gawk at him.

"Are you okay?" Salwa asked, seeing his pale face and shaking body. She reached toward him, but he stiffened and moved away.

"What just happened to me? What was all of that about?" Salim asked, angrily wiping the sweat from his face with his napkin. He leaned his head back to the chair, closed his eyes.

"I don't know what happened to you," Salwa replied.

"Something just happened to me a minute ago, I don't know what it was. It started the moment you touched my hand. What did you do? It was a nightmare … or something. It took me right out of here, I thought I was drowning!"

"But you looked fine sitting with me. You just seemed a little sleepy."

"No, no, I felt overwhelmed by violence, as though some strange force had snatched me away from reality. I thought I was going to die. How long was I out of it?"

"Well, you never looked out of it at all. You looked normal, nothing wrong at all, and just a little sleepy."

"Well then, how long did I look sleepy to you?"

"Maybe a minute or so."

"It seemed to me to be going on for hours," he said, still unconvinced.

"Are you sure you're all right? Do you want to go home?"

"No, I'll be fine, just give me a few moments to get my mind back together."

Salim laid his head back on the chair, and gradually felt himself regain his normal senses. The first time he met Salwa at school, his logical mind told him she could be bad news. Then, after they were introduced, Salim was convinced that there was something deeply wrong with her. Now in the cafeteria, he questioned whether she somehow, mysteriously overwhelmed him with a sinister black sorcery. Now that he was back to normal, he could detect no logical connection between the innocent-looking young woman sitting across from him and the bizarre episode he had experienced. Still, it had started when she touched him ... and he was convinced she had somehow triggered the nightmare. Salim's breath was coming in gulps, and he pulled extra napkins from the dispenser to mop his sweaty forehead.

Salwa sat across from him, looking a vision of innocent young womanhood. Still, in his deepest mind, Salim could not separate her touch from the nightmare he had just experienced. He apologized. "I'm sorry. I feel better now. I don't know what came over me."

For the next few minutes, time seemed to slow down and their conversation was sparse. In Salim's mind, doubts flourished. Was this innocent-appearing young woman some kind of a medium for the dark spirits that haunted him? He decided to cease contact with her. "Salwa, please, it would be best if you and I do not speak again. And now, I need to go home."

As he stood to leave, he heard her saying, "You might as well go on, Salim, with what you have been doing. Do what pleases you. But be careful, because someone is watching you."

Salim gave no thought to her warning. He thought Salwa was referring to Almighty Allah, who always watches over the believer. Upon recollection, Salim realized he had raised his voice when arguing with her, and he felt ashamed. He wanted to tease her and he smiled while exclaiming, "I pity the man who marries you, Salwa. You'll give him a hard time."

Salwa did not care much for his joke; she frowned in irritation and snapped, "To hell with the husband who does not seriously respect his religion!"

The following days, when Salwa showed up for class, she acted as if their argument had never happened. Before long, she was asking again whether he attended Friday prayer at the Mosque. "My father and brothers join the congregation every Friday," she said. "The blessings of Friday prayers are doubled for true believers."

"Maybe I will do it *some* Friday. I don't have time to go to pray on *this* Friday. The day is short and time flies."

"But you find time for *other* pleasures, don't you?" She was almost shouting.

Salim grew angry and spat out his reply, "Salwa, you're just terrible. What's your problem? What you have just said is obscene!"

She glared at him, and then began whispering in heated anger, "Do you know what, Salim? I'll be frank with you. I'll tell you what I feel about you regarding your disrespect to your faith; I wish you to be banished from the face of the earth because you're nothing without practicing your religion. You're only a deceiver. You pretend to be an honorable man but you betray the godly people who taught you how to live."

Salwa rose and stalked away. Salim never saw her again. But Salwa had made it clear to him that she was one of the Dervishes. His fear mounted, and he vowed to remain vigilant.

A few days later, Salim contracted the flu. He had to stay in the dorm and miss classes. One evening, Ekram returned to the room and found him with a high fever. Ekram asked if he could take Salim to the hospital. Salim said that he only needed Ekram to go to the pharmacy before it closed, and buy him some cough syrup and medication to relieve his fever.

"Sure, my dear friend," said the smiling Ekram. "I'll be back soon." As Ekram left the dorm, two young men rushed out of the dark, attacked him with jagged knives, stabbing him relentlessly. In bed, Salim heard Ekram's cries for help. Despite his high fever and drowsiness, Salim sprang to his feet and looked through the window. He saw the attackers. They looked like Salwa's two brothers, slashing their knives at Ekram, who was already prostrate on the ground. Salim threw open the window and yelled for help, but the attackers got away. Ekram died within moments. People rushed to encircle Ekram's lifeless body. Salim stumbled downstairs, staggered to Ekram's body, and collapsed in shock.

Hospitalized, Salim lay delirious for days, crying and begging for Ekram. He mumbled over and over again that he was to blame for his best friend's murder. Salim had asked him to go to the pharmacy. If he hadn't asked Ekram to go out, his friend would still be alive.

Eventually the police came to question Salim. More stable, Salim told them he had seen the killers, but now could not be positive they were Salwa's two brothers. The flu may have distorted his perception. He couldn't be sure.

Guilt continued to swell inside Salim. He decided he was obviously the one they wanted to kill. They took the life of a kind, innocent young man instead. Salim began to realize the truth of Salwa's warning. He now understood more clearly than ever: Salwa and her brothers were Dervishes, and they were on a mission to execute him. The day after Salim was discharged from the hospital, he received a phone call at the dorm. A student in the next room came knocking on Salim's room. "Hi, are you Salim?" The young student asked.

"Yes, why, what is it?"

"Somebody wants you on the public phone down the hall."

Salim walked down to answer it.

"Hello, who is this? Is this Salim?" the female voice asked.

"Yes, and who is this please?"

"Never mind that, just listen; we have killed your friend just as a warning to you, to let you know that we could kill you anytime we want. There will be no intercessor for you, and you should reconcile with your old masters, the Dervishes. Woe to a sinful liar like you, if you don't reconcile!" The woman hung up. Salim knew the voice. It was Salwa. Now, anger and resentment swelled in him. If they were going to kill him, then it could be only by Almighty Allah's decree. But they would have to come for him. Salim told himself that nothing was worth returning to his past life with the Dervishes. That was Salim's final decision.

The years passed. One evening of his senior year, Salim sat alone in the dormitory garden, writing a letter to his friend Abdul in Nasiriya,

Dear Abdul,

I hope this letter will put me in your thoughts again. I have begun to feel that all of you already have forgotten me. I am so sorry I've taken so long to write back to my father and to you since my last letter. These months have rushed past. It seems like yesterday when I was leaving for Baghdad and saw you in the railway station to say goodbye. Remember? Now I'm a senior, and I've only a few weeks to go. It's been a very fast four years—between studying hard in school and having a little fun here and there. It seems that Baghdad knows what kinds of misery people like me have gone through, and offers help to anyone who appreciates some taboos.

Thank you for teaching me about life. I'll never forgive myself for joining the Dervishes without letting you know first. Never! They are still after me, destroying my happiness and the best friend I ever had besides you. While I appreciate all the things you have done for me, I should have had the decency to let you know about my stupid decision. I chose the wrong people to associate with. I chose the most ruthless people who, unfortunately, will never forgive me for living my own life. You are my great friend and always will be. I particularly miss sharing my thoughts with you in person. I was just reflecting as I prepared to write to you. One day, perhaps, a person might be too old for almost everything. All that may be left is to remember and talk about the good old days with sighs and hidden tears.

Most of the time, I'm still enjoying life in Baghdad. Life here is extremely different from Nasiriya. Now, after the four years living in Baghdad, and accustomed to things here, I doubt that I would be able to live elsewhere. Most of the time, I feel happy just to be living in this lovely green environment among so many beautiful faces. Baghdad is altogether amazing. At first sight of the stunning beauty of the environment and the unfamiliarity of the streets crowded with cars and people, I felt sort of intimidated. I was knocked out by Baghdad's clean streets, and by the many stores, restaurants, movie houses and big buildings. Even the appearances of people were different from those in my hometown. In Baghdad, they mostly appear clean, neat and healthy. It's also not like Nasiriya where you can just look at a person and know most of what you need to know about him. In Baghdad, you need to study in many more ways than that to figure out the truth of a person. During these four years, I've discovered many interesting facts about the people of Baghdad. I suppose it is as with people the world over, there are some good and some bad among them. But, most interesting, people here are no more industrious than the people of Nasiriya. Most seem accustomed to doing just enough to survive. As you know, Iraq is among the top countries in oil production, giving Baghdad a wealthy population. I was surprised to find that, on the whole, the men and women here tend toward the hedonistic. In spite of the pleasures that accompany wealth, most people here are no less sad than those in Nasiriya. How can it be that those lifted up by wealth find ways to be just as discouraged as those who are dragged down by want?

In this great prosperous city, drunken, miserable people and homeless beggars haunt even the neighborhoods of grand homes and elegant shops. Could human nature be the great equalizer? If I study for another twenty years, perhaps I will discern the mechanism that propels even the wealthy toward sadness, notwithstanding the bright cloud of possible fates? Somehow, the baseline of human trajectories seems to curve toward misery.

I don't accept that the impoverished and drunken among us have fallen by accident. There must be compelling reasons for them to languish so short of their goals. The myriad possibilities of

Baghdad seem to encourage people to achieve their maximum potential, to achieve any immediate satisfaction, happiness, and comfort. In spite of the playground of goodness in which they find themselves, so many of my neighbors are like donkeys that refuse to take one easy step to the carrot that dangles before them.

What could be more ironic than the way they compete with each other for success and happiness, yet deflate at the end of the day and fall back into pits of defeat, sorrow, and pain.

Maybe their sense of the possible has been warped by living under ruthless dictators and corrupt judges. Perhaps the scales of possibility have been lubricated by the excrement of deceitful governors and the spittle of treacherous Dervishes. Political unrest has become a sickness to which even good people awake on too many mornings. The result of these plagues seems to be that the people of Baghdad suffer an unremitting nervous disease that irritates every sense and provokes every pore. Yet, God help me, everything here is fascinating and worth watching closely.

Hidden underneath so much disruption and social malaise, there is a layer of daily duty and activity in Baghdad life that is not unlike everyday life in Nasiriya. In the market stalls, bartering goes on without end. In the mosques, men whisper their fears and hopes, at the well, and women gather to brag about their children. Just as in our squares, children dance to the sound of musical entertainments.

Are our fears created mostly within the dark corners of our overactive brains? Are we each guilty of birthing our individual devils? Perhaps even well-intentioned parents launch skiffs of doubt within the imaginations of their beloved children, when wishing only to teach some lesson of self-control? Why have our people never launched a great expedition of discovery to another continent across the seas? Are we genetically ill-equipped to delve into sciences, to peel back the layers of assumptions with which our temples are painted? Is there a general lack of willingness to test the limits of understanding about our own selves and our world, such as we read of in the news from afar? Maybe we've not been guided precisely during our individual and national growth. Or perhaps the fault lies in the decades of political chaos, wars, and unrest in Iraq and the region that have quashed our curiosity and killed our happiness.

I always asked myself why most of us rush to order the carving of our tombstones even when we are still young and healthy. We fail to appreciate life. Don't you think, Abdul, that we should challenge our heritage of pessimism and sadness? How can we begin, Abdul? Let us increase in faithful worship of Allah. Let us trust in Him, that our fortitude may be enhanced.

As I graduate from college next month, I wish again to invite you to come for my graduation. I've decided to continue studying for my master's degree this summer. The dean welcomed the idea. I miss you all every day. On many occasions, feelings of loneliness and homesickness paralyze me. The life of a bachelor is a sad one. Sometimes, I think seriously about getting married and making a home with a woman. My prayer is to live the few years I have left in peace and tranquility in this beautiful city. Now, I still live in the dorm and use the bus to get to school, a fifteen-minute commute.

Abdul, I wish you were here with me to talk daily and help me discern my path. It would be a blessing to live near each other in Baghdad, where most things we need are a short walk from home. I mainly am missing our sharing of thoughts in person.

One day, every man becomes too old for engaging conversation. Then, all that may be left is quiet remembrance and contemplation of days gone by with sighs and tears. Tonight homesickness makes me think of you and all my family. Everything here hangs weights upon my heart, so I decided to write to you. How is your wife? Does she still bring you treats each afternoon, with tea? How are my brothers and our father? Hug them for me. Please write and tell me about your patients, our neighbors, and news of the streets.

Thank you, Abdul, for your several letters to me. Imagine my surprise, when I read in your last letter that the last of my brothers has married now and has his own home. That news makes me jubilant. So did the news that my father still spends his days on the road. Is it true that he has remarried and bought a house in Basra for his wife? That's incredible. I never thought he'd give up on Mom's memory! Anyway, how nice to hear that the government finally plans to build a big bridge over the Euphrates in Nasiriya, connecting the two parts of the town. Thank you much for the money you have been sending me with each letter. I have been able to save for the day when I will have a wife and, God willing, a little home of my own.

I look forward to news that you will come to my graduation. My best wishes to you and your family. I miss you all.

Your friend,

Salim

After the decision to study for his master's degree in English, everything in Salim's life seemed new and exciting. Two days before his graduation, Salim returned to his dormitory in the evening and found a welcome surprise. Waiting patiently in the lobby was Abdul. Salim embraced his mentor and cried out, "I don't believe my eyes! Abdul, is this really you?"

"I'm so happy to see you, Salim. Look at you! You're a man now. When you left Nasiriya, you were small and without a full mustache. Now you are tall and handsome."

"Thank God, Abdul. Thank you for taking all the trouble to come to Baghdad and witness my graduation from college," Salim exclaimed with tears in his eyes.

"Thank you for writing to me about your graduation. A herd of gazelles could not have held me back from watching your graduation procession and congratulating you with a hug," Abdul replied. His wrinkled eyes sparkled with happiness.

"Thank you again and may Allah bless you and your family," Salim replied while hugging his best friend again.

"I want you to remember Salim, that I have loved you more than your own parents. I love you as much as my own, departed son. And I would like you to have this golden necklace as a present for your graduation and to remember me by. Don't sell it unless you have to. It will bring you luck, complementing the stone necklace you already have." Abdul looked at Salim, who was weeping. The two had dinner in a quiet restaurant.

The day after the graduation ceremonies, Abdul arose at five o'clock in the morning and left without waking Salim, who slept the sleep of the accomplished. Abdul took a last look, whispering, "Goodbye, Salim, and good luck." Abdul tiptoed out of the dorm room and walked slowly out of the dorm, disappearing into the foggy morning.

CHAPTER ELEVEN

His Lovely Professor

As TIME PASSED, SALIM GRADUALLY BECAME MORE COMFORTABLE, in spite of the murder of his best friend, Ekram. Most evenings he felt homesick and sat alone in his room, studying the novels of Kurt Vonnegut, Jane Yolen, and Judson Hout for his graduate work in English. Often, he put the books down and drowned his alienation in music. On those nights when sad memories of Ekram over-whelmed him or boredom crept into his concentration, Salim forced himself to go downstairs to play ping pong with other students. Salim continued to suffer from disturbing nightmares. Since adjusting to life in Baghdad, the dramatic dreams which had devastated his earlier life had returned less frequently. Still, almost once a week, he would awake sweating, beating his pillows as if fending off dark characters from his earlier life. Almost every one of these recurring dreams brought back threats from the Dervishes and their cronies. He would awake with vivid scenes of their grim, gaunt faces circling him, shouting at him, ordering him to return to their ranks, and threatening to stab him in the back if he would not rejoin them soon. Their threats were painfully realistic, and their promise to make him suffer an agonizing death even haunted his daytime dreams.

Often in dreams, Salim saw Ajil and Chief Omran, waving their sharp skewers and warning with vivid threats, of their plans to cut him to pieces. They promised that no one could save him from their wrath. While in other times, they tried to lure him by offering him a monthly allowance and higher position among the ranks, telling him that "We so much cherish loyal people, but we hate those who deny us." They taunted Salim, reminding him that his friend Ekram was killed on account of Salim's own departure from the group. They filled Salim with remorse by telling him that his friend would still be alive if he, Salim, had remained loyal to the Dervishes.

"Think ... Salim, think about that deeply," shouted Omran angrily. "Why did you kill your dearest friend? Will you now continue to kill everyone you love? Is that what you intend to do, to kill all of your family and beloved ones? Does that picture make you happy? Or will you accept the love of Allah and return to the Dervishes, acting rationally and responsibly? Just remember your past days of peace and serenity, when you lived happily among us."

As Salim contemplated his dreams during his daily solitude, his nightmares increased in frequency. Now they haunted his sleep several nights each week—sometimes for three or four nights in a row. The torturous vision of the blonde woman who kills herself returned more frequently. Usually, she twisted and grasped at him, covered in her own blood. With both hands, she gripped his arms and would not release him. To his horror, he watched as her blood spattered across each wall. Her blood now became matted in her hair. As her hair radiated from her contortions, the flying blood spotted his clothing, his skin, and dripped from the woman's eyebrows and chin. She tried to say something to him, but he was so scared that he wouldn't dare come nearer to her. His mind was split between wanting to hear her message and wanting to escape from her grasp. What was it that she intended to tell him about? Who was this woman who has been terrifying him all these years of his life, consuming his nights?

Alternating with the nightmares of the bloody blonde woman were very different dreams in which Salim saw his friend, Ekram, as if he were still alive. It was as if they were still roommates, living in peace and friendship. Yet there was something macabre about the Ekram of these dreams. One moment, the two friends would be living as they had while Ekram lived: jovial, full of energy, and in high spirits. They would exchange jokes with each other as they used to in real life. Then, without warming, Ekram would turn pale, exhausted, and sad. At those times, even if the friends were chatting about their prosperous futures, Ekram became turbulent and shut Salim out of his thoughts, his eyes turned away.

After every such dream, when Salim awoke, he was faced with the reality that Ekram was gone forever. Salim was then so miserable that he asked his dead friend about things known only to the deceased. On those mornings, Salim cried bitterly as he washed his face and brushed his beard. Those dreams were, in a way, more traumatizing to Salim, because they reminded him of how dearly he had loved his friend, and how responsible he was for Ekram's murder. Those dreams ruined whole days, as they befuddled his concentration, leaving him unable to absorb the poetry of Wendell Berry. Salim had no recourse to emotional support, being so far from his brothers and his mentor, Abdul. In his agony, Salim rested his head against the wall of his room, took many deep breaths, and told himself to be patient, accepting the life granted by Almighty Allah. Resigned to his fate, Salim asked Allah for forgiveness and the grace to live out the life assigned to him. Since Ekram's murder, and during those extreme nights of sadness, worries, and fears, Salim had to stay home instead of going out the way he used to with his friend. He feared that, in his emotional state, he would be an easy target for the Dervishes who may be stalking him to murder him in the street. Of course, Salim told himself, the Dervishes were powerful enough to break into the dorm and attack him viciously in his room.

Salim, however, would never bow to the Dervishes' threats nor would he ever return to associate again with those terrorists. Maybe he was alone in this big city and had no one else to help him out against these inhuman monsters, but he depended on Allah, determined to stay away from them and to remain vigilant. Salim's fears for his life had forced him to go to the police to ask for protection from those who threatened his life. He explained to the police chief what had happened to his friend Ekram, and that the following day he had received a phone threat from the same terrorist group through a classmate in the college. But unfortunately, since he had no witness to confirm the threat, Salim wasn't granted the protection he requested. The kindly middle-aged chief was sorrowful having to reject the request, and inquired, "How can we protect you from bad people when you have no idea who they are? If you could describe specific people, giving us a photograph of those who threaten you, perhaps including the addresses of their residences, we would surely bring them in for questioning. Believe me, son, we wish to help you, but how could we go out and search for some people whose descriptions we do not know? Your story concerns us, but you have given us no useful information to work with, so how do you expect us to help you? You're not even sure of their identities or their addresses. I'm sorry, son."

"Unfortunately, as I said, I have no hard proof of their threats. Still, I thank you, sir, for your gracious interest," replied Salim, as he looked down at the floor while shaking hands with the man. Salim returned to the dorm, hanging his head the whole way.

Salim enjoyed his flexible graduate college schedule. Some days, when he had no classes, he would stay in his room at the dorm to work on his critique of John Steinbeck's early novels. Other days he spent in the university library, studying the mysteries of the English language. Salim worked hard in college, giving his professors reason to admire his dedication to the study of the English language and the variety of literature composed in the language. He read *The Lord of the Rings* in its original language, and savored the poems of Robert Frost. In the English Department, Salim counted at least sixteen professors, including both men and women. His studies as an advanced student were taught by professors who had advanced beyond mere grammar, which was taught to undergraduates. Graduate professors had more time in their offices and each one had indicated a willingness to help him. It was not uncommon for Salim and perhaps one or two other graduate students to cause a professor to stay in the department offices later than usual, spending extra time with their most earnest students. Salim was known among those dedicated educators for the quality of his questions. Sometimes, Salim would leave those sessions asking himself who his favorite professor might be. On one such occasion, Salim admitted to himself that Dr. Henan, his lovely drama professor, often looked at him in a special way, causing his face to flush. Salim showed an exceptional interest in her class. And he was not without interest in her, either. She often rewarded his excellent scholarship with a flash of her brown eyes, which peered out just beneath a coiffure of short chestnut brown hair. And he had to admit that when she turned to write on the board, he took notice of her feline grace and her slender figure.

His only female professor, Dr. Henan was probably in her late twenties. She was an intelligent person who clearly explained every point of instruction, and stressed her individual interpretations of theater. But Salim was cautious, fearing that the brown-eyed beauty could be another Salwa, ensnaring him on behalf of the dangerous Dervishes. Had they sent her, under cover of beauty, in order to lure him to a private spot and kill him? Salim had to be cautious. While he tried to avoid the risk, his eyes and heart kept returning to the graceful young woman.

Usually around noon, Salim would go to the university cafeteria for lunch. He regularly noticed some students with short beards, accompanied by a couple of young women, at a nearby table. Salim often felt them staring at him. He listened to them talking in English, with some Arabic words mixed in. Their accents told Salim they were from Saudi Arabia and Iraq. A short middle-aged man with wispy white hair and a professor's appearance sometimes joined them. The man's features suggested he was Middle Eastern, but he spoke fluent English. The group tended to listen intently when he talked, his voice seeming carefully low. Occasionally, he would pass to everyone some photocopies to keep. As the man spoke, his eyes quickly included Salim. Annoyed by this, Salim, decided to find out whether those glances were intentional. Therefore, when their eyes met again, Salim smiled politely. He was surprised when the man only shook his head mournfully, returning his smile with a frown. Salim became angry. He left the cafeteria and went to his class, but kept thinking about the man's negative reaction. Any educated person should have returned his polite smile. What was going on?

Whenever Salim had some time between classes, he would sit on the campus' stadium benches, either to study or to watch the soccer team training and students playing around. Once, Salim noticed a student playing with her big black German Shepherd dog. The young woman was not far from him, and when she seemed to intentionally pass by very close to where Salim was sitting, she gave the dog a verbal command. The dog rushed toward Salim, and sniffed him. Thinking it was innocent, Salim smiled and patted the large dog. Salim smiled at the young woman and she smiled back. Then she called to her dog and left without speaking.

A few days later, as Salim was leaving school, walking to the bus station to go home, he sensed a car following him. He turned to see a dark sedan slow down and then stop at the curb. The car door opened, and the huge German Shepherd dashed toward him. Suddenly, with a menacing growl, the dog leapt at Salim, who turned too slowly to run away. The flying dog struck Salim's back, knocking him to the ground. Salim cried for help, covering his head and face with his book bag and hands, while the dog slashed him, its flashing teeth trying to rip at his neck and throat. Then, just as suddenly, a University Police patrol car appeared, it's lights flashing. An officer jumped from the car and yelled, trying to distract the dog. The dog wheeled and sprang toward the officer, who swiftly pulled his pistol and shot the dog dead. The dark sedan, by then, had sped away.

Salim, bleeding and still shaken, sat in the hospital emergency room, receiving an anti-rabies shot and stitches on his neck, arms, and shoulder. He could not give the police any description of the car's occupants, nor any explanation about why anyone might attack him.

Back in his dorm room, Salim stayed in bed for a couple of days, panicked and puzzling over who would want him dead ... except for the Dervishes.

When Salim resumed his schoolwork, he went to Dr. Henan's office to show her his paper on Shakespeare. The woman welcomed him with a smile, studied his bandages and fresh scars, and asked him what had happened. She sympathized with his story. She read the paper, and then raised her head to look at Salim. "Nice job. I like it. You need to work on some grammar, but the paper is good."

"Thank you. I'm glad you find it acceptable." Salim got up to leave, and so did she.

"I'm through with my day and might as well go home," she said.

"I'm going to the library to borrow a book."

"Do you need help in the library, Salim? I can give you some research tips and introduce you to the graduate research librarian. I'm not in a big hurry."

"I would appreciate that, if it isn't too much trouble." Salim warmed to the idea of being in Dr. Henan's company a bit longer.

"No, no trouble at all. Glad to do it," she said with a bright smile.

Salim and his professor walked slowly down the sidewalk. The wind was blowing slightly, and many students were sitting about talking or standing in couples or small groups. The Baghdad University library housed its special collections for graduate studies in a cavernous room where twenty long tables afforded seclusion for serious scholars. It did not take him long to learn the process of borrowing books or periodicals from the graduate collection. Then, thinking about how he could detain Dr. Henan a little longer, Salim asked, "Would you like a cup of tea?"

She studied him for a moment with a thoughtful look in her eyes, then said, "Okay. There's a place not far from here." After glancing at her watch, she added, "Let's take my car."

The quaint coffee shop held perhaps a dozen small, round tables covered with white tablecloths. A few students sat on stools at the counter. Dr. Henan and Salim selected a quiet corner, and sat facing each other, drinking their tea and nibbling on date-nut cookies.

"How do you like the drama class, Salim? Do you think it's interesting? Are you learning anything?"

"The class is excellent. I am interested in many aspects of theater in the English-speaking world. I've been learning a lot, and I think you're a good teacher. But, honestly, there are some things that make the class even more interesting."

"Like what?" she asked smiling.

"Your beautiful voice, your wonderful personality, the way you express your feelings about things so enthusiastically."

"Thank you, Salim. That is very considerate of you." Dr Henan thought for a moment, then she asked, "How old are you?"

"I'm twenty-four, twenty-five in September. How old are you, Dr. Henan?"

"I'm twenty-eight."

"I guessed you were younger than that."

"I'm flattered, Salim," she said softly, her eyes suddenly cast down at the tabletop. Then, looking him directly in the eye, Dr. Henan asked, "Are you from Baghdad, Salim?"

"No, I'm from Nasiriya, and I live in the dorm."

"Do you miss your family in Nasiriya?"

"I do. Sometimes I am lonely and at other times, life is not so bad. I love Baghdad, but I have to tell you that some fanatics have harassed me on a couple of occasions. They even killed my best friend, thinking he was me. They have told me that they intend to hurt me someday. In fact, that dog incident was carried out by someone from their group."

"That attack—when the dog jumped you—was in the news. My family and I saw a report of it on television. That kind of incident is frightening. But why would fanatics want to hurt you, Salim?"

"Because I no longer affiliate with them, they have sworn to hurt me. I made the mistake of joining a fanatic cult back in Nasiriya, thinking that it was a way to learn more about the faith and Allah. After they became violent and played dangerous games at the meetings I attended, it was plain that I had misunderstood their goals. Then I withdrew from them when they turned out to be false and deceptive. I think they are hunting me here, too, after they hurt me while I was in Nasiriya. They have already established a powerful organization against all who they think are not practicing Islamic rules."

"Are you anti-Islamic?"

"No, no, not at all, I'm a believer; although I don't exactly practice the faith. Yet, I have a great respect for my religion. I love Allah, but those thugs … I am against *them*. They're bad Muslims, spreading terror and falsehood on earth by using the name of Islam falsely."

"That's terrible. Why don't you go to the police?"

"I went to the police and found that it wouldn't do any good. These fanatics are sly and professional. Besides, I have no witness. Last time, I almost got killed by them with that dog they sent!" Salim was now feeling upset.

"Look, I have many good friends who are lawyers and judges and I can help you. Don't you worry, okay? I'd like to help you, you amaze me a little," she said as her bright eyes flashed.

"Thank you Dr. Henan, I appreciate your kindness, and I'll let you know if I need some help like that."

The repeated meetings in the official manner between Salim and Dr. Henan had strengthened their relationship and they had become friends. Salim wasn't only a bright student, but Dr. Henan also recognized his civility and his gracious manner toward her, both in class and now when they were together outside the university. It was apparent to her that Salim truly cared for her as a person.

At the end of their first academic year as professor and student, Salim's conscientious study habits and enthusiasm for his studies had enhanced his stature in Dr. Henan's esteem. When the time came for him to begin writing his thesis, Salim naturally chose Dr. Henan as his supervisor. This added dimension to their relationship and brought many welcome opportunities for professor-student interactions. Neither was disappointed.

Salim began to think seriously about Henan as a prospective wife. Henan became his principal source of happiness. Any day that did not include a one-on-one interchange with Henan was a disappointment to Salim. But, how could a mere graduate student expect a university professor to consider him a serious candidate for marriage? Dr. Henan had not mentioned any romantic interest, but was she just coddling his delicate feelings? Surely, Salim thought, Dr. Henan must notice the way his eyes followed hers, the way he lingered as each of their academic consultations drew to a close. Salim decided to divulge his true feelings. "Nothing ventured, nothing gained," his brother, Nadeem, would have said. Had he, in fact, already demonstrated his intentions? Recently, when Salim was with Henan in her office, he had suggested that they go to the movies. And was it not something of a Baghdad tradition that a young man who was in love with a young woman should invite her to go to the local cinema? Yes, Salim knew that a movie date was the most common expression of sincere interest.

So it was that Salim, finding himself in Henan's office one afternoon as the sun first considered the possibility of setting beyond Baghdad, brought his chair just a bit closer to hers and cleared his throat. The music of their soft voices had led Salim to fantasize that Henan might, possibly, maybe, admire him just as much as he admired her pretty face with the flashing eyes, her bent fingers tapping study papers just inches from his own hands, and her long, brown hair half-hiding her gorgeous smile.

So he asked.

"Would you accept my invitation to go to the movies?"

"Why? If … I may ask?" Henan's soft response held a hint of a challenge, yet she was unable to sequester that full smile, which now increased in wattage.

"Because, I love you, Henan," Salim exclaimed, his sudden boldness surprising even himself. "I cannot remember when I did not love you. I feel like I have known you forever, but have only just now found you. Surely, no man could love any woman more than I, Salim, love you, Henan. It is no longer possible to hide this big love. Surely, my legs will cease to bear the weight of my heart, now that it is so filled with love for you."

Henan gasped, her face flushed, and she smiled radiantly. Henan lowered her eyes, and then after a long moment, she lifted her face and her eyes locked upon his as she replied, "I love you too, Salim."

"This is the happiest moment in my life," Salim said. His mind was cataloging all of his happy—or at least pleasant—memories. He thought of his mother preparing his favorite meals, his father arriving home after a month of absence in his truck, of the delights among the Sheikh's maidens, of Abdul leading him into the secret rooms of his house. Nothing compared to this moment, and he banished all of those earlier moments from this one, which contained his beloved and her declaration of affection for him.

"I love you, Henan, more than anything in this life." Incredible! He had said it again!

———

The next weekend, Salim took Henan to the movies. A romantic film ignited more flames of passionate fire into both hearts. During the movie, when Salim took Henan's hand in his, she gasped, but made no move to withdraw. Her reaction to his touch was pure acceptance, pure love. Salim, feeling her small hand trembling with joy, could hardly breathe quietly enough to hear the movie.

Salim and Henan talked of their feelings, because nobody had ever explained to them the presence in the universe of feelings this intense, this joyous. As Henan felt the tips of Salim's fingers rest agains the palm of her hand, she could not imagine a more intense joy. And as Salim felt Henan's fingers locking between his own, he was quite certain that no two other mortals, in all of Allah's creation, had ever experienced such intimacy. Perhaps each was right to think so. Had any authority risen to challenge these sublime feelings, surely they would have declared that authority no wiser than a bush that had died from overexposure to the desert sun.

Salim would need to finish his master's degree before the lovers could allow themselves to contemplate any more thrilling conjugation. Salim would finish the degree this summer.

Salim and his fiancé now saw each other almost every day. They touched … almost every day. Usually, they met after school, dining in a restaurant, grabbing sandwiches at a deli, or enjoying ice cream under a date tree near the Tigris River. Sometimes they walked to the stadium, where the electricity of their bodies was subsumed among the crowd cheering a soccer match. On the field, the running athletes shone, their bodies sweating from heroic exertion. In the stands, Henan and Salim were surprised that the power coursing through their bodies did not attract as much attention to themselves. They were truly falling in love with each other.

For almost three months, Salim and his lovely professor had been seeing each other almost every day. Yet, somehow they felt invisible to others around them. Other professors, upon stopping at Dr. Henan's office, did not acknowledge Salim as her beloved. How could this be? After school, when dining by candlelight in a restaurant, waiters and fellow diners did not withdraw their tables to protect themselves from the lovers' molten aura. When holding hands beneath the date palms along the Tigris, families did not stop to shield their toddlers' eyes from the glare of true love. The city around them seemed unprepared to acknowledge the power that each felt in the presence of the other. Science had not yet articulated the magnetic force that erupted when their eyes met, when their fingers intertwined, when their shoulders ground into each other. Salim and Dr. Henan decided to crown their great love with the eternal pledge, to get married. They planned to be engaged to each other for a few months until Salim's advanced degree would be conferred this summer.

———

Friday had always been Salim's favorite day of the week. The Friday after falling in love with his professor, Salim's life had grown more interesting. Because he had no classes on that day, he and Henan would be together all day long. His pleasure was reflected in the generous way he greeted other students at breakfast, in the simple elegance of the clothing he chose, and in the loving respect that eminated from his voice as he addressed others in the dorm and on the street. This Friday was even more special because this evening Salim would walk to the home of Dr. Henan's family, there to meet her siblings, her mother, and her father, whom Salim would entreat for the honor of her hand in marriage.

Salim woke up early that Friday morning feeling lighter than air. While his shoes did touch the ground, that fact seemed improbable when compared to the ecstasy in his heart. Salim made himself fold clothes and dust his room. He polished his shoes, proofread a paper on Ralph Waldo Emerson for another professor, and then went to buy groceries and a newspaper. It was the longest day Salim ever remembered.

When Salim arrived at Dr. Henan's house that evening, her family greeted him with smiles and handshakes. A handsome gray-haired man in his mid-fifties, wearing a blue business suit and silk tie, shook hands with Salim and hugged him. With a gentle yet authoritarian voice, the man introduced himself, "Alssalam Alaikum, Peace is upon you, I'm Haj Abbas Mahmud Haider, father of Dr. Henan. Her mother and I have the honor to bring you among us tonight. The man then introduced his family, pointing first to a lady of about the same age wearing a long modest dress, saying, "And this is my wife, Hajja Meliha." Then Haj Abbas pointed to a younger couple, "This is my son, Ali, and his wife, Rania ... and this is, of course, Dr. Henan, to whom we think you may need no introduction. You are most welcomed in our house, son."

Salim returned Henan's warm smile and offered his hand to shake with them all while saying, "My name is Salim Wissam Jawad. I come from Nasiriya. Thank you very much, sir. It is my honor to meet each of you."

"Please, have a seat, son. Make yourself comfortable."

Salim sat on the comfortable couch, noticing that the living room was decorated in a light sky blue matching the new furnishings and the intricate design of an oriental Persian carpet. It was a genuine, hand-knotted wool silk blend with a torque blue color. According to the Iraqi tradition, the blue color protects against evil spirits. Salim was impressed by the fireplace mantle, bearing a collection of crystal figurines. Above was an oil painting of a mountain waterfall, a scene that looked so real, he could almost hear water crashing over the rocks. He felt as if he had been in that mountain vista before, although he did not remember how or when.

Salim chatted happily with Haj Abbas and with the rest of the family for a few minutes before he changed the subject and addressed Haj Abbas directly. "Haj Abbas, sir, I'm here to ask for the permission … that is, for the honor of having your daughter Henan's hand in marriage." It was not a question, yet Salim felt he had asked a question.

The Haj smiled broadly, looking at his daughter and her mother before replying,

"Son, my wife and I have taught our children to have their own free decisions in all life's matters so that they're able to choose what they think best for themselves. Therefore, I'm going to ask our daughter about her answer for your request."

Henan's face flushed, she smiled but could not find the words to reply. She just nodded her head in assent.

"I think that's all that we need to know. Congratulations to both of you!"

The Haj's voice became more serious, as he said, "We want you to promise to honor our daughter and treat her with dignity, decency, and respect the rest of your life together. Henan is a great woman, and you're a wonderful man. We think that you two are deserving of each other. We've done a little research into your academic record—and into your family. Everything was satisfactory. Again, Henan's mother and I congratulate both of you."

Salim's spirits were flying with happiness. His heart was filled with overwhelming joy as he responded, "I promise you that I will always respect Henan, that I will honor her in all that I do, and in the eyes of our children." Blushing then, Salim concluded, "I will treat Henan with the same respect that I give to the morning light that tells my eyes of Allah's desire that I live another day." Salim stood and came forward to shake hands with the Haj, and to kiss him on both shoulders in the Muslim tradition. Then Salim shook hands with Hajja Meliha, Ali, and his wife. Then Salim drew a deep breath and turned to Henan. He looked deeply into her eyes, held both of her hands for a long moment, and then reached into his pocket for an engagement ring, which he slipped on her finger. The newly engaged couple hugged and whispered to one another, "I love you."

Henan's face flushed again, and she smiled happily. As the elders stood beaming with pride and joy, Hajja Maliha and Rania expressed themselves in loud ululations. Their cries of joy were loud enough to raise the curiosity of neighbors, who then appeared, inquiring about the cause of the joyous cries.

Upon returning to his dorm room that evening, the first thing that Salim did was write to his friend, Abdul, telling him the great news of his engagement to Henan. "Since I met Henan and became engaged, I feel an overwhelming happiness for the first time in my life. The love of a beautiful woman—a woman whose kindness, gentleness, and purity make me feel as if God has decided to be gracious to me. You, my friend Abdul, can understand what a new feeling that is to me. After feeling tricked by Allah during my internship at the Sheikh's house, then after feeling fooled by those who drew me into the ring of Dervishes, this love of Henan is a wondrous experience to me. Henan is the most precious human being on the entire earth to me. She is the only hope left to me in life. She's everything to me. I mean everything. My heart has been so overwhelmed by Henan's love and kindness that I no longer know who I am or what I am without her. She has made me forget all my former misery. From now on, it is only Henan who I'll live for. For her, I am ready to sacrifice my own life. I could never dare to wish for anything more than her at my side."

———

Married life brought many blessings to Salim, who adored Henan and gave her both the affections of an eager young man plus the adoration that so often enters a marriage only late in life. She returned his physical affections enthusiastically, realizing a hunger that surprised even her and giving Salim nonverbal assurances of security that far exceeded what any words could convey.

Despite Salim's happiness with Dr. Henan, he remained very cautious about Salwa's riddle. Its mystery continued to mystify him, causing unpredictable fits of worry. The object of his worry was most often the young woman, Salwa, who had cursed him after he turned from her romantic advances. Whenever he found himself brooding, worrying for the safety of his wife, Salim's brother, Nadeem, in a telephone conversation, would inquire, "What exactly is the story of this Salwa? Could she have anything to do with the cafeteria incident in which you hallucinated in her presence?"

Salim's mentor, Abdul, also showed concern about Salim's state of mind. "Young love can be demanding, even draining a person's emotional stability, Salim. Perhaps you are only tired and need a few days of rest?" Abdul pointed his questions at the former girlfriend, "Where did this Salwa come from, and what caused her to show up in the school suddenly? Why was she acting so indecently with you, pushing herself into your schedule. Did she plan to harm you? Could her attentions have been a kind of baited hook, hiding some sinister purpose to trip you?" Abdul's questions often mirrored Salim's own concerns.

"Please, God, help me to discern which powers are at work in my life! Surely, you, Almighty Allah, want me to know whose love to trust and who may wish me ill?" Salim's prayers, while not offered at the mosque, were sincerely voiced by a troubled heart.

While Salim was counting his blessings in the joy of Henan's agreement to become his wife, his bliss was usurped by the arrival of an unsigned letter from the Dervishes. Appearing under the door of their apartment seven days following his marriage to Henan, the letter read:

> Just remember that we've always warned you that we could never leave you living happily while you refuse to maintain attendance at our fellowship. Your recent engagement will be the beginning of a new misery that will occupy your heart for many months and will cost you the imitation joy you revel in today.
>
> So, why don't you try to understand your fate, Salim? No one could give up on us except snobs, especially a brat like you since you know us better. We still love you and want you to come back to us before it's too late. We ask you to keep your body from the knowledge of women and your soul as pure as gold so you may return to communion with us, where your immortal soul will be safe in our company. We hope your soul never gets rusty.

As Salim read the letter, tremendous anger surged through him. When Henan came into the room, she found him shaking with fear and anger. Salim could not escape; he had to reveal the ugly contents of the letter. Henan encircled him with her soft arms and kissed him tenderly. "Don't let these savages ruin our happiness. You can't live with such torture. We will see a lawyer that my friends know and perhaps even a judge my father has known since childhood. They will help us."

"All my worries are for your safety," Salim answered. "I don't care anything about myself. Besides, if I lose you, Henan, my life is over, you're all that I have left."

He took her in his arms and held her for a long time.

CHAPTER TWELVE

Welcome to Misery

SALIM FAILED TO RID HIMSELF OF SADNESS THAT DARK NIGHT. He tried to forget about the letter, but the Dervishes' threats kept stabbing deep into his heart. Despite his gloom, he forced himself to accompany Henan to dinner at a friend's house, but within thirty minutes of their arrival, Salim's joyless brooding pervaded the whole dinner party. A quiet withdrawal was the only possible course.

After they returned home and went to bed, Salim was unable to sleep. Had his eyes been fitted with lasers, the ceiling above their bed would have been incinerated. Finally, around three o'clock in the morning, Salim drifted off to slept, only to begin an awful dream. He and Henan were captives in the Dervish circle. Abdul was there as well, so sad among the Dervishes with their menacing glares, savage scowls, and inhuman visages. Abdul studied Salim before turning his face away, in a failed attempt to hide convulsive sobs. Every muscle in Salim's body burned and flinched. Henan clung to him for protection as she trembled and cried. Drums pounded, and the Dervishes gyrated in their joyless dance. Chief Omran stood up and approached his captives, who recoiled from his shouts while holding each other tightly. He rasped his indignation:

"Salim? Why didn't you try to love us? Why do you refuse our loving kindness and continue to barter your heart with the devil? What have we done, Salim, to make you hate us? Look what will happen to you and the woman you love if you keep shunning our invitations. When will you understand? The blood rushing through your veins is our blood. The power you squander in worldly pursuits belongs to our godly circle. Even your very life is a daily dispensation from your brother Dervishes!

"When will you discover that communion with us is your inevitable fate? You can't indulge forever in your sins and evil desires. We're bonded, Salim. You can't forsake us forever! Can a fish live without water? Can a man peel his own skin? Or tear out his fingernails? Neither can you live without our blessings and mercy.

"Salim, we have always been good to you. We have fed you since you were only a few days old. Remember? We protected you when your little heart was grieved, lonely, and full of fears. We demonstrated our secrets, our mysteries, and our wonders for your edification.

"In return, you walked away from us. You betrayed us. You followed your passions. Now we must stop you, Salim. We must hurt you with the same fire you once danced around in joy. We will destroy the love in your heart. Hurl you into a pit of bitterness and remorse. Your sinful heart will know only darkness, emptiness, and despair for the rest of your short life!"

The Dervish turned, nodding to his followers. Their drums grew in ferocity, their flutes wailed mournfully. Slowly, four young men rose and surrounded Salim and Henan. Two muscle-bound Dervishes grabbed Salim, holding him immobile on the ground. The other pair grasped Henan—one by the arms and the other by her feet—and carried her writhing toward the fire. She was struggling, shaking, writhing, and crying hysterically. Salim tried to break free, but couldn't overpower his captors. The merciless hold against which he fought caused bruises on his arms and legs. It felt as if his bones were being snapped and crushed.

Salim cried out to Ajil to stop them, "No! Ajil! Don't hurt my beloved wife! Don't hurt Henan!"

Then Salim felt someone shaking his body. He jerked, sat up gasping, and glancing around in confusion. Henan sat beside him on the bed, astonished. Henan held him tightly until his breathing slowed, and then dried rivulets of sweat from his face.

"Oh, sweetheart," she whispered. "I'm so sorry you're going through this."

"It was an awful dream," Salim stammered. His mouth was dry, his body convulsed, and his eyes refilled with tears as fast as Henan could dab them with the corner of a bedsheet.

"But it was just a dream," she consoled. "You're all right. I'm right here beside you. We are safe in our own bed."

Salim did not believe that it was just a dream. It scarred him emotionally and physically. He agonized through a high temperature, with head, chest, and stomach pains causing him to vomit throughout that day. He sensed the dream was a warning, that it was too late to protect Henan.

Who could help? Who would believe his story? People might think he was insane. Only Henan knew his background, his past with the Dervishes. He would never be able to tell her about the dream. Doing so would only frighten her. Besides, Salim knew he could not stand it if her reaction was to laugh at him, if she should chide him for being superstitious.

But wait! There might be a way to protect her. He could move to another place, away from her. Then the Dervishes would have nothing against her. They'd leave her alone. His wife had done nothing to them. The fault for their predicament was all his—why should Henan have to suffer for his juvenile foolishness?

But how could Salim explain a decision to live apart from his bride? Hours passed. Salim remained torn. Finally, he decided what he must do. He would tell her. Then he would act. Henan was in low spirits and seemed preoccupied. Each time Salim began to initiate a conversation about the crooked path that had brought him to this dilemma, the deep sadness he saw in her eyes caused him to turn away. Nonetheless, Henan still smiled and kissed him, trying to reassure him that nothing was bothering her. That evening, she suggested they go out, enjoy a nice dinner, and let off steam perhaps by taking in a Western action movie.

Salim hated to decline Henan's innocent suggestion. He acquiesced, feeling sure that the outing would, at least, improve Henan's state of mind. Besides, he reasoned, the change of scene might lift the dark clouds from both their spirits. It also might allow him to tell her about his decision.

As Salim drove his car into the city, the rain poured. The narrow road was slick. His preoccupied head and pelting rain limited his ability to see, so Salim slowed down. At a curve in the road, an approaching truck crossed into their lane, bearing down on their car, its lights blinding him. As Salim reacted to avoid the much larger truck, their car was struck from behind by a powerful force that addled his mind. Out of nowhere, two arms—neither his nor Henan's—grabbed at him and the steering wheel. Henan screamed as other arms—apparently from the back seat—wrapped about her neck and shoulders.

The oncoming truck smashed into Salim's car, causing both vehicles to careen off the narrow roadway. Salim felt his car, now out of control, hurtling down a steep cliffside, rolling over and over, catching fire. Then it exploded.

When he awoke, Salim learned that he had been thrown from the car. A policeman had found him, lying unconscious, with a broken leg and a dislocated shoulder on a rocky ledge, about fifty feet from the car's scorched hulk. Henan's remains were sealed inside it. Salim learned that he had been in a coma for more than eight weeks. His arms and legs had lost most of their muscle, and his ribs protruded ominously from his formerly smooth chest. After waking from the coma and coming to terms with the fact that he was confined to the hospital bed, Salim assessed the strength of his mind. He found that he was strangely calm. Why was he not raging with anger? Shouldn't his sadness at the loss of his beautiful young wife be driving him to fits of tears? Reality and fantasy seemed a single, flawed vision. He left the world around him.

Abruptly, Salim found himself wandering down long, empty streets in Nasiriya. "Nasiriya, you haven't changed much, but I still love you the way you are." He looked upon a few new houses. He ambled to his childhood home, recognizing a few neighbors and recalling the past. Then he stopped to contemplate an old house that seemed abandoned. Salim recalled accompanying his mother to this house, when it was inhabited. His mother would buy hot and delicious bread from the widow Sabiha, who lived here during his childhood. He remembered that Sabiha took relish in blending a special salad with meat just for him. He remembered sounds of Sabiha's voice and industry, which seemed absent in the dream. The word *void* came to mind.

Finally, Salim approached the house of his childhood family, where he hesitated a few moments, studying the faded paint. Stalled there, Salim gazed blankly at his friend Abdul's home, then at the house of Fahima, the woman who had been cast from the city for having an affair.

Then, he knocked on his door. When his mother's delighted face shone before him, beaming as she stood in the doorway, Salim felt contented. Monira called out joyfully, "Salim is here! My son is here. Thank God for the mercy." She stepped up and encircled him in her fleshy arms. His brothers ran from different rooms to welcome him, and his father peered over his mother's shoulder. Then, behind him, Salim heard Abdul arrive. Everyone was vibrant with life and laughter, gathering around him, asking questions of his life in Baghdad. Salim told them about his life as a university student in Baghdad, about his dorm room and his best friend, Ekram.

The family dined on Salim's favorite meal, which his mother cooked. Okra soup and lamb, plus "Umber" Iraqi rice. The family carried on, laughing in a cocoon of love. After dinner, they all went to bed, except Salim, who crossed the street to visit Abdul in his house. Abdul fixed the Turkish coffee that had been Salim's favorite. They sat and chatted for hours.

Then, Salim found himself standing before the Ur temple, reconstructed as it had been in his dream the night his mother had died. Salim climbed the stone-paved staircase and entered the temple. The sacred courtyard with vividly-painted walls was still standing. About eighty worshippers sat in its center. A young woman played her Santur, producing delicate music to the rhythm of which a cadre of dancing women moved gracefully.

Salim toured the temple, passing groups of people who whispered meaningfully among themselves. Six men marched in from the courtyard, shouldering a decorated coffin. Following in procession was a long line of men wearing dark robes and carrying torches. The people sitting in the courtyard's center stood up and strolled to the prayer area where the coffin was placed.

Salim watched the prayer ceremonies from a distance. Two men bathed the dead man with rosewater-scented towels, then dressed him in fine clothes and lightly splashed eucalyptus-scented oil on his face, hands and feet. Then the two men joined the others. After the prayer ceremony, the men carried the coffin to a large cemetery outside the temple. Before burying the deceased, they placed inside the coffin some of the man's personal things: his sword, armor, robes, and food. No one cried out or wept. All of the ceremony seemed appropriate, honorary, and customary.

Salim did not remember when he left the Ur temple or how he arrived at the great, unknown sea. He found himself standing on its shore in the early hours of morning. The shore was completely empty. The sun was rising gradually, introducing a beautiful new day and promising new hope. Salim breathed deeply, filling his lungs with fresh air.

Salim bent and picked up a stone, hurled it, making it skip nine times across the water before it sank. After skipping a few more stones, Salim noticed something moving between the rocks along the shoreline, not far from where he was standing. As Salim walked closer, he saw that it was a woman. Only her long black hair covered her nakedness. As she stood staring at him, Salim realized he had seen her somewhere before. She was the woman on the mirror in Abdul's special room. "Morisona!" he could only whisper. "Abdul told me your sad story with your husband, Soberian. Yes, it is you, my God," he continued to whisper. She took one more look at Salim, then stepped from the shore and disappeared into the water. Salim tried to speak. He wanted to rush and stop her, but instead he lost his balance and fell to the ground, feeling a sharp pain.

Opening his eyes, Salim found himself in a small room, lying in a bed. The tube of a life support system filled his mouth. His left shoulder and leg were in slings. Two men and a woman stood beside his bed. They all were smiling. "Ain Ana?" he asked in Arabic. "Where am I?" Their smiles broadened.

The two doctors took turns explaining what had happened. "You are lucky, Salim. You have been in a coma for about two months. It is a miracle that you have regained consciousness after all these weeks."

———

Salim's life with his beloved wife Henan was over. She was gone forever,

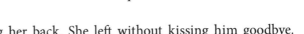

and nothing could bring her back. She left without kissing him goodbye. Their wonderful life together was now no more than a memory.

Henan was burned to death, just as the Dervishes had threatened. With Henan's burnt body were buried all of Salim's dreams for success and happiness. She had embodied all of Salim's ambitions and hopes. Not only had he lost his wife, but his lifetime lover and friend. During their courtship and brief marriage, Henan had come to life inside him, breathing within him, thinking and feeling within him. How could she be gone? How could he go on?

Salim cried hysterically for seven days and nights. He began to suffer from seizures, which choked him and drew him closer to death. His appearance had morphed dramatically as he lay comatose. Now that the coma was past, his behavior changed rapidly. His eye movement became erratic, he suffered from spasms which made him appear insane. In unpredictable spells of vomiting, he frequently soiled his bed, which would have been upsetting enough, were those episodes not followed with hysterical laughter, which ended in fits of deep and painful crying. Salim lost all appetite for food or drink. His eyes remained wide open, never closing in sleep. Salim's cheekbones were as clammy and sunken as those of the dead. He lost his ability to recognize people.

Then one day he tried to commit suicide, fighting with attendants, desperately attempting to throw himself from the hospital's second floor. After that, a nurse stayed with him constantly. He sometimes called her Henan. Most of the time he begged her to kill him and let him die peacefully.

For six months Salim underwent mental, physical, and psychological therapy. He had to resign his teaching job. It was impossible for him to continue living in Baghdad. The city reminded him of his wife, Henan, and the home that they had shared so joyously, if briefly. His life with her was in Baghdad, and that was why needed to leave. The anguish of losing her overwhelmed him, draining every bit of his enthusiasm for life in the city.

After Salim was discharged, he decided to go to Mosul for a change of venue. He took the bus to the center of Mosul, and rented a small room in an old hotel. Alone again as ever, Salim was entering a new and unknown period of his life.

CHAPTER THIRTEEN

A New Destiny

ONCE AGAIN, THE PASSAGE OF TIME slowly raised the blue-black cloud that blocked the sun from Salim's drowning soul. After four months in Mosul, Salim one day realized that it had been two whole years since he had last suffered the constant tearfulness over the death of his his wife. Then he reached a startling acceptance about the prospects for his existence.

Salim became gnawingly aware of the little time he had left. Suddenly, he found himself waiting for the end with no hint of patience. He clearly understood now: He was a man on death row. There would be no relief or mercy for him, or if there was, it would surely be temporary. Continuing to live could only lead to more dread, shock, and destruction.

Why should a person like Salim care about living anyway? His life was only day after day of suffering. What had he accomplished? He had brought sadness to his family, to his friend Abdul, and now death to Henan and grief to her family. He had lost the only true love of his life. Where had those few days of happiness with Henan gone? Why was their joy cut short? How could life be so dark and ugly?

Perhaps his lost happiness was caused by leaving his hometown and loved ones. But that could not be. The fault lay in his fate, the prophecy of his death and torture. In reality, only the fear and agony of death remained. Even the sun, which used to warm his face with sweet nectar scents, now only parched his lips with the stink of rotten fruit and bitter berries.

Without warning, Salim recalled Abdul's sad voice: "I'm afraid that

you will die lonely after you feel your life is not worth living anymore ....."
Now, Salim was indeed lonely, feeling unworthy of life. Abdul's prediction
had come true. Haunted, Salim wondered when and how he would die. After
a week of restless nights contemplating his impending death, Salim decided
that nothing could cause more suffering than waiting for an imminent death.
But wait he would, and his internal torment would remain his constant
companion.

For the next few weeks, Salim stayed in his hotel room, contemplating
his lonely, miserable, and hopeless life. During the rare nights when he slept,
Salim found himself trapped in an interminable delerium. Slowly, Salim
began to accept his fate. Outwardly, he adopted a facade of calm acceptance.
At times, with great effort, he achieved a nearly-cheerful persona. Salim
decided to start walking tours of the city using a guidebook someone had left
behind in his hotel room. Occasionally he stopped at the hangouts near the
University of Mosul—markets and cafes where the chatter of students seemed
to lift his spirits.

Salim rented an apartment just a few blocks from the University. The
city was the second largest in Iraq, and it's botanical treasure was an aromatic
green park, a grassy expanse where young families gathered to listen to music
and watch their children play. Often, a family group, sensing Salim's need
for familial embrace, invited him to share in a modest meal, spread out
on a ground cloth. The people were more than cordial, but he felt none of
the vibrant energy of Baghdad. Still, Salim daydreamed of Mosul as a suitable place where he and Henan might have raised healthy children in a safe
environment.

Then he chased those thoughts away.

Mosul University had established a solid academic reputation and
attracted a substantial number of students from other countries in the Arab
world. But the town retained the air of all provincial places, conservative
and much less open than Baghdad. From his many walks, Salim had become
familiar with the layout of the city. The Public Library was his favorite spot to
read information about the history of the ancient city, its founding, and the
highlights of its history.

Salim learned that the ancient city of Nineveh (its ruins are across the Tigris River from the modern-day city of Mosul) had been the third capital of Assyria. Now a part of Iraq, it had once become the home of the global traveler and British archaeologist, Austen Henry Layard. His 1845 excavations at Tel "Quintin" in the ancient Assyrian capital of Nimrud, south of Nineveh on the Tigris River, revealed the lost palace of King Sennacherib. According to Wikipedia, it included what may have been the prototype of the legendary Hanging Gardens of Babylon, or even the actual Hanging Gardens. Layard also discovered the Ashurbanipal palace and library, which included more than twenty thousand cuneiform clay figures. Among them were discovered a book of Nineveh and the great treasures in this archaeological site. Salim learned about the original name of Mosul. Because Mosul was between Syria and Khorasan and between the Tigris and the Euphrates, it was long ago described as "the door of Iraq" and" the key to Khorasan," which later became Azerbaijan.

Finding himself something of a surprise to locals, Salim also recalled how, in his hometown of Nasiriya, people would be curious when encountering a tourist on the street. He had not found this curiosity in Baghdad, where the complexity of life and variety of ethnicities was taken for granted. Still, Salim welcomed the quiet atmosphere of Mosul. He usually stayed home, watching television or listening to music, a lifestyle that was not questioned by his affable neighbors in the apartment building. A young man called Hadi and his wife Samia, both in their early thirties, lived in an adjacent apartment. A happily childless couple, they taught at nearby public schools. An elderly couple, Abdul Majid and his wife Fatima, occupied another. Abdul was a retired military officer and his wife was a retired nurse. Salim introduced himself to neighbors when they passed in the building's narrow hallway, and invitations to afternoon tea were frequently extended.

Salim bought a used sky-blue Chevy, affordable and adequate, and enjoyed driving himself around the city. Two months after his purchase of the auto, Salim was awakened by an insistant knocking on his door shortly after midnight. He rushed to open the door, where he found his neighbors, Abdul Majid and his wife, in urgent need. The husband was suffering from a terrible pain in the abdomen, and begged Salim to take him to the hospital. Immediately, Salim dressed, found his keys, and led them to his car. Salim felt like a trained ambulance driver as he negotiated the dark streets to the hospital. Abdul Majid was diagnosed with a case of acute appendicitis, requiring emergency surgery to avoid certain death.

Three days following the surgery, Abdul Majid's incision was sufficiently healed and he was discharged. Again, Salim felt the weight of responsibility and competence as he chauffered the retired gentleman and his worried wife from the hospital to their apartment.

The next weekend, Fatima fixed a famous delicious Mosuli dish, *Kubba,* inviting Salim for supper at their apartment, and Salim gladly accepted. During the elaborate dinner, Salim and his hosts chatted happily, cementing their nascent friendship. Abdul Majid, it turned out, was originally from Baghdad, and his wife was from Mosul. Their two sons were married and had left home to live with their families. "After retirement a few years ago, we moved to Mosul just for a change," Abdul Majid told Salim. Then his host inquired, "Do you work, Salim?"

"No, I'm not working right now. I hold a master's degree in English Literature and I was teaching at Baghdad University before moving to Mosul about two months ago."

"Are you intending to find a teaching job at Mosul University?"

"Not really. Not right now, anyway. I had a good teaching job at the University of Baghdad, College of Languages, but I resigned before moving here."

"We love Baghdad, it's a charming city," his host continued. "What brought you to Mosul, Salim?"

Shifting in his seat, Salim wished they hadn't asked. However, his mother had trained him to respond as helpfully as possible, even under duress. He hesitated, then, began to explain, "We had a terrible automobile accident and I lost my wife. I was in the hospital for two months. Then, after I was discharged, I decided to come here because I couldn't bear living in the familiar city anymore. I like Mosul, and I'm still here."

Abdul Majid sensed Salim's discomfort and immediately changed the subject. "We're very sorry to hearing about your tragedy, Salim. We hope you get over it soon."

"Thank you," Salim said, unable to mask the deep sadness in his voice.

"Are you from Baghdad too, Salim?"

"No," Salim answered. "I'm originally from Nasiriya, but I finished my schooling in Baghdad."

"Oh, Nasiriya, it's a nice city." Abdul Majid looked at his wife, smiled and said, "By the way, one of our best friends lives with his family in a suburb of Nasiriya. His name is Rahim, a truly fine man. I would like very much for you, Salim, to meet him and his family when you visit your folks. I'll give you his phone number when we meet again. Rahim and his family visited us here a few months ago, and they forgot some things here—including a golden necklace, which we found after they left. If it would be no trouble, we would appreciate it if you would take the small package to them whenever you would go to visit Nasiriya?"

"Sure, why not? I'll give him a call when I visit there."

"Great, much obliged, Salim. May Allah bless you."

Their talk rambled from life in Baghdad, Abdul Majid's military experience, to the charms of Mosul—especially its balmy springtime weather. Abdul extolled the many beautiful places in Mosul before their conversation devolved to evaluation of popular television shows and favorite films. Salim then thanked his generous neighbors for sharing the tradition Iraqi dish, before excusing himself and returning to his own apartment.

Salim found himself spending more time with the neighbors. The following weekend, he invited Abdul Majid and his wife to a restaurant for dinner. They accepted with delight and spent the evening conversing animatedly. Salim and the Majid family developed warm feelings for each other, resulting in even more evenings spent together.

Abdul Majid and his wife discovered Salim's consistent gentleness and intelligence, and they joked about adopting him as a son. They tried their best to help him forget the tragedy that had caused him to flee Baghdad. Soon, they were offering to introduce him to their relatives and friends whose families included eligible women, from whom he might choose an attractive and attentive wife. Salim was appreciative of their intent, but not interested in meeting new women. At least, Salim told himself, he had made excellent friends, souls with whom he could talk and share his deepest feelings. For Salim, the prospect of abandoning the memory of Henan's tenderness was an impossibility. Salim tried to explain to his new friends that he could not love again. What he did not add was that he felt sure that he would never even love himself again, that he would always blame himself for Henan's death at such a young age. In his heart, there was no space for any other woman.

Yet his new friends—both husband and wife—gently persisted in trying to persuade him that he should forget the past and launch himslf into a new life. They implored him that death is Allah's ultimate decree to every soul, not a choice we can make for ourselves. They spoke of other friends who had found the strength to re-marry after the loss of dear spouses or children. Fervently, they asked him to consider putting aside even the most harrowing of circumstances, and reach out for the joy that a gracious Allah surely held in store for him. We should, they said, wait patiently for His mercy and the revelation of new hope.

Salim drove his friends to a number of tourist areas in and around the ancient city of Nineveh. On one occasion, they arrived at a place called Hamam Alil, "the bath of ill people." The ancient, communal bathhouse was located about thirty kilometers southeast of Mosul. It is now famous throughout Iraq and the world, for naturally-heated waters that emerge from the ground, near-boiling in summer and winter. The water is pumped by large engines, from the thermal features near the Tigris River to a large water bath in the form of a basin, divided into two parts, a bath for men and bath for women, surrounded by ruins of the ancient bathhouses.

Hamam Alil was established as a regional bathhouse for the healing of those suffering diseases such as psoriasis, rheumatism, swollen joints, open sores, and wounds that refuse to heal. In addition, many use the healing waters to revive normal aches and pains, or simply for relaxation. The sulfur water springs were also used in the treatment of other diseases and to stimulate blood circulation in women. The healing effects of the thermal baths have been known for centuries, even going back to the ancient Greeks, who utilized the baths in the treatment of skin diseases and battle wounds.

The thermal springs were the first attraction in the area, leading to the earliest settlement in the region, which grew into the city that we know today as Mosul. In modern times, builders established fine restaurants and hotels to serve affluent visitors to the thermal baths. Since then, the waters have become an important tourist destination. In addition to health tourism, the waters have been bottled and shipped around the Mideast as healthful, pure drinking water.

Salim, Abdul Majid, and his wife joined with tourists from throughout the Mideast to bathe in the warm waters of the springs. Salim and Abdul Majid bathed in the men's pools, while Fatima went to the women's pools. After bathing, the three friends relaxed together, basking in the release of tensions for which the waters are famous.

Besides Hamam Alil, Salim and his friends also toured a formation called the "Hill Saturday," or "Tel al Sebat," which rose out of the surrounding flat plain to a height of about sixty feet. The Hill is revered regionally and honored in myths as a sacred place which draws pilgrims—mostly young women who have been unlucky in love, and their families. The myths generally advise young women to process up the hill in a state of reverence in order to enhance their prospects for receiving marriage proposals.

Fall turned to winter, bringing cold weather, gray skies, and barren trees to Mosul. Strong winds stripped the trees, ruthlessly denuding their branches, leaving only a gnarled nakedness everywhere. The frozen season set in a reign of gusty winds, frozen precipitation, and slick sidewalks throughout the city. Having never lived in the north of the country previously, Salim had no acquaintance with the onslaught of such weather. Snow covered the city, changing its image completely. Salim had no idea why, but the snowfall made him homesick.

In that winter, temperatures dropped to below zero and blowing icy winds from the north settled in for weeks. Cold rains made driving and even walking unpleasant and dangerous. Several decades ago, this kind of pronounced bitter cold was common for Mosul's winters, but in recent decades the city had enjoyed more moderate winter weather. People walked tentatively on the frozen ground, cracking a layer of transparent ice that breaks and snaps underfoot, while listening to the foreign sound of freezing rain. Doors and windows were bombarded by wind-driven hail and sleet, disturbing children and evoking panic among many.

On one Monday in November, when the temperatures in the city dropped to twenty degrees below zero, the governor of Nineveh ordered the closure of primary schools and kindergartens for the day, fearing for the children's health in the cold wind and sleet. The unbearable weather made Salim decide to travel south to Nasiriya, where the temperatures were warmer and the winds gentler. After packing, Salim went to saying goodbye to his good friends, Abdul Majid and Fatima. Explaining that he needed relief from the weather in Mosul—and that he was heading to Nasiriya—he renewed his offer to deliver the possessions of their friends who had visited from his hometown. Abdul Majid gave him Rahim's phone number and a small box of the things they had forgotten upon departing from their visit. Salim assured Abdul Majid and Fatima that he would extend their hearty greeting to the family.

Telephoning his friend Abdul in Nasiriya upon arising early the next morning, Salim pointed his blue Chevy south toward his hometown. After continuous driving for ten hours, punctuated only by a short break in Baghdad, Salim arrived at the house of Abdul in Nasiriya. It was five o'clock in the afternoon. Received by his friend and his family with hugs and cries, Salim couldn't hold his tears, and he cried out, "Abdul ... they have killed her ... the Dervishes killed my wife, Henan, they killed all my life, I don't have any life left within me."

With tear-filled eyes, Abdul was unable to respond with anything other than a fatherly hug. Once the men separated, Abdul stood in sadness, his eyes downcast. Following a few moments of silence, his voice rattled, "O my dear son, your fate is only the will of Allah alone. It is not the will of anyone but Him. Our travail in this life is only the Almighty Allah's will." Continuing weakly, Abdul said, "You look very exhausted. Follow me to the room we have prepared. You need some rest."

Salim walked between Abdul and his wife into the house. They sat around the table for a brief visit, and then Salim was shown to the shower, while Abdul carried Salim's bag to his bedroom. Abdul explained, "I made the first room down the hall from the front door into my clinic. Your room will be next to it, over there on the left."

"I would like to take a nap after the shower, if that's all right."

"Absolutely, Salim, make yourself at home. I'll be close by if you need anything. Are you sure you don't want to eat something before napping?"

"No, not now. Thanks anyway."

After the warm shower, Salim stretched and relaxed. He went to his room and rested on the bed. The room was spacious, carpeted, and nicely furnished. Large, colorful (and surely expensive) Persian Kashan rugs were hung on two walls of the room. The bed and nightstand were comfortably arranged. Though he intended only a short nap, Salim slept soundly until the evening.

Anticipating Salim's visit, Abdul had already concluded his appointments at the clinic for the day, in order to focus on his guest.

After the nap, Salim awakened in good spirits. Abdul gave him a nice gown to wear. The gown, similar to what any man in Nasiriya might wear, meant that Salim would not stand out when encountering townspeople. In it, he felt more comfort and relaxed than wearing the jeans that were his normal attire in larger cities. When Abdul noticed that Salim still wore the necklace of polished stones that had been his gift so many years before, Abdul relaxed. "I am so happy to see that you still have it, Salim! That makes my day. Please, always wear the necklace, it's blessed by an honored exorcist to provide strong protection. Those stones will keep you safe from all evil spirits. That garland was my special gift to you, and I have asked you to wear it all the time. By Almighty Allah's leave, it will abrogate your anxiety and cast off calamities from your soul. The necklace is your intercessor, and you must always regard it with respect and love. By Allah's will, it will help you restore your health and well-being. It also will aid us to fight Dervishes and defeat them." Then, sitting back in his chair, Abdul fixed his eyes on Salim with joy and exclaimed, "I'm so happy for you, Salim, that you thought of me and came a long way. It pleases me to see you now satisfied and content."

"I'm grateful for you, Abdul."

After supper, Abdul exclaimed, "Salim, son, I was talking with my wife about how genuine a man you are—one who loves his culture, his friends and folks, and owns the freedom to choose where to be, yet, you came all the way to visit me and honoring my family by staying with us and not to go to your own brothers. We think that a great honor in our culture." Abdul's eyes filled with tears as he went on, "As you may know, in our culture parents raise their children in a certain way of life. The parents expect their children to revere their parents, treat them with dignity, with love and respect. It would be an honor for any good person to defend his family with blood if anything happened to them. They ought to keep making sure that their bonds with their family always remain strong and dignified, and should keep viewing parents as the ultimate authority. And you, dear Salim, have been offering all of those great values and virtues for your family. Still, you also treat other people you love with same level of dignity and respect."

"Thank you, Abdul for your reminder. I am honoring you and your family because you helped me become the man I am now. You deserve my love for you and your family."

"Do you know that just a few years back," Abdul continued, "adult men, married men who are fathers, could never dare to smoke a cigarette in the presence of their parents, especially the father? The father might already know that his son smokes cigarettes, but respect required the son not smoke in the presence of his father. Back in our culture, friends might die happily for their friends. Well, I could assume that life might have been changing, and the new generation was behaving oddly, but, some people could not give up their precious tradition and virtues toward their parents." Abdul's voice sounded more emotional at the moment while saying, "I have known you, Salim, for many years. I have observed what an honest, kind, upright, and determined man you are. I would be honored to die for you and for your revenge. Your horrific tragedy and the blatant repression the Dervishes inflicted upon you by killing your wife, must be never forgotten. After all, what could life be without trust and loyalty between friends?" Abdul was sad, his eyes glittered with tears. Salim remained mute, considering what his friend had said.

"I know how ruthless they can be," Abdul continued, "And they will be after you until they kill you too. That's the way they treat those whom they consider their enemy. But, I'm with you all the way, don't worry son, I wouldn't let anything hurt you. You may trust me."

"I'm sure of your word. In fact, you're my only real friend in this life."

At Abdul's house, Salim had no doubt that he was welcome to stay as long as he liked. The next morning, during the breakfast hour, Salim took Abdul across the street to his own family's house, where he was pleased to find his father at home, and to see all of his brothers present to honor their late mother. In the living room, where his family had lived since his childhood, Salim, his father, Abdul, and Salim's brothers all sat at breakfast. Salim was especially happy to find his oldest brother Nadeem, his wife and five children, visiting their father and honoring their mother. Shortly, they were joined by his other brothers, Nori, Sabir, and Saif, who came on foot from their residences in different neighborhoods. They all sat with their families and children to learn of the exploits of their younger brother. Each one praised Salim for his studies and invited him to return to Nasiriya to live among them, regardless of all the troubles he had gone through with the Dervishes during his early years.

Salim listened, taking pleasure in the stories of his father's life in Basra after he had remarried, and in the good fortunes of his brothers here in the city of their birth. Reverently, Salim entered his mother's special room where she had performed fortune telling, remembering how the room used to overwhelm him with a sort of strangeness. Vividly, Salim remembered his youthful confrontation with his mother when she told him about his destiny, admitting to himself that she had been mostly correct about his future. His eyes filled with tears for the difficulties he had encountered, especially for the loss of his dear wife, Henan.

Abdul also took Salim to tour the city. Sadly, Salim noticed very little progress in terms of buildings, bridges, traffic patterns, and public utilities during the years of his absence. He realized that the dictator, Saddam Hussein, would never think of the Iraqi people as human beings deserving of modern improvements to enhance their lives. Salim had heard many reports about how the tyrant has wasted the wealth of Iraqi oil entirely upon construction of his seventy-eight palaces throughout Iraq, and also on his wars against Iraq's neighbor, Iran.

CHAPTER FOURTEEN
The Uprising

SADDAM HUSSEIN'S MILITARY FORCES HAD INVADED AND OCCUPIED KUWAIT. The tyrant still refused to end the occupation despite the mediation of the Arab League and the heads of several Arab countries. The United States and many other nations had recently announced that their armies were planning to assemble in Kuwait against Saddam. The dictator's forces, the fourth-largest army in the world, prepared to defend Iraq against a coalition led by the United States. The people of Iraq dreaded the coming clash between Saddam's army and the forces assembling in Kuwait.

Meanwhile, the leaders of the Shi'a had set up a plan to free Iraq from the notorious Saddam Hussein through an internal public uprising. The Shi'a leaders, however, faced a wall of non-cooperation from every unit of the Iraqi army. Tensions mounted as Saddam's government defied the Shi'a faction within the country, as well as the massing armies of Coalition nations, landing in Kuwait. The situation remained bleak, as every element of Iraq society feared the devastation that would be unleashed in their cities and towns, should Saddam's army defy the much-larger international force. Soon, it became apparent to all parties that the dictator would not bend to powerful forces in his country or to those preparing to invade.

After Saddam's invasion of Kuwait, the Iraqi people were boiling in rage against the tyrant Saddam Hussein. It was discussed in the tea rooms. Saddam's irresponsiblity seemed to invite the international coalition amassing in Kuwait. It became clear that Hussein was prepared to toss the people of Iraq into a new cauldron of bombs and missiles.

In about three weeks, the Iraqi army was devastatingly defeated, the bitterest humiliation proud Iraqi soldiers had known. The United States, leading the United Nations troops, had kicked them out of Kuwait and were now pouncing upon Baghdad with a terrible war of "Shock and Awe." The Iraqi people were extremely furious at the apparently easy defeat of their army. Although the majority of Iraqis had disagreed with Saddam's occupation of Kuwait, the humiliating defeat of the Iraqi army united them in furious rage against the dictator who pushed Iraqi faces into the mud.

The war in their beloved capital added fuel to the fire that was Saddam's long, corrupt rule, during all of which he treated his people like slaves. He dishonored them, stepped on their pride, and belittled whole regions. Yet, for decades he had repeatedly gotten away with blatant humiliations. Saddam had proven his insensitivity to the worries of his own people. When his taunting of the international coalition brought war to Iraq, Saddam's much-touted army folded like a card table. Not only did his generals achieve no triumph, they leapfrogged over one another to retreat in shame and disgrace. Saddam, the sadist and selfish braggart, demonstrated his failure as a military leader, just as he had already proven himself a spoiled toddler when it came to the distribution of oil income during peacetime. In peacetime, he proved himself heartless and in war he showed himself to be no better than a savage chieftain, who runs from spear-throwers with no thought to the women and children whom he leaves behind. In defeat, Saddam left the country to the invaders and allowed his own people to be bombed, shot, and taken prisoner in their own homes. Those who suffered the worst were the Shi'a minority.

The uprising plan was developed in a network of secrecy, for fear of government reprisals, but the Shi'a's leaders sought some assistance among the Iraqi army friends who hated Saddam despite the deadly risk. It was not an easy task for anyone to speak in such taboo especially among the army officers. Among civilians as well as military, fear was everywhere, and trust was nowhere, not even among family members. Saddam offered wealth for anyone who would reveal a conspiracy against him. The Shi'a's leaders finally, however, decided to undertake their plan under diversionary cover of the war of the international coalition against Saddam's troops in Kuwait. The conspirators expected multitudes to parade in the streets, grateful to join the movement against the dictator, Saddam. The time seeming right, Shi'a leaders seized the moment, and worked seamlessly to execute their plan as soon as possible.

Salim was greatly worried for the safety of his two brothers, Nori and Sabri, who he was told were helping inspire the rebels. Salim reflected on his dismay at his brothers. He had never expected that his own brothers would become leaders of the fight to unseat Saddam. Salim feared for their lives at the hands of government soldiers. Salim knew that Nori and Sabri had gone to Baghdad—on business, they said. To his surprise, his friends said they had not gone to Baghdad, after all. He was later told that his brothers were now actually in the holy city of Najaf, about 90 kilometers to the southeast of Baghdad.

In Najaf, Nori and Sabri first paid a visit to the Holy Shrine of the Imam Ali; the cousin and son-in-law of the Prophet Mohammed. In the crowded shrine, the two brothers prayed to Almighty Allah to assist them in a difficult mission, to light their way, and to bestow power upon them to overcome adversities they were about to face. Nori and Sabri had to wait until dark before stepping into the streets, avoiding Saddam's security forces that were on high alert due to rumors of clandestine meetings. Saddam had prohibited assemblies of any kind, fearing the development of a sophisticated conspiracy against his rule.

At the stately home of a Shi'a party leader, the expansive living room was crowded with leaders representing the Shi'a communities in every Iraqi province. All wore long faces. A tall middle-aged man with a light gray beard and wearing a white Turban started the meeting by announcing:

> Dear brothers, we are meeting here today for the most honorable cause that any man could wish to die for. We, the pious believers, who wish to honor our generations of the Shi'a, are called to be the pioneers in sacrificing our lives for our great faith of Islam, by rising up against the tyrant sinner, Saddam Hussein. Each one present assures the man at his right elbow and the man at his

left that he will, if necessary, sacrifice his wealth, his lands, and his life to free our families, our communities, and our country of Saddam, the great usurper both of worldly power and of the true faith.

We dedicate our mortal lives to one another and to our great cause in this historic meeting. Saddam has brought great mischief upon our beloved Iraq, upon our Shi'a people, and upon our families. Saddam has raised his gigantic sword in an attempt to cut down our fathers, our sons, and ourselves, murdering our best Islamic religious scientists and leaders, and continually pouring his wrath, endless oppression, and false holiness upon us all. We gathered in this place to pledge our readiness, if necessary, to martyr ourselves in this great cause. So doing, we write history today. What our Shi'a brothers and sisters have suffered all these long years under Saddam's oppression must end.

Enough is enough, and we have decided to deal with it this time, no matter what the loss may be. All members in this room have confirmed readiness, each in his own province, to begin disruption of Saddam's unholy forces in the streets, in the police stations, municipal buildings, and wherever we find them. We have established tomorrow as the day of our uprising, and each will begin at daybreak next.

We all pray to see other brothers in Tikrit, Mosul, and Al-Unbar provinces joining us in our great revolution. Yet, since Saddam has held rifles to their heads, we have to exempt them from joining us at the outset of our honorable revolution. In fact, those provinces have been key to Saddam's control of his secret services and agencies, perpetuating his rotten regime. Nevertheless, all our Shi'a brothers in Baghdad, who are the majority, are supporting us. For their sakes, we fear that if they act first, they could be crushed by the concentration of Saddam's forces in Baghdad. That is why, brothers, we must act first. This is our situation. Now, let any member who disagrees with our plan for the first move, raise his hand and let us hear it."

As the speaker sought and received the expected unanimous agreement, he continued, "Okay, if all agree on the stated day to begin the uprising, please raise your hands. Perfect," the man again said, as he saw that the agreement was unanimous. Then he went on, "Then our plan shall be implemented. If any have comments or objections, let them get heard this moment. Otherwise, we're done here. We will be sending telegrams to each province while you are on your way back home. Now, we need to perform our covenant with each other." Afterward the leaders pledged their covenant, one to another that they'll fight unpityingly against Saddam's regime in all fourteen provinces until the tyrant is ousted. The men shook hands and embraced each other. Few by few—in order to avoid suspicion—the men departed quietly into the night. Leaving the host's home, Salim's two brothers returned to pray at the holy shrine of Imam Ali, supplicating almighty Allah to bless their difficult mission, and to lighten their way. They asked Allah to bestow power upon them to overcome all the adversities they were certain to face soon. After the prayers, Nori and Sabri returned immediately to Nasiriya.

CHAPTER FIFTEEN

Rahim's Wife

A WEEK LATER, SALIM PHONED RAHIM, THE FRIEND OF ABDUL MAJID who lived in the suburb of Nasiriya, and asked for a convenient time to deliver the things that were forgotten in Abdul Majid's house at their last visit. Rahim's phone voice sounded pleasant, as he welcomed Salim back to Nasiriya and told him that Abdul Majid had called, asking if he had met with Salim yet, and that he wished to meet soon. Salim offered to bring the things to his house, but Rahim insisted that he would come to Salim and save him the extra driving. The next morning Rahim arrived at the appointed time. Salim and Abdul welcomed their guest and the three sat, talking mainly about the defeat of the Iraqi army by the coalition in the amazing Hundred Hour War. Rahim appeared to be in his late thirties, with choppy hair that hid his ears. Salim decided that the gray in Rahim's hair made him look older than his true age. Salim kept staring at Rahim, brooding on where he had seen this man before. Unable to remember, Salim had to ask him, "Have we met before, Rahim?"

"I don't think so," Rahim replied after a pause, forcing a smile as he added, "but you *do* remind me of somebody I used to know, and the resemblance is incredible." After some seconds, Rahim added, "It maybe be true as some say that Almighty Allah creates resemblances in every fortieth individual. Have you heard of such a saying, Salim?" The three men laughed. They kept talking for about an hour, when Rahim excused himself, inviting Salim to be his guest that afternoon. Rahim insisted on that, saying, "Listen, Salim, since Abdul Majid and his family cherish you so, they would never forgive me if I failed to invite you to my house. Right now, I've to go to meet a friend. Then I will come back to pick you both up in less than two hours."

"I'm so sorry," Abdul interjected. "I have an engagement with a patient, and will not able to join you this afternoon."

"I am so disappointed to know that you won't come with us, Abdul. That's really regrettable," Rahim retorted.

"Well, then, it'll be only you, me, and my wife, Salim."

"Could we postpone it to some other time, I would like for Abdul to be with us as well?"

"Well, it's too late for that," Rahim objected. "My wife has been up since early today, cooking in anticipation of your honored visit. And probably you don't know, Salim, that we regard Abdul as if he were the "Chief" of the city. He is the friend of everyone in town, needing no invitation to have supper at any home. As a matter of fact, over the years, Abdul has healed, counseled, and saved dear ones in so many homes that everyone sincerely wishes to host him at their homes anytime. However, we'll invite him once again soon. I promise."

"Well, if you insist then," said Salim.

"I do insist," Rahim laughed as he shook hands with Salim and Abdul before departing.

Salim hated that Abdul would be unable to join them. While he admitted it only to himself, Salim was assailed by anxiety by the invitation to Rahim's house. He didn't know why, but he wished he could apologize to Rahim and remain in the security of Abdul's familiar home. Still, thinking that he might upset Rahim who was—after all—trying to be hospitable and make him feel welcome, Salim resigned himself to the dinner.

That evening, in Rahim's car as it snaked through the narrow city streets, Salim's feeling of discomfort increased the closer they got to Rahim's house. Salim kept thinking about where he had seen Rahim before. Then, in a split-second of unwelcome clarity, Salim recalled a profile view of Rahim dancing with the Dervishes one evening years ago. Alarms went off in every part of Salim's consciousness just as the car stopped in front of a newly-built hilltop home. Unhappily, Salim followed his host into the open jaws of the house.

————

Walking toward the glow of a yellow room, Salim felt as if he was crawling into the throat of a sleeping beast. Inside, just a few steps ahead of him, stood a shapely young woman, tall, statuesque, and focused upon him. Reality assaulted Salim. Welling up in his memory, worming up through his esophagus, came the memory of a woman who looked just like the one he was about to meet. In fact, he was quite sure that the remembered woman and the tall blonde who stood before him were one and the same.

A subtle smile moved across her face as her head rotated slowly to focus upon Salim. He stopped, gazed wide-eyed at her in shock, and the room began to spin. Salim knew her from his nightmares. He wanted to scream and run out of the house, through the gate, down the street, all the way home to his safe family house. But his legs buckled, and he melted onto the floor, unconscious.

Rahim carried Salim to a bedroom, laid him out and crossed his arms over his chest. With a cold, wet cloth, Rahim wiped Salim's face and neck. Then Rahim massaged Salim's forehead and wrists. Finally, Salim brought his hands to his eyes, as if to wipe away a troubling dream. Panic flushed his eyes, pricked the backs of his hands, and teased the bottoms of his feet with nails. Salim was sure he was drowning, though the mysterious water in which he found himself was thicker than syrup and it radiated incandescent orange.

Rahim grabbed the writhing man, but to Salim, Rahim's face was distorted by the orange waves in which he was drowning.

"Salim, it's all right! You're here with us. What happened? Please tell me!" Rahim seemed genuinely concerned and entirely unaware of the part he had played in his guest's anxieties over the years.

Salim nodded his head, breathing heavily. He looked around to see the blonde woman, from whose knowing smile emanated every evil Salim had ever dreamed. Salim quickly turned his face away. He had recognized her immediately. He had dreamed about her all his life. She was the blonde woman who had brought him nothing but endless horror. She was the blonde woman who filled him with shock and misery, the one who endlessly shot herself in his nightmares. As she concentrated on his eyes now, he saw blood soaking her garment, smeared across her nose and cheeks. Was it her blood ... or was it his own?

I'm just delirious, or out of my mind, Salim thought as a cold sweat covered his face. He looked up, trying to apologize, even while knowing the threat was very real. "I don't know what's happening to me. I'm sorry. I am feeling very sick. I've been sick for a long time. I'm sorry for the trouble I've caused." Salim turned his eyes quickly toward the blonde woman, who now stood next to her husband.

"Salim, this is my wife Mona."

"I know Salim," the blonde woman replied from a frightening calm.

"Nice!" exclaimed the unaware Rahim. "Salim, I bet you met her before we got married, when you used to live in Nasiriya, right? What a small world!"

Salim was trembling, and his eyes filled with tears. He could not form words.

"I hope you will be better soon, Salim," Mona said softly, almost in a whisper, looking deep into his eyes. Fearfully, Salim jerked his face away from her gaze.

"I think we need to let him rest," Rahim said. They moved from the room. Rahim walked normally, but Mona moved like a reticent electrical storm, withdrawing only after having sucked all of the energy out of those over whom it has passed.

A fever overcame Salim. He vomited once and was certain that he would vomit again if he tried to eat any of the bloody steak Rahim had grilled. Salim was petrified, seeing the recurrent prophecy walking before him, abruptly and starkly. The epitome of his lifelong suffering, the source of his nightmares and madness, was now right beside him, in flesh and blood—if, in fact, any human blood remained in the strange woman whose face had terrorized him since childhood. Suddenly, the reality of her was indisputable. She sat just a few feet away, flexing her evil just as a normal woman might push her long hair from her eyes. Mona smiled at him, though it was not a loving smile. Only Salim had seemed to notice how her eyes burned with hatred and devilish purpose, as her soft words lightly teased him.

Seemingly without effort, she focused on his fear. "What miserable fate invited you to our home, Salim?" she inquired discreetly, when her husband left Salim to bring a freshly cooled towel. Only Salim heard her.

His fright mixing thickly with sadness, Salim continued to ponder the course his life had taken. He wondered if unknown other persons in the world were being tried daily and nightly as he was. Could there be others whose survival despite similar entangling traps might be causes for relief—even if only for camaraderie in his darkest moments of fear? Could others have dreams so entangled as his own? Could their strivings to claw their way through days that appeared normal to others give him encouragement? Could he somehow reach out to them in love, offering hope?

Salim could barely see himself now as a living person since life itself had lashed him down, disrupting his childhood innocence, and leaving him dispirited and bewildered. How could death be much worse? How could this be a life? His nightmares and brutal experiences had ruined his hopes, buried his dreams, and stripped him of his will. Alone as ever, he again had to fend off the fanatics' ruthless skewers and simulated reverence for religion. They had wrapped themselves tightly with Islamic cloaks, but were in fact worse than sadists. What love had they for God? Where was the love they professed for others? All they knew was how to seek revenge, how to ruin lives and kill.

He had learned well. The Dervishes' immorality meant that no one could cross them and publicize their perversions. They never stopped coercing him to subsume his Godly spirit and cower among them, submissive and obedient to their savage rule. The Dervishes had surrounded his life with terror and pain. Now, Salim shook as he faced the terrible reality of renewed exposure to Dervish terror. It seemed to paralyze his chest, pressing air from his lungs. He knew that there would be no escape, no avoidance, and no sanctuary. The tragedy that had smothered his dreams every night for years was now unfolding before his eyes. It was his fate, foretold in the old prophecy his mother had once read on his forehead. His inevitable destiny was finally here—right before his eyes. The fulfillment of the divine predictions was at hand.

"For every matter there is a decree from Allah," the Holy Qur'an says. And elsewhere, "Say: nothing shall ever happen to us except what Allah has ordained for us." Salim had also read that in the Holy Qur'an. He was no longer a devout Muslim, but he believed in Allah. That was the way he had been raised. But the big question, whether he was ready to leave life, was all that mattered to him in that hour. Deep in his heart, Salim had never felt, not once, prepared for the final moments. Yes, he might often have wished to die, but whenever he felt death was near, he had crumbled. He had hated the thought of dying, even though death would bring the ultimate release. He knew that his death now would bring such cheer to the Dervishes. His dying would inspire them to sow more evil. Salim stirred in agony, helpless against the fear that blackened his thinking. Boundaries between truth and fantasy were demolished. His mind drowned under waves of premonition. As often as Salim had thought of his end, as frequently as he had considered abdicating all control over his earthly life, he was unable to abandon it now that the opportunity arose. His confusion mounted, logical thought was impossible. He fought a threatening darkness.

Twice before, just after his mother had died and again when Henan was killed—murdered in the car "accident"—he suffered lures of a terminal psychic trap. In both instances, Salim's fervent wish for death was genuine. Loneliness and fear had stood before him, almost as real as Mona was now. Now as then, he reasoned that if he was not dying, then he must be going insane. On that very hot summer afternoon, years ago, when Salim had knelt alone in the graveyard atop his mother's grave, sobbing and confronting the uselessness of his feeble life, he had totally surrendered to bitterness. His mind had seethed with hopelessness as the blistering sun seared his brain. He had shivered, overtaken by the peculiar idea that the scorching sun was tormenting his mother inside her grave. At that moment, his puzzlement disarmed his normal senses, and he desperately felt he should help his mother. Salim had actually taken off his shirt and covered the grave! He then had experienced deep relief, having shaded his dead mother from the blazing sun.

The same mad thoughts assailed him today, the minute he laid his eyes on Mona, the blonde woman of his nightmares. Scything through him, illogical convictions told him that the woman standing before him was not real, that he was suddenly swirling in another nightmare. Now Rahim appeared, interrupting his reverie. Stumbling after Rahim, Salim padded outside only to stand beside him, watching the fiery sun setting behind the tall date palms that surrounded the town. Their eyes were lost in the boldly painted red and orange sky.

Rahim put his arm around Salim's shoulder, causing Salim to flinch. "Sorry, man, I didn't mean to startle you," Rahim murmured.

Salim did not reply.

Rahim then inquired affectionately, "Salim, what exactly is the matter? Please tell me. What has happened?"

Salim sighed, turned to face his host. "It's an old story. But I think my time is coming to an end," Salim muttered with downcast eyes.

"What story? What do you mean? Could you please tell me about this story that's tearing you apart? Why don't you tell me, Salim?" Rahim was obviously upset.

"I'll tell you … I will tell you, but not now."

"Why won't you tell me right now? Do you want to keep me in the dark? You are my guest and it is painful to watch you grieve while I have no idea what is distressing you. Again I say, you are my guest!"

"I just … I want to see first about certain things. Please, give me a little time. Then I'll tell you everything," Salim lied. He knew there was no time left. Nothing he could say or do would change that. He tried to smile as his eyes found Rahim's, but he instantly felt a shiver. Salim's eyes closed, he was unable to lie to anyone.

Salim wanted to go home, but hesitated to sound rude. Making up his mind to face his fears, Salim determined to investigate this blonde woman and examine his fearful dream. Could he be mistaken? Maybe Mona was not the woman of his dreams. But … why did she say she knew him? She *is* the same woman, Salim though, *I saw her birthmark on her neck. I know she is the one. I must face my fate and see what will happen.* He remained outside with

Rahim, watching the sun set behind the thick date palms.

Salim went to bed early, still sick and apprehensive. He lay awake for a long time, sure something was about to take his life this time. Then he began to drift off, half awake and half asleep. Although conscious of things around him as he lay in bed, he seemed to move through a foggy dream.

Salim saw himself with the blonde Mona, both naked in the barn beside Rahim's house. Mona moved to him passionately and started kissing him all over his body. Passionate and lustful, Mona whispering in his ear, "What took you so long, Salim? I've been waiting. All these years I've been waiting for you. Take me, take me Salim." The woman aroused his manhood, and he found himself making love to her in the barn.

Then, his dream was abruptly shattered by a gun blast. Salim jumped out of bed in horror, realized it was daylight, and ran outside clad only in his underwear. Instinctively, he dashed into the barn. Inside, he saw Mona lying naked. She had shot herself in the head. Blood drowned her blonde hair in liquid crimson. The pistol lay nearby. Without thinking, Salim picked up the pistol and stepped to the woman. She opened her eyes and looked at him. She struggled, grabbed his hands and pulled him toward her. She breathed out harshly, "Der ... vishes ..." The stench of blood filled Salim's nostrils as she struggled to keep him near her. She whispered in a choking voice, "You're dead ... Der ... vishes ... will ... revenge ..."

At that moment, Rahim dashed into the barn. He froze in his place, unable to speak. Then Rahim's hysterical shouting shattered the silence.

"You killed her! You shot my wife, my Mona! Why, Salim?! Why?"

Salim realized how guilty he appeared, standing there holding the pistol over a bloody body. Standing speechless and trembling, Salim looked down at the pistol in his hand. Rahim grabbed him, pulled the gun from his grasp, and threw Salim to the ground. Then Rahim ran for help. Within moments, the police arrived, followed by an ambulance. Mona was pronounced dead. Salim was handcuffed and taken to jail.

CHAPTER SIXTEEN

Consequences

THE RUMOR OF SALIM MURDERING RAHIM'S WIFE SPREAD QUICKLY THROUGHOUT THE CITY. The woman's death coincided with the popular uprising that took place the next day, a confluence of big news stories more significant than had occurred in Nasiriya for decades.

Immediately upon hearing of Salim's arrest, Abdul rushed to the police station. Finding the police headquarters a vortex of excitement, Abdul asked discreetly to meet with the chief of the police, whom he asked for a meeting with the prisoner, Salim. When Abdul was taken to Salim's cell, he found his friend miserably distraught. Salim appeared pitiful and disarrayed and was going through utmost fears. And as soon as he saw Abdul, Salim made sad, painful croaking sounds.

In his grief and torment, Salim cried out, "I didn't kill the woman. Please, Abdul, try to believe me and understand that I never touched her. Someone else killed the woman while I was sleeping in the guestroom bed. I was dreaming of her, that much is true, but it was only a dream. Can anyone to be accused of a crime that they saw in a dream? I was in a state midway between sleep and wakefulness when I heard the shot. Thinking it was still night, I left the bed and rushed by instinct to the barn, where I found the woman already was shot and dead."

"I was petrified, not knowing what to do, and in that shocked state, I saw the pistol beside her. Foolishly, I now see in retrospect, I picked it up without realizing what I was doing. And there I stood, not yet awake, when

Rahim showed up. He saw his wife dead, me holding the murder weapon, and thought I was the killer. But I was not! I couldn't kill her—nor could I kill anyone. I'm innocent, Abdul please, trust me, please, believe me, I swear by my mother's grave. There is no way that I would ever murder that woman. I was not in the barn when she was shot."

Abdul saw the difficult position his dear friend was in, and knew that proving his innocence may never be possible. Still, Abdul spoke kindly to Salim, "I believe you, Salim, I believe you, and I'm very sure that you could not kill anybody. I have known you many years and I know you're not a killer, but tell me the story from the very beginning. Start with this: why did you have to stay overnight at their house and not come home?" Abdul was astonished that Salim had put himself in such jeopardy, first of all, by his unfortunate choice to spend the night at the home of a family he did not know well.

"Thank you, Abdul, thank you very much for believing in me. Allah be praised for sending my best friend in my hour of need." After taking several deep breaths, Salim went on, "You know about my very long troubles with the dream of the blonde woman killing herself. Well, here I was half asleep, while it had come true.

"Entering Rahim's house last night, who appeared as his wife but the very woman who has haunted my dreams all of these years! Even while I was in Rahim's car on our way to his house, I had a bad feeling. A sickness came over me even before I saw the woman, even before we arrived at his house. The more I worried, the more unhappy I became. Then, as we entered Rahim's house, there, suddenly, a tall blonde woman with a subtle smile etched on her face stared at me. I stopped in my tracks, and gazed at her in shock. Rahim's blonde wife was the same woman of my many anguished dreams. The room began to spin. I wanted to scream and run away, but my legs buckled, and I fainted onto the floor, unconscious. Then, after I regained my consciousness, Rahim tried to calm me. He asked what happened to me, and introduced his wife, Mona.

"I saw the blonde woman with her evil, knowing smile. Though I turned my face away without hesitation, I had already recognized her. Yes, Rahim's wife was the very woman about whom I had dreamed all my life. There before me was the blonde woman who had brought me endless horror for so many years. She was the woman who filled me with shock and misery, the one who shot herself in my nightmares—over and over again for so many years.

"Last night, I tried to apologize. I told Rahim how I've been sick for a long time, and I'm sorry for the trouble I've caused. But the woman repeated that she 'knew me.' I trembled when I heard her say that while at the same time looking deep into my eyes. Then she said that she hoped that I would be better soon. Rahim said that I needed to rest. So I accepted their kindness when they placed me on their guest bed to calm down.

"Later—still last night—I developed a fever, vomited once and could not eat any food. I was petrified, seeing the old prophecy abruptly and starkly before me. I was sick from wondering what miserable fate had brought me by invitation to their home. However, later on at night, I tried to sleep. All I remember is drifting, half awake and half asleep. I seemed to move through a dream. I saw myself with her, the blonde Mona, both of us naked in the barn beside Rahim's house. Mona held me passionately and started kissing me on the lips, on my ears and throat. Her nipples touched my chest as she asked, 'What took you so long, Salim? I've been waiting. All these years I've been waiting for you. Take me! Take me, Salim!'

"The woman aroused my manhood, and I found myself making love to her in the barn. Then, I was abruptly awakened from the dream by the sound of a gun. I jumped out of bed in horror, and without really realizing that it was daylight, I ran outside clad only in my underwear. I dashed into the barn because I had been dreaming of her in the barn.

"Once in the barn, I saw Mona lying naked. She had shot herself in the head. Her hair was soaked with blood. Without thinking, I picked up the pistol that lay beside her body. Weakly, Mona opened her eyes and looked at me. She struggled, grabbed my hands and pulled me to her. All she said was, 'Der ... vishes ... revenge.'

"The stench of blood filled my nostrils as she struggled to keep me near her. She whispered in a choking voice, 'You're dead ... Der ... vishes ... will ... revenge ...'

"At that moment, Rahim appeared in the barn. He froze. His eyes were on fire. Then Rahim's hysterical shouting shattered the silence. 'You killed her ... You just killed my wife! Why man? Why?' I stood speechless and trembling, still holding the pistol in my hand. Rahim grabbed me, pulled the gun from my grasp. I was on the ground. He ran out. The police arrived ... the ambulance."

"Don't worry, Salim, you'll be just fine," Abdul replied, while puzzled awfully. He then added, "I'll hire the best lawyers in Iraq to prove you're innocent. Trust me, my good friend, and do not worry. There is something behind these events, and we need to uncover the truth. However, I'm going to bring your pajamas and some of your clothes that you need while you're here. And I'll be contacting you every day, just to make sure you'll be all right. Don't worry."

At midnight, however, four Dervishes whose faces were hidden with masks, broke into Salim's jail, overpowered the guards, tied them up, and beat Salim mercilessly, before escaping just as a new shift of jailers arrived. When Abdul heard the news, he immediately called Salim's brothers, Nori and Sabir. Abdul told them that the Dervishes had beaten him after breaking into the jail and overpowering the guards. The brothers were sad to hear of Salim's distress. When Abdul told them that Salim had been treated by three nurses, Nori and Sabir were fearful for his life. Abdul urged Salim's brothers to come right away to his house to discuss Salim's fate.

"If the jail rats don't get him, the Dervishes will finish him—unless we act. We must hurry to do something to save his life." Abdul sounded very angry. The two brothers were aghast to learn the depravity of the Dervishes' attack. The three drew up a plan to set up a watch outside of the jail entrance to save Salim's life.

Nori suggested attacking them at midnight since the Dervish base was in the woods. "Attacking them by grenades and machine guns while they are dancing will do the job perfectly."

But, Abdul had to warn him, "I think it's a good idea, yet we must be careful. They're sly. They even use witchcraft on their enemies."

"We will see what their witchcraft can do against our machine guns and grenades!" Nori was still fuming. With the plan set, the friends waited to put it in action.

On the day in March that the Shi'a brotherhood had set in secrecy, the entire city of Nasiriya awoke with hundreds of full-throated calls angrily demanding the downfall of the tyrant, Saddam Hussein. While anxious crowds milled about in the streets, many townspeople were taken by surprise, and looked on in awe. In secret, a hundred men hid the weapons that the city's Shi'a leadership had accumulated—the weapons of Iraqi Army deserters who had either joined the popular uprising or, at least, had donated after returning to civilian life.

While the revolutionaries' eyes were wide open in the main intersections of the city, their comrades assigned to keep watch were vigilantly and cautiously observant from their positions on rooftops overlooking critical streets. Keeping watch near police stations and Army barracks, the lookouts watched for any movement that might portend a possible strike from Ba'ath party thugs, police, or the Army units stationed in the city. Amid the tense anticipation and caution, occasional shouts arose from the courtyards surrounding some homes, from which high-pitched voices of women's loud, joyous ululations could be heard for blocks. Altogether, the mixed sounds of newly-released joy was interlaced with shouts of passionate anticipation for relief from the dictator's harsh rule in a cacophony of tense hope, longing, and heartburn. To many residents, most of whom did not venture far from the safety of their walled homes, the courage of the rebels was received with enthusiastic—though often mute—hope.

At dawn, an hour earlier, the calls to prayer had been sung from a network of minarets, serene and almost subliminal, enticing languid souls and comforting worriers with the promise of Allah's peace. As the lilting chorus of the callers continued floating over the city, inviting the dawn with faith and tranquility, Salim's brothers, Nori and Sabri, rode on the back of a bouncing pickup. Using hand-held loudspeakers, Nori and Sabri joined other revolutionaries, imploring the people to join the popular uprising against Saddam Hussein's regime. Some people peeked from their windows, trying to figure out what was going on. Soon, many dressed hurriedly and rushed to join the rebels.

For the last three weeks, the Iraqi people had been in a boiling rage against the tyrant, as he had foolishly led them into the mouth of another foreign aggression. Their army had suffered a humiliating defeat, as the U.S.-led Coalition troops had kicked them out of Kuwait. Most Iraqis had disagreed with Saddam's occupation of Kuwait. The latest defeat—this time at the hands of the Coalition united against the dictator—had dragged their army through the mud.

Undefended by Saddam's Army, the people of Nasiriya waited impatiently for the thousands of Coalition vehicles that would enter their city, almost as if invited by the buffoon, Saddam, who—in his long rule—had treated the people of Iraq as his personal slaves. He dishonored them, stepped on their pride, and drafted their children into his Army. Why did he always get away with it? The tyrant had proven that he was only capable of hurting his own people, and when it came to fighting his wars against foreign armies, he shamed and disgraced the Iraqis. Saddam, the wrongdoer, sadist, selfish, and arrogant, had proven his failure in adversity, whether as an idiot-leader or a savage human being. However, it was time for the Shi'a to pay him back for their suffering, and his treatment of them.

The popular uprising against the dictator, Saddam Hussein, had begun and the rebels declared their cause to the people of Nasiriya, urging them to join in deposing the tyrant. Undaunted by the possibility of arrest or death, should their rebellion fail, the plotters declared their cause before the public. As night fell over Nasiriya, the conspirators' anxiety was long and tortuous—amounting to a group panic among the Shia leadership. The hours of the night crept toward them, like a platoon of stealthy assassins in the dark. Their beloved Nasiriya was covered with a blanket of horror. The ominous unknown, tomorrow, crouched like an unseen enemy before their blinking eyes.

Like other leaders, the brothers, Nori and Sabir, spent the inky hours anxiously contemplating the enormous commitment that they and their neighbors had undertaken. Although the leaders were disappointed by the failure of any promise of support from the Iraqi Army, they had no choice but to proceed with the uprising plan, regardless of all consequences. What was going to become of them all, since they were the first Iraqis to rebel against Saddam's dictatorship? The fearful puzzle of their fate hung in the darkness like a marksman's target placed out of range.

Awake all night, struggling with their heavy responsibility, Nori and Sabir replayed any number of outcomes in the sweaty theaters of their anxieties. Exhausted and yearning for sleep, they remained in this state until brought back to the present by the harmonious call to prayer as the sun rose. In the fragile serenity of the morning, Nasiriyans heard the melodic invitations to prayer, comforting them with at least the gloss of a peace that, however real, may be only moments from breaking like a perfect eggshell held over a hot frying pan. The two young men had no desire to remain in their nervous beds. Although deprived of the peaceful rest that night had falsely promised, they hastened to perform their early prayers.

After their prayers, the few minutes that Nori and Sabir spent under a warm shower refreshed them so that, as they sat at the breakfast table in silence, still brooding, the scent of black tea being poured into their cups was a pleasurable distraction from heavy thoughts of the day ahead. Sabir took a sip before adding fresh milk to his cup, and abruptly, inquired anxiously, "Are you sure brother, that we're ready for the big mission, I mean even without the support of the army?"

Before answering, Nori looked at his younger brother with a smile. He sighed and quietly replied, "Absolutely, we're ready, everything's set and our best men are armed."

"I'm talking about the innocent people who will be endangered. Could our latest recruits be setting themselves upon a suicidal path?"

"We don't have much choice. Now we rely upon Almighty Allah first and then upon our people. What more do we have? The job must be done, no matter what." Nori replied confidently, and then he added, "Whatever today brings, brother, it is only our fate. And if we are today to be honored in martyrdom for the sake of our people's freedom from the vicious Saddam, then is not ours an opportunity that might never occur twice?"

In the street, the crowds were both full of enthusiasm for their cause and also absolutely fearful of the dictator's retribution. Rallying to help overthrow Saddam, the crowds shouted for guns and ammunition. Meeting in the tent that sat in the middle of the street, the leadership of the uprising agreed that Nori and his brother Sabir should lead an attack on the main police station, to steal the handguns and other weapons cached there. Nori immediately formed a team of ten combat-trained soldiers. Seven of them were armed with light carbines, including his assistant, Sabir. Because of the lack of sufficient weapons, the remaining three carried only pistols. Nori, their leader, was equipped with a Kalashnikov rifle and a grenade.

Nori set off in his pickup with his team, speeding toward the main police station, located in the building adjacent to the governor's office. This morning, the governor's office was empty, as the staff remained in their homes after learning of the uprising. As they approached within three blocks of the station, Nori and his men fanned out to surround the place. Once his team was in place, Nori shouted to the police staffing the center, urging them to surrender and come out with their hands up.

"We are the rebel uprising, and this is the day of freedom," shouted Nori through a hand-held loudspeaker. We order you to surrender in order to keep your lives. We are rising up against the tyrant Saddam, who destroys our beloved Iraq. We do not invite clashes with you, unless ...."

Nori had not finished his warning when the police began shooting from inside the station. Nori ordered his men to return fire, and the skirmish between the two sides was characterized by assorted gunfire. Suddenly, Nori shouted to his group to cover him, and he sprinted toward the police building, spraying the doors and windows of the police station with heavy fire as he ran. He took shelter behind three police cars parked just outside of the door. His right arm swung wide as he pitched the one hand grenade in his possession at the window from which most of the police fusillade came. The pomegranate explosion tore a large hole in the wall where the window had been. As debris settled from the explosion, screams and cries of distress, pain, and anguish were heard within. Nori immediately led four of his cadre into the smoking building, taking advantage of the confusion and opening fire on survivors inside. Once the building was cleared of policemen, Nori led his men to a large, triple-bolted door. Nori ordered two men to open the arms storeroom with iron bars. The prize of automatic rifles, carbines, handguns, grenades, and large boxes of ammunition required three loads per man. All of the weapons and ammunition were loaded into the police cars, which were now used to return to the center of the uprising in Haboobi Street.

Nori and his brother Sabir, after their victorious attack against the police station, presented the new supply of weapons to the leadership, which immediately nominated them to be in charge of the city's safety. Still feeling the excitement of overcoming the police station, the brothers began their new responsibility to oversee the protection of the city. Nori chose the same team who assisted him in his police station mission and deputized them as officials at critical checkpoints throughout the city. He addressed various gatherings of townspeople, advising that the criminals and thieves who may take advantage of the lawlessness to loot the property of the people would meet Allah much sooner than anticipated. By Nori's stern words, chaotic behavior and assaults upon citizens were minimized.

At sunset, small celebrations broke out as the rebels gained confidence following dissemination of the police weapons throughout the cadre of original revolutionaries and trusted recruits. Using the afternoon and early evening light to raid a number of lesser police stations and the headquarters of the Ba'ath Party, the rebels commandeered hundreds of additional weapons and the ammunition required for them to fulfill their promise. Nori used his newfound authority to establish new rules to ensure the protection of the town. Pickup patrols were begun throughout the city. A trusted lieutenant was charged with establishing sniper groups over the rooftops of critical buildings and intersections. A corps of small groups was established to police the streets in systematic intervals. However, in spite of all these precautionary steps taken to provide security, many good people worried, feeling their neighborhoods on the edge of some new abyss.

The greatest concern of the rebel leadership was the continuing silence from the Shi'a authority in the province of Najaf, led by Ayatollah al-Khoei, whose promised statement of support for the rebellion was critical to its stability. When the people heard from the Ayatollah, their hearts would be with the rebels. Until he spoke in authority, the rebel's only certainties were the weapons in their hands.

The popular uprising had begun in Basra, followed on the next day by the rebellion in Nasiriya. Thereafter, the uprising spread quickly to Mosul and other cities of northern Iraq. However, because no central spokesman communicated with definitive authority, the rebellion in each city stood on its own against the Iraqi Army of Saddam Hussein. The stability of the uprising was in the hands of the Ayatollahs, whose voices could cement its legitimacy across Iraq, establishing the rebels groups as something more than random gangs in the streets of disparate cities, each standing against Saddam's army without any support. Meanwhile, Saddam Hussein was still alive in Baghdad, or in one of his seventy-eight palaces throughout the silent country.

CHAPTER SEVENTEEN

Like Paper Dolls

IN HIS JAIL CELL, SALIM WAS FOCUSED ON THE INVESTIGATION OF HIS CRIME as it stagnated while authorities kept their eyes upon the civil unrest which threatened their livlihoods. Interrogations showed the conflict between Salim's testimony and Rahim's statements. Rahim told the police that in all the years of his marriage to Mona, he had never seen a pistol in her possession. He asserted that Mona had indicated she and Salim were acquainted. She had said so in front of him. Rahim was suspicious of Salim, and now also suspicious of his dead wife. Something was going on between them.

A public defender tried to work with Salim, who meant to be cooperative, but jail life magnified his anxieties. He became delirious. He seldom slept. He could not discern between reality and his near-constant dreams. At one point, Salim thought that the autopsy revealed he had engaged in sex with Mona just before she died. Believing he could not defend himself against such physical evidence, he became more and more hysterical. He saw no salvation. He felt no one believed him, not even his lawyer and a famous defense attorney that Abdul hired to save him. Salim was certain that, to everyone, he was an atrocious murderer who deserved no pity. Abdul and Salim's four brothers, Nadeem, Nori, Sabir and Saif, came to encourage him and to offer help, but nobody could do anything for his complicated case. Despair slashed its sword, cutting Salim's heart to pieces. Death was creeping toward him. Sadly, he examined his life. *How can any truth survive when no one wishes to hear it? How can justice be served, when the truth is denied? Why is everyone attacking me? What is my sin? Why have I, since my fragile childhood, been forced to battle for survival? Why do ghastly events constantly pull me down? As long as I can remember, my life has always been assaulted by an angry fate, forcing me to face down fears that even the toughest men would avoid. Is the present agony more than anyone can be expected to live through?*

Why do people find me such helpless prey, so easy to exploit? Why am I considered weaker than anyone else? I have never been intimidated by anyone; and have never wanted my life to be run by anybody else. From the Sheikh on down, every one of these Dervish bastards have claimed themselves my savior, but the truth has shown them to be evil. They all wanted to see me either submissive or dead. They desired only to control and run other people's lives, and to hunt for victims to exploit. But why me? Why was I chosen to be a victim? Why not one of my brothers instead? Why me?

The Sheikh had humiliated him, stomped on his pride and left his wounds open and unhealed, all the while claiming piety and religious reverence. After him came more deception: the Dervishes pretending to be worshippers of Allah, yet their falsehood revealed them to be a sadistic and evil group. They had entangled him with their odd words; and when he had sought his freedom, they tracked him down to kill him. They had pursued him here to the end.

At that moment, Salim was left with only one choice: to submit to Allah. In supplication, he knelt and begged forgiveness, "Allah, my great God, and my Omnipotent King, why are such wicked evildoers given power? Why do they dare to disobey your Majesty? My God, I seek refuge with you. You are the Oft-Forgiving, the Most Merciful, and I'm begging your forgiveness for all my frailty and faults. For all the struggles of my life, and for my pain and calamities, I'm asking you, my Lord, to give me your pardon and to absolve my sins. Men are accusing me of murdering a woman who had terrorized my life, but only you, Allah, the Omnipotent King, know the truth, that I didn't kill her. It would have been a great relief if I had killed her; but I could not, because I know killing is a sin. As my life is about to end, I ask for your great mercy. My great Allah, please recompense me with your forgiveness. You're my great God that I rely on, and you're our Allah, the most merciful and the most gracious.

"No one will believe me now, just as no one believed me before. No one ever listened to me or led me to safety in my entire life. I'm fed up with living, and I can't take any more pain and hurt. I will end up in prison for a crime I did not commit. All of my life I've been hurting, but I've hurt no one. Nobody in the entire world has been destroyed the way I have been. I won't wait for a trial and then be executed. What's the difference if I kill myself now or I'm hanged later? There is nothing left for me in this ruthless life, and death is inevitable.

"All my life I have been a person on death row. I spent each day searching for the meaning of this dream and its intent, and finally it has become reality. I've seen it happen with my own eyes, exactly as in my dreams. I know I did not kill her, not a chance. I hate what she has done to me in my dreams, but I did not kill her. Although she has been terrifying me all my life, I still couldn't kill her—or anyone. I couldn't do it. I couldn't do it. The only person I can kill is me, myself only. Yes, I can do that. I can do it now, and there will be no more pain, tears or misery. I must stop all tortures right now."

Salim rose, looked at the single light bulb bulging from the wall of his cell. He moved toward it. He would remove the bulb and end his life. Then Salim suddenly heard a familiar rhythm from afar. The glaring light bulb went out. The small cell became dark. Frightened, Salim clearly heard the familiar rhythm coming from the depth of the earth, the old Dervishes' drums. The beat became louder and louder, and the darkness gradually began to fill with the familiar ominous glow. The bonfire appeared again as a great symbol of a mysterious death. The view became clearer to Salim.

Suddenly, Salim saw that four men had broken into his cell, gripped him from his shoulders, and covered his head with a dark cloth sack. Up the stairs they carried him, outside to a waiting car, and drove away with him.

The next day, after the cover was removed from his head, Salim found that he was in a small room. It was empty. There was no window. The only opening was a tiny space just large enough to insert a plate of food. Leaning his back against the cool wall, he listened to his breath and waited to see what would happen next. After about two hours, the door opened. Omran and Ajil entered the room.

"Al Salam Alaikum brother, Salim, how are you doing? Have you slept well last night?" Omran questioned, a cynical note to his voice.

"What's this all about?" Salim inquired angrily. "You ought to be ashamed of yourselves. Have you not done enough to me yet? Now, instead of helping me, you're accusing me falsely of killing the woman? And now you are kidnapping me? Are these the manners or virtues of true Muslims?"

"You deserve all that has happened to you, Salim, and you know that!" It was Omran who spoke.

"Oh, is that right? are you hearing yourself?" Now, Salim was cynical. "But, why is that? Is this how you force people to be back with you?"

"Yes, that's the reason," Ajil retorted. "Why is it so difficult for you to return to the Dervishes? Could you tell us why?"

"Are you sure you don't know my reason for rejecting you? Well, I'll tell you why then. It's because you are false Muslims! You are nothing but sadist killers who could commit all kinds of sins! Yet—amazing as it is—you still see yourselves as good Muslims! Because you are fanatics using the religion as a means to control people's destiny! By contriving false and deceptive principles of Islam, you limit their freedom and eventually destroy their lives. No matter how hard you pretend to a genuine intention by wrapping yourselves tightly in the cloak of religion, you are still the ones with the most to hide.

"You are the terrorists who have been murdering innocents and destabilizing the peace throughout Iraq. And while you could hide your sinful attitudes from people, you could not hide from Almighty Allah, the all-seeing, the all-hearing. Haven't you killed my best friend, Ekram, that innocent young man? Haven't you killed my beautiful young wife? Now, you have killed Rahim's wife and thrown her blood on me, accusing me of your heinous killing!"

"Salim, Salim! If you know all this about us, why do you think that we're not going to kill you, too?"

"I'm sure you're going to kill me. But, I no longer love this life, where sinners like you could control the lives and destinies of innocent people. I hate you and despise you all."

"Is there anything else you want to say before we kill you?"

"There are many things to say about your sinfulness, but words are too small a mirror to hold up to your infinite worthlessness, your savage emptiness! You took a good life and made it cheap. You took God's gift of life and, in your ruthlessness, you make it ugly. Peace and serenity, in your hands, become horror unending. You take utopia, and gut it like a diseased camel. Your insane passion for random killings in the name of Islam have made honest men distrust Allah. God's people become unnaturally frightened when in your presence.

"Regardless of what you people might possess, whether it could be exceptional luck, daring, or merely recklessness and disrespect for everyone, it seemed that you could make all the difference in the world, yet, all at the cost of Islam and its true values. You don't deserve to live in any society, because you Dervishes are a scourge, an epidemic, no more and no less," Salim exhaled, drew his shoulders back, and stood immovable as a bronze of the Prophet, himself.

"Listen,' said Omran, "We are here to inform you that tonight will be the last evening of your life. You'll be executed tonight in front of everyone." After Omran spoke his last, the two men walked out, not looking back.

After confirming the plan to save Salim's life from his kidnappers, the Dervishes, Nori suggested that Abdul should wait home as his group went to do the job. So it was that, before midnight on Thursday, Nori and Sabir led fifteen men armed with semi-automatic rifles walking down an empty street toward the date palm plantations. The night sky was serene, an indigo-velvet canopy studded with millions of the twinkling stars, and a sliver of moon slowly setting to the horizon.

As the men entered the woods where the Dervishes were known to dance, they confirmed that their arrival preceded their prey. "Everyone, immediately take position, except the sniper, who will remain with me. We'll wait for the Dervishes in silence," said Nori in a hushed voice, before he and the sniper disappeared among the date palms.

Moments after midnight, the Dervishes showed up at their ritual place. Their captive, Salim, walked among them with eyes downcast. He seemed horrified with fear of death, as if his legs could barely carry him forward. Nori's men in hiding slowly released the safety of their machine gun and levelled it in the direction of their targets, ready to fire at Nori's order.

The Dervishes encircled Salim in silence. Raising his head, Salim recognized each one of them. He knew their names, their gaunt faces, and their antagonistic eyes. They crowded together, following customary rituals. Somewhere beyond the circle, Salim heard the drumbeat rhythm begin slowly and softly. Gradually, he heard it increase in speed and volume. He assumed this was the Dervishes' way of heralding his final ordeal. Having already consigned his soul to Allah, Salim watched the scene of his own execution as if from the eyes of a vulture circling high overhead. The Dervishes, having constricted their circle, focused upon a huge fire. Their faces hardened, but otherwise they were immobile.

From his vantage point perhaps sixty yards distant, Nori could see his brother, Salim, seated within the circle of men, near the fire. For a moment, Nori reflected that it almost appeared as if his brother was an honored guest. But then the drummers lurched into a wild rhythm, faster and louder. His finger barely touched the trigger of the machine gun, as Nori—hidden among the dark undergrowth surrounding the Dervishes—was suddenly overcome with an incredible hatred, an overwhelming desire to murder them all, an impulse he fought with every ounce of his being. He must wait until the right moment.

Powerless and petrified, Salim focused his mind upon the reality of his situation. He was surrounded by the Dervishes, those who had forced him to join them and then threatened him when he sought to follow the dictates of his own soul. Everything was real now, live and tangible. He was fully awake. The drums halted. Silence. Then suddenly the drums again, and the old Omran began dancing to their violent rhythms. His skewer was shining in his hand. He grimaced in pain, and danced wildly. He then started singing, and all the Dervishes joined in his sad song, their voices an ominous chorus of impending doom:

> *You, who our souls planted in you,*
> *It's time now to pay us everything that you owe.*

How much you hurt us before as you know.
We initiated you a brother, but you turned a foe.
It's time for your sinful blood to mix with the soil and no regret when you go.
And when a tree with demon face tomorrow will grow,
We curse you with morning's dew.
No memory for a sinner's life, but so much shame and hate flow.

Another Dervish stood up and jumped into the circle, joining the leader. Then another. One-by-one they all stood to dance around Salim. They weaved maniacally to the pounding of the drums. One after the other they danced in the circle. The fire raged, and the skewers shone in its angry glow, ugly and frightening.

Three men broke off from the circle, rushing toward Salim. They grabbed him and forced him to the ground. Salim resisted but they were too powerful. For a split-second, time stood still as Nori's crack sniper squeezed the trigger of the precision rifle. The drums went silent at the sound of the rifle shot. Silence reigned for a long moment until the Dervish whose sword was raised menacingly over Salim emitted a soft groan and slumped to the ground, beside his intended victim. Salim was surprised to find that he was still breathing.

Horrified as seeing their chosen executioner lying in a pool of his own blood, the Dervishes released Salim and rose to scurry away in fear. However, before they were able to take two steps, Nori's machine gunners swept the circle of Dervishes, crumpling the figures like paper dolls made of tissue.

From his observation spot, Nori shouted for Salim to stay down and take cover, but Salim understood the sound of the machine gun and lay flat on the ground, listening to the spray of automatic weapon fire as bullets flew less than an arm's length above his body. Dervishes were falling to the ground on all sides of him.

A cadre of the Dervishes who survived the withering machine gun barrage sought refuge in a small mud hut partially protected by trees on the far side of the circle from Nori's position. Tumbling inside the hut and slamming its heavy wooden door, six or seven Dervishes survived for the moment, escaping the continuing fire from Nori's raiders. Peeking from the hut's only window, they saw that most of their fellow Dervishes lay dead around the fire, which continued to rage.

The Dervishes inside the mud hut shouldered the carbines that had been stored there and opened fire on Nori's position, intending to provide cover for any of their number who may yet be seeking safety behind trees or rocky outcroppings. At a pivotal moment in the exchange of slaughter, a Dervish bullet injured Nori's machine gunner at the same moment that three determined Dervishes made a suicidal attack upon the rebel position. It appeared that luck was on the side of the intrepid Dervishes for a moment before Nori shouldered his automatic rifle and dropped the intruders without further injury to his men. As the battle continued, the Dervishes seemed to embody a collective death wish, jumping up to advance just at the time that the machine gun sprayed their position or otherwise disclosing their vulnerable position behind nothing more than leaves and fronds. The battle raged much longer than Nori had expected, and he was relieved that Salim had taken advantage of confusion early in the fighting to crawl to safety behind a low rock formation.

The remaining Dervishes fought untiringly until Nori determined that only two of their number remained in action. One was returning fire from the mud hut, which the machine gun had reduced to an oversized anthill, and another continued passionately replying from cover behind a group of trees. In the end, the last survivor among the Dervishes was Omran, whose precise carbine fire almost earned Nori's admiration until a precise shot from the sniper found the side of his head, and dropped him in silence. Omran's body seemed to morph into the shapes of tree roots which resembled elbows and knees in their snaking forms.

The rebel contingent arose man by man from their shooting positions behind trees, rock formations, and depressions in the ground that served as natural foxholes. Nori was proud of his fighters and happy to find that they were all alive, although many had been injured by grazing bullets or flying rock chips. He, himself, was bleeding from a shoulder injury, where a bullet might have killed him had it flown a few inches nearer his heart. Salim stumbled from his hiding position and was met by opened arms from the rebel fighters, especially his brother, whose hugs nearly suffocated the weakened refugee.

Nori and his proud cadre mounted their pickups, with Salim in the position of honor behind the cab of the lead vehicle, and paraded to Abdul's house, where the old man waited anxiously to hold his young friend in the flesh, seeing him saved.

CHAPTER EIGHTEEN
Mr. Nothing

THE NEWS OF THE REBEL'S BATTLE WITH THE DERVISHES to save Salim's life spread throughout Iraq by word of mouth and through occasional news items in those newspapers which were not silenced by the dictator. Nori was the hero in these narratives, which—as rumors will—morphed slightly with each retelling. In some versions, the Dervishes began floating like angels when struck by the rebels' bullets. In other versions, the bleeding Dervishes slithered away like wounded snakes seeking refuge in the dark forest. The editor-in-chief of the Nasiriya newspaper, a storyteller at heart, listened intently to the recountings of the heroic rebels and captured their exciting details in his long account. Then, he continued to divulge many truths from the history of the Dervishes, including the following:

"In Nasiriya, after the mysterious murder of Sheikh Gupta and his mistress, Adela, by an unknown assailant, a man later identified as Omran proclaimed himself to be the new Sheikh. Omran's notorious scams, loan-sharking malaises, and evil schemes that left many ordinary people penniless were told from one household to another as the atrocities he fostered among the people of Nasiriya were unveiled. Omran and his Dervish followers exploited small business people and citizens greedily. They were known to threaten and terrorize people with impunity. The Dervishes, it was agreed, reserved their most gruesome horrors for those who rejected affiliation with them. Omran had threatened to kill former Dervishes and their families, or at least to expel them from town.

"Omran's background was not as vague as his predecessor, Sheikh Gupta. A few close associates who knew Omran as a vicious criminal told the story of his imprisonment of seven years for the hideous murder of a man and woman during an alcoholic rage, which—apparently—was not an uncommon state for the young Omran. In due time, Omran's wealthy merchant father, Khalil Abdul Allah, attempted to save the family honor by bribing the judges. Omran was released from prison.

"Omran, who had proclaimed himself a believer in the Truth Faith, had been an ugly person even during his youth. Reliable reports show him to have been maliciously self-centered, greedy, and vicious. His carelessness resulted in a tense relationship with the police. But since he was the only son of a wealthy father, the family provided him with expensive legal defenses on many unhappy occasions. The young Omran was devoted to dissipation in an unbridled search for thrills and pleasures. His nights were spent among the tents of gypsies, boozing and leading a chorus to encourage gypsy women dancing and undulating before his peers. Reliable sources say that his father used to taunt him, calling him, 'Mr. Nothing.' Then, all of a sudden, Omran turned to religion. He married his cousin, Huda, who gave birth to their daughters, Sabah and Mona. Huda was later killed by Mona.

"After the killing of his wife, Omran briefly returned to his dissolute ways, before his father, Khalil Abdul Allah, who owned a garish Baghdad casino and large farms in the countryside, decided to send Omran abroad. Abdul Allah decided upon a medical career for Omran and sent him to the United States, where medical schools welcome students from abroad. Abdul Allah favored the idea of his devout becoming a respected and wealthy doctor. But Omran, who was spoiled, never took his studies seriously, and was eventually expelled by the dean of the medical school, who was himself already a respected and wealthy doctor, and careful with his reputation and that of his school.

"Omran remained in America, living happily in a stylish neighborhood near the medical school. There, in a popular pizzeria, he met Vicki, a tall American beauty, to whom he introduced the hypodermic instrument with which God had endowed him. Before the American holiday of Thanksgiving,

Vicki and Omran were married in an infidel worshipping house. Soon, Vicki gave birth to an infant girl they named Amanda. After living many years in America, Omran, Vicki and Amanda returned to Iraq. But Vicki could not bear living in Iraq more than four years. The lifestyle and political situation frightened her. Vicki divorced Omran and returned with Amanda to the United States. Vicki, however, maintained her relationship with Omran after the divorce because he provided her with enough money to maintain the infidel standard of life that pleased her. Confidants report that Omran continued to love her, especially her fine body, and he often yearned for her in his heart and elsewhere upon his person.

"As Omran experienced himself aging, he became a conscientious man of the Truth Faith. Indeed, the Islamic Religion became his main concern. After the death of his wealthy father, Omran took his inherited fortune and moved to Nasiriya. He built a fine house and bought more properties. Omran also formed a group of religious fanatics calling themselves 'the Dervishes movement.' This movement attracted many people, mostly because of money that Omran generously offered members. Impartial observers were curious about the slogans of Islamic faith that the movement proclaimed, as there were many questions about the sincerity of the group's faith. Was Omran deceiving recruits by the employment of the True Faith and its scriptures? Were the Dervishes enticing young people by selective quotations from texts we should cherish? However, the movement's success—not to mention the flow of money that the Dervish activities generated—was, no doubt, due to the strict rules that Omran imposed on members. In a short time, the Dervishes became a powerful organization. The Dervishes were strong enough financially to bribe officers of the Iraqi government, thus avoiding the officials' move toward dissolution. It was learned that even Saddam himself tried to destroy their movement through secret savagery. His Republican Guards killed Dervishes in large numbers and buried them in mass graves. By doing so, Saddam indirectly increased popular sympathy for their movement.

"It could be only by the wrath of Allah that Omran's family was inflicted by many kinds of problems. Omran's daughter, Mona, from his cousin, Huda, committed suicide in Nasiriya and a local man named Salim was wrongly accused of the killing. Mona was mentally ill, having been born with mental problems which had never been resolved. She suffered a kind of phobia about people, a condition doctors never fully diagnosed. Mona's successful suicide was at least the fifth attempt that doctors recorded during her life. Mona was a problem to herself and to everyone in her family. She one night even attempted to kill her grandfather Khalil Abdul Allah during his asleep. Afterword, however, Mona was kept in her room chained to her bed, because family feared that she may do the worst. Such serious problems, when found in Iraqi families, were handled discreetly by the family to hide the scandal and to block rumors that might cause bitterness, embarrassment, and harm to the family reputation. For that reason, Omran had steadfastly refused to send his daughter, Mona, for treatment in Baghdad. His prohibition continued until the day that her mother Huda, Omran's first Iraqi wife, was in the foyer washing clothes, where Mona tiptoed behind her, sliced her skull open with a heavy meat cutter, and killed her.

"On that sad day, Omran was compelled to send Mona to Baghdad's mental health hospital for treatment. At the time, Mona was twelve. After two years in the hospital, her health improved and she was discharged. However, Mona suffered periodic mental crises. Her instability compelled her father to prolong her treatment. After years of treatment, Mona's health and life turned much better.

"Again rehabilitated, and with a new certificate of likely sanity, Mona enrolled in school, where her work was promising. Then she met Rahim. The young couple fell ecstatically in love and got married. Mona had been—mostly happily—married to Rahim until the fateful day when she inconvenienced her houseguest by committing suicide. Salim was accused of murder in her death, but it was later determined that Mona had committed suicide. Judges finally ruled that her suicide was related to her mental illness, since her history of instability was peppered with occurrences of unexplained anger and unannounced depression.

"When trying to detect plausible motives behind Omran's adoption of a fanatic cause, his biography revealed dishonorable hints. For much of his life, Omran made lifestyle choices that would make a camel herder blush. As he approached old age, he was overcome with guilt, and tried to atone for his early crimes and shortcomings. Or perhaps it was his criminal history which would later provide models for larger terrorist movements, such as Al-Qaida.

"But it also could be that, since Omran and other fanatic Muslim groups were connected to some Islamic governments, the Dervishes may have profited by millions of dollars from national 'donations' to destabilize Iraq and other countries. It is now a matter of public record that these Islamic governments encouraged these groups to establish militant Islamic states in the Middle East so that Bin Laden and other terrorists might have a safe harbor from which to threaten the West. But strangely enough, during the Iraq-Iran war, when Saddam Hussein ordered to deport all the Shi'a population of Iranian descent, only Omran and two of his assistants remained in Iraq. No one has determined why those three men were allowed to stay by Saddam Hussein in personally-signed orders. To compound the mystery, Omran himself later called for jihadists to join with his movement of fanatics against Saddam's regime.

"The Dervishes were extremely sadistic murderers who took pleasure in killing people in the name of Islam. Their rules were *never to forgive or forget*, and *we can easily eliminate anyone who dares to cross us.* They perverted honorable interpretations of the Qur'an, twisting them to coincide with their own agenda. These fanatics were against every modern idea anywhere, especially in the Islamic world. They regarded good Muslims and believers of other religions to be their worst enemies. Good Muslims threatened them because they might expose the Dervish lies to the world. These fanatics accuse good Muslims of spiritual weakness, often calling upon them to join the Dervish in 'defending Islam,' though the fanatics know in their hearts that they have betrayed the True Faith. In fact, anyone who joins the Dervishes—and Omran himself knew this—forever abdicates his honorable apprenticeship to Allah.

"The Dervishes have prospered by dancing upon the souls of their converts. They have survived because of the financial donations of Saddam and other rotten tyrants who pretend to love Islam, but who actually love their own wealth and glory much more."

If you have enjoyed this book, please visit:
www.parkhurstbrothers.com
for more titles that spotlight humanities, folktales, and storytelling.